# Where the Bones
# Are Buried

**Books by Jeanne Matthews**

The Dinah Pelerin Mysteries
*Bones of Contention*
*Bet Your Bones*
*Bonereapers*
*Her Boyfriend's Bones*
*Where the Bones Are Buried*

# Where the Bones Are Buried

A Dinah Pelerin Mystery

Jeanne Matthews

Poisoned Pen Press

Poisoned Pen Press
6962 E. First Ave., Ste. 103
Scottsdale, AZ 85251
www.poisonedpenpress.com
info@poisonedpenpress.com

Printed in the United States of America

# Acknowledgments

I would like to thank the following friends and writers for their helpful suggestions: Sal Gordon, Jeanne Kleyn, Joseph Massucco, Sandra Wainer, Mary Brockway, Judy Kimball, Sylva Coppock, Ronda Taylor, Theresa Zimmerman, Susan Schmidt, Katherine Berryman, and Gaylloyd Sisson. I'm also indebted to Joseph Winston for creating my website and for trying against all odds to teach me how to maintain it.

Particular thanks go to Barbara Peters, my editor at Poisoned Pen Press, whose careful reading and acute insights always raise my game, and to my husband and first reader, Sid DeLong, whose inspirations and sense of humor pull me through.

It's like a lion at the door;
And when the door begins to crack,
It's like a stick across your back;
And when your heart begins to smart,
It's like a penknife in your heart;
And when your heart begins to bleed,
You're dead, and dead, and dead, indeed.
  —From "A Man of Words and Not of Deeds,"
    Anonymous Nursery Rhyme


"In a utilitarian age, of all other times,
it is a matter of grave importance that
fairy tales should be respected."
    —Charles Dickens

# Late September 2013

# Chapter One

Dinah Pelerin wasn't used to waking up happy, and it scared the daylights out of her. She pulled the blanket to her chin and snuggled close under Thor's arm. They had known each other for almost a year, but had moved in together just three weeks ago. With every passing day, her confidence grew that she'd made the right decision. She cared about him more than she'd cared about anyone in a very long time, but the people she cared about had a habit of turning into liars or dying. Thor was too honest to lie.

She said, "I wish you didn't have to go. It's not fair. I haven't learned my way around the city yet, and the only person I know besides you is the wacko across the hall."

"You have a dozen Berlin guide books and street maps and Geert isn't a wacko. He's the resident caretaker. If the lights go off or the furnace dies, tell him and he'll take care of the problem. Anyway, I'll only be away for five days. Norwegian Intelligence can't function without my unerring wisdom."

"Can't you send your unerring wisdom to them in an email?"

"I'm glad you'll miss me, *kjære*, but I have my orders." He looked at his watch and sat up. "I need to be at the Embassy in an hour. I'm picking up two diplomats who will join me on the flight to Oslo."

"Just my luck to fall for a latter-day James Bond, forever charging off to save the nation." She placed a hand over her heart. "I could not love thee, dear, so much, loved I not honor more."

He kissed her in a particularly melting way, then rolled out of bed abruptly and headed for the shower. "Hold that thought."

"You're a tease, Thor Ramberg."

"Like Bond, I leave them begging for more."

"Them?"

He didn't hear. The bathroom door snicked shut and she slipped on her robe and padded into the kitchen to make coffee. Rain pelted against the windowpanes, and the pedestrians on the Niederwallstrasse down below carried umbrellas and wore their collars turned up like KGB operatives. Until the Wall fell in 1989, this street and the area for miles around was Soviet-dominated East Berlin. Since that time, the Germanys had reunified and Berlin had reinvented itself as the cultural and financial hub of Europe. The only thing that hadn't changed was the KGB weather.

She shivered. If September was this cold and dreary, she didn't want to think what winter would bring. But in spite of the gloom, she'd never felt so happy. It seemed that the stars had aligned and, for the first time in living memory, every aspect of her life clicked perfectly. Thor was wonderful, her new job as guest lecturer on Native American cultures at Humboldt University was a plum, and the weather aside, Berlin was one of the most exciting cities she'd ever visited. She tried to put the thought of all this happy synchronicity out of her mind lest the gods grow jealous and snatch it away.

She brought in the *International Herald Tribune*, brewed a pot of the local Einstein coffee, and sat down at the kitchen table to read about the turmoil in Greece and Pakistan and Kenya. The world seemed fragmented, a jigsaw of violent factions that refused to fit together and fanatics willing to do anything in furtherance of their causes. She worried about Thor's work carrying out counterterrorism missions on behalf of his native Norway. He'd almost been killed in Greece last June while investigating a ring of arms-traffickers. She had encouraged him to go to law school or return to a less hazardous police job in Norway. But he was a patriot and he craved adventure. She had learned not to try to argue him out of his dream job as an international sleuth.

He breezed into the room in a dark suit and tie, bringing with him the ferny scent of Fitjar soap. With his deep brown eyes and almost black hair, he did look a bit Bond-like—a cross between Sean Connery and Genghis Khan. Descended from the Sami people of Arctic Scandinavia, he loved cold weather as much as she hated it. He poured himself a cup of coffee and glanced out the window. "Museum weather. You should go to the Pergamon this afternoon. The Gates of Ishtar will start your anthropologist's juices flowing."

"It's on my list."

"And there's a market in the platz with local fruits and vegetables and flowers."

"I'll check it out." His tie didn't need straightening, but she pretended it did, standing ready for a kiss that would have to last her for five days. "I'll probably spend the day preparing for my first class. I know that most Germans speak English, and the ones who sign up for my class will be fluent, but I don't want to use too many Americanisms."

"Most Germans under the age of fifty have studied English in school. Even those who say they speak 'only a little English,' can talk politics like a senator, which by the way, is the German word for senator."

He was so relaxed and reassuring. Too relaxed? She felt a frisson of superstitious fear. "You will be careful, won't you? Don't let the bad guys sneak up on you."

"I'm off to Oslo, not Kabul."

Her iPhone burst into its ringtone of imperative plinks.

Thor took a quick swallow of coffee and set down his mug. "Answer your xylophone. I've got to run."

"No, wait…" she turned toward the phone.

"I'll call you." His kiss landed in her hair somewhere in the vicinity of her left ear and he hurried out the door.

Frustrated, she picked up the phone. "Hello."

"Dinah, is that you? It's your mother. Your friend Margaret and I are in the Hartsfield Airport in Atlanta waitin' for our flight.

What's that number, Margaret? Here it is, Air France, eighteen thirty-four. Do we change planes somewhere, Margaret?"

"You're coming here? To Berlin?"

"We stop over in Paris, but we don't change. Good heavens, that's too little for me to read, Margaret. Anyhow, we'll be arriving this evening at…what? Can that be right? All right, *tomorrow* evening at eight-thirty at TXL, which we think is the name of the airport. If you can come get us and put us up for a few days, that'll be just lovely."

Dinah fought back a groan. "How long do you plan to be here?"

"That depends, baby. We have a little detective job we need you to help us with."

# Chapter Two

Dinah watched in frozen fascination as the two former Mrs. Dobbs passed through Customs at Gate A of Berlin's tiny, soon-to-be-retired Tegel Airport and into the baggage area. Margaret Dobbs, the taller of the two, had aged considerably since her murder trial. The skin beneath her owlish eyes pouched and the pleats around her mouth had deepened. She still wore her blond hair sleeked back in a tight bun and the sharp point of her widow's peak resembled an approaching arrow.

Swan, the second Mrs. Dobbs, had made several treks to the altar since her divorce from Cleon Dobbs, once with Hart Pelerin, Dinah's father. Her *nom du jour* was Mrs. William Calms, a name distinctly at odds with the effect she had on Dinah. Black-haired, with high cheekbones and an inscrutable half-smile, she appeared as crisp and unwrinkled as if she'd stepped out of the pages of a ladies' wear catalog. In stockings and blue kitten heels, no less. She spotted Dinah and held out her arms. "Hey, baby, you look lost as last year's Easter egg." Her drawl was thick, but not cloying. She radiated an air of nonchalance and Chanel No. 5. "Come give us a hug."

Dinah embraced her mother, but she felt instinctively on her guard. Their relationship had been on a tentative footing for the last four years. "It's good to see you, Mother. Couldn't Bill take time away from work and join you?"

"Poor Bill is strictly a land animal. I couldn't coax him onto an airplane if I tickled him with mink mittens. Us girls will have to make our way in the big city as best we can, right, Margaret?"

Margaret's lips twisted into the shape of a crowbar, demolition end up. "You're the one who said he'd be useless."

These two women don't inhabit the same planet, thought Dinah. What conceivable circumstance had brought them together? She held out her arms to Margaret. "Long time, no see, Margaret. How are you?"

"Lousy." She waved Dinah off. "I won't hug you. I caught a cold on that damned flying petri dish. They ought to quarantine the snufflers and coughers in the rear of the plane. You pay a thousand dollars for a ticket and they throw in a passel of crying babies and a case of the flu for free." Her breath smelled faintly of gin and her voice was scratchy.

"Great heavenly days," said Swan. "I can't believe it's been over a year since I saw you." She held Dinah at arm's length and studied her face. "I expect you're wonderin' why Margaret and I buried the hatchet, and what gave us the notion to come to Germany."

"I admit I was surprised by your call." Blown bang away would have been a more accurate description. Forty years ago, Cleon Dobbs had divorced Margaret to marry Swan, and the two women had cordially hated each other ever since.

Margaret said, "Of course, we wanted to spend some time with you and meet your new boyfriend, but I confess we have other fish to fry."

Swan hooked an arm through Dinah's and began walking. "Let's collect our bags, shall we?"

It wasn't much of a walk. The baggage carousel was just a few feet beyond the customs booth.

"What fish?" asked Dinah. "What is this detective job you mentioned?"

Her mother gave her hand a little squeeze. "We'll tell you all about it when we get home to your apartment. I can't wait to meet your beau."

"Unfortunately, Thor isn't in the city." Dinah now thanked God he had been called away to Oslo. An impromptu dive into her family shark pool would give him the bends. But if her luck held, Swan and Margaret would be off to Paris or Madrid by the time he returned.

Margaret frowned and blew her nose. "Smart girl. You've always known how to clear the tracks when you see a train coming."

Swan smiled one of her enigmatic smiles. "Mercy, this is a little bitty airport for a big city, isn't it? Our bags are here already."

Dinah helped them load their suitcases onto a trolley and they proceeded to the parking lot through a mizzling rain. She should have remembered to bring umbrellas. Margaret appeared to take the elements in stride, but Swan brought out a plastic rain bonnet and tied it under her chin. Dinah searched for clues in their body language and facial expressions. But Margaret was as tight-lipped and self-contained as a clam and Swan was unreadable, as always. She kept up a steady patter—the awful fodder the airline had served them, the dreadful airport security checks, "and some of the stewardesses are boys. Can you believe it?"

"They're called flight attendants, Mom."

"And the way the passengers dressed. Not a shred of glamour. One man wore pajama bottoms and bedroom slippers."

"A lot has changed since nineteen sixty-nine," said Dinah as they arrived at the car. She popped the trunk, hoisted her mother's heavy, wheelless bag and slid it in. "Most suitcases today have wheels, for example."

"I've seen them. But those big ol' handles take up so much room. I can fit a lot more outfits in my old-fashioned American Tourister. I used it many times during the seventies. Cleon took me to Rome and Paris for our honeymoon."

Margaret's eyes narrowed, but she didn't comment. Maybe she had finally conquered her jealousy, or maybe she was reluctant to speak ill of the man she'd killed. She collapsed the handle of her rolling Pullman and swung it into the trunk next to Swan's. "Is the weather always this raw in September?"

"It's not that cold," said Dinah, feeling the need to defend her new turf. "I finished my dig in Turkey at the end of August and it was sweltering. The cool weather is a relief." She slammed the trunk lid closed while Swan automatically settled herself in the front seat. Margaret climbed into the back. Dinah took the driver's seat, untangled the straps of her mother's handbag from around the gearshift, and checked the rearview mirror. "Fasten your seatbelt, Margaret."

"Damn nuisance. What's the point? We're all going to die one way or another." She pulled the belt across her broad bosom and stabbed it into the fitting. "This car's no bigger than a matchbox. Don't the people who design airplanes and cars know we have legs?"

Swan scooted the front passenger seat forward. "Is that better?"

"A little. Is there a heater?"

Dinah started the engine and turned on the headlights. It wasn't cold enough for heat, but she turned that on, too. Margaret exuded a bitterness that lowered the ambient temperature like a block of dry ice. She had never been a bright-sider, but she hadn't sounded this morbid when she was in jail awaiting trial. And what had she meant about having other fish to fry?

The rain was coming harder. Dinah turned the windshield wipers a notch faster and waited for the climate control to dispel the interior fog. "Don't keep me in suspense, Margaret. What brought you and Mom all the way from South Georgia to Berlin?"

"We need you to help us track down a tax cheat."

"What?" Dinah let out a startled laugh. "Somebody from Georgia?"

"A German."

"What does someone who cheats on his taxes in Germany have to do with you?"

"Cleon cheated your mother and me out of at least two million dollars we didn't know he had when we divorced him and he dragged both of us through hell. This German Judas that we're after was his accomplice. He's got money that by rights belongs to us."

Dinah had been on tenterhooks all day and she couldn't stifle her irritation. "Come on, Margaret. Cleon left you some money and anyhow, by law, you're not entitled to any of his other assets, let alone money he entrusted to a third party."

She sniffed. "There are more important things than the law. Who knows that better than you? You've been sitting on Cleon's illegal drug money for the last four years."

Dinah ground the gears as she shoved the stick into reverse and jerked the Golf out of the parking space.

"For goodness' sake," said Swan. "You've gone and upset her, Margaret. You should have waited until after we've kicked off our shoes and had a nice glass of merlot. She probably hasn't told her young man about that drug money yet. Didn't you tell me he was in some branch of law enforcement, baby?"

Dinah's stomach took a roller-coaster plunge. Was that an expression of concern or an implied threat? Her fingers clenched the steering wheel as the implications sizzled through her brain.

Swan didn't wait for an answer. She chattered on, seemingly oblivious. "Your brother Lucien sent you a sweet little watercolor of the pier on Cumberland Island that he painted for your new home and I smuggled a jar of your favorite kudzu honey past the TSA guards."

"How'd you do that?"

"I showed it to a young man and asked very politely if he could please let me through with it. He apologized like a gentleman and put it in a barrel on the far side of that machine that takes naked pictures and when I walked through and saw his head was turned, I grabbed the jar back and put it in my carry-on."

"You could've landed yourself in trouble, Mom."

"But I didn't. And I brought you something else. I've decided it's time to pass on your grandmother's sapphire pendant. She always wanted you to have it."

"It's no use trying to inveigle the girl with honey and geegaws, Swan. She's no fool."

Swan sighed. "It's sad to think everybody's some kind of an inveigler, Margaret."

"Sad, but true." Margaret blew her nose as if to trumpet her contempt.

And I'm in the company of two of the best, thought Dinah. If she could, she would put them out on the side of the road and make a break for it. But blood and history held her. She was tied to these women, and to the ghost of Cleon Dobbs, like a tin can to the bumper of a speeding getaway car. She could imagine cutting the cord, but in the crunch, she couldn't go through with it. Instead, she bottled her anger and followed the signs out of the airport on the Zugfahrt Zum Flughafen.

When she had nosed the Golf safely onto the road and reached cruising speed, she took a deep breath and asked, "Who is this alleged tax cheat and how did you find out about him?"

# Chapter Three

Dinah retraced her route, doglegging onto Tegeler Weg, a four-lane highway divided by a median. The now-bucketing rain obscured visibility, but traffic didn't slow. Cars slalomed in and out of their lanes like Olympic racers as brake lights flashed and horns blared. Driving in Berlin was not for the faint of heart even in good weather, and this rain turned the road into an obstacle course. If she could make it back to Bismarckstrasse, she could wend her way across to the Tiergarten and from there, she knew the way home.

Thor had leased a townhouse in an upscale neighborhood near Hausvogteiplatz in the central part of the city, the Mitte. The owner had painted their unit lavender, which made her feel a shade conspicuous, but the location was convenient to the Norwegian Embassy and within walking distance to Humboldt University on Unter den Linden. Proximity to the Tiergarten, a magnificent park with miles of walking paths, was an added bonus.

The car in front of her braked and she took the slowdown as an opportunity to elicit a bit more information. "Who is this man you want to find, Mom? Who was he to Uncle Cleon?"

"Don't let's talk about it until everyone is bright and fresh in the morning."

Dinah didn't expect a refreshing sleep, or any sleep at all, for that matter. But her mother refused to elaborate and there was nothing she could do but stew. She felt cornered, like a mouse without a bolt hole. Her thoughts darted every which way. She had no idea how much Swan had known about Cleon's crimes while they were married. She had always claimed ignorance. But truth-telling didn't run rampant in Dinah's family. Everyone she'd ever loved lied, except maybe Thor. He'd bent the truth once when he neglected to inform her that he was working undercover in Greece. But that was a matter of national security. He'd had no choice. In personal matters he was honest almost to a fault. He would freak if he found out that she had inherited one of the last numbered bank accounts in the world, a financial dinosaur built on the sale of illegal drugs.

Some people aspire to crime. Some have crime thrust upon them. Dinah considered herself to be in the second category. She hadn't wanted to come into possession of a pile of dirty money. She hadn't wanted to be stuck with a dead drug lord's millions or become his posthumous accessory-after-the-fact. But Cleon had held a gun to her head. Literally. He had pointed a gun and reeled off a summary of his sins against the world, against her, against his ex-wives and their grown children, and against his current wife and her young children. To spite them all, he had exhausted his legitimate assets. There was nothing left but a nefarious bank account in Panama and if Dinah didn't assume control of it, his minor children would be out in the cold, reduced to rags. He had stated his terms and then he'd turned the gun on himself. Ironically, he didn't have the guts to pull the trigger. Margaret had done that for him.

When he was dead and his betrayals revealed, Dinah felt bound to do what she could for the sake of the people he screwed. She had traveled to Panama, met with Cleon's shady "personal banker," showed him the number and code Cleon had given her, and withdrawn money to pay for Margaret's defense lawyers. No questions asked. Thereafter, she periodically took out money for the ongoing needs of his children. She had never spent a penny on herself, although she'd been tempted once or twice. She would gladly have washed her hands of it if she could. If she explained the situation to Thor in that way, would he understand? Somehow, she didn't think so. He was as incorruptible as salt. He would never allow himself to be maneuvered into an illegal bind.

The jam up ahead cleared suddenly and traffic spurted ahead. A bus in the left-hand lane sloshed a cascade of dirty water across the windshield. She gave it a couple of squirts of washer fluid and boosted the wiper speed.

"I'll bet you're a sensation here in Berlin," said Swan. "The Germans are positively obsessed with us Injuns."

Dinah had a master's degree in sociocultural anthropology and zero teaching experience. But no one at Humboldt University had alluded to her ancestry and she attributed the offer to teach a survey course in Native American cultures to Thor's connections. She said, "I haven't met anyone who's obsessed."

"Well, I have. Online. You could've knocked me over with a feather." She laughed and wiggled two fingers over her head. "It seems there are thousands of Indian clubs. A man named Florian Farber who calls himself Thunder Moon found my name in the Seminole tribal registry and asked me to friend him on Facebook. He collects 'friends' from every native tribe in America. I'm his first Seminole, but the main interest over here is in the Western tribes. Apaches and Comanches."

"Weird," said Dinah.

"A little. But Florian is so enthusiastic you can't help but like him. He and his club hold powwows in the woods every summer. He posts pictures of their parties on the Internet, everybody with painted faces and animal skins dancing around a fire whoopin' like in an old Western movie. It's the funniest thing."

"Sick," Margaret croaked from the backseat.

Dinah didn't know if she was referring to the whooping German Indians or herself. "Should I take you to a pharmacy, Margaret? Most Germans speak some English. They could tell you what medicine you should take."

"All I need is a stiff nightcap and a soft bed to stretch out on."

"We'll be home soon. I booked you into a bed and breakfast that's practically next door to our apartment."

Swan looked hurt. "We can't stay with you?"

"You'll be more comfortable at the Gasthaus Wunderbar. Friendly as you and Margaret have become, I didn't think you'd want to share a bed. And our sofa is hard and short, more of a loveseat really."

"I don't care where we sleep as long as we get there soon," said Margaret.

Swan swiveled her head and recited. "'Don't Care was made to care; Don't Care was hung; Don't Care was put in a pot and boiled till she was done.'"

"What's that supposed to mean?" asked Margaret.

"Nothin' at all. It's just a silly verse about caring."

Swan had a rhyme for every occasion. Dinah knew that the "silly verse" was a not-so-oblique gibe at her. For her lack of hospitality. For throwing cold water on their cockamamie plan to track down one of Cleon's accomplices. For not caring. She might have pointed out that caring was a two-way street. But reasoning with Swan was like jousting with smoke. She changed the subject. "Do you plan to meet Mr. Thunder Moon, aka Farber, while you're in the country?"

"I do. He invited me to one of their powwows. I told him my daughter is a cultural anthropologist who knows simply everything there is to know about native rituals and beliefs. I promised I'd bring you along to—"

Something whammed against the left rear of the Golf, knocking it sideways. Swan screamed and a loud crack exploded in Dinah's ears. She gripped the wheel and steered the car back into its lane, but a black hulk in her blind spot rammed them again. She couldn't correct and swerved into a concrete guardrail. The right fender and doors scraped along the rail, metal screaking. Dinah stood on the brakes and the Golf skidded to a stop. The red taillights of the car that hit them surged away in the left lane and disappeared.

Heart racing, Dinah reached for her mother. "Are you all right?"

"Yes. Just scared."

"Me, too." She turned on the overhead light and looked in the backseat. "Margaret?"

"I think so, except I've got a lap full of glass pebbles from the broken window." She unbuckled her seatbelt and tried to open the rear door, but it was too close to the guardrail. She started to brush off the glass with her hand.

"You'll cut yourself," said Dinah. "There's a snowbrush under your seat."

Margaret found the brush and swept the rubble off her slacks onto the floor. Dinah squinted through the downpour and took stock. They were in the middle of a bridge over one of Berlin's many canals. She looked for an emergency phone box. They appeared at intervals all along the autobahns, but apparently not here. A blur of red lights whizzed past them. Where was a cop when you needed one? She took out her mobile.

"What are you doing?" Swan asked.

"Calling the police."

"Do we really need to bother the police?"

Dinah stared at her mother in disbelief. "Some lunatic tried to run us off the road, twice, and then fled the scene. Of course, we need to *bother* the police."

"They won't catch him. He's already ten miles gone by now."

The whoosh of traffic made the Golf shimmy and wind rushing through the broken rear window whipped Dinah's hair across her face. Since she'd been in Germany, she hadn't seen a single jaywalker or litterbug, and while Berlin drivers were aggressive, they adhered to the rules of the road and honked when others did not. This was bizarre. She dialed 1-1-0, the police emergency number, and asked for assistance in English. The dispatcher responded fluently, asked her location, and advised her to wait for help.

Dinah hung up and turned on the emergency blinker. "It shouldn't be long."

Margaret sneezed explosively and Swan jumped.

Dinah took off her sweater and handed it over the seat. "Put this around your shoulders and move away from the window so you don't get damp."

"Thanks." She blew her nose and scooched into the middle seat. "Has your boyfriend been in any shoot-outs lately?"

"What?" Dinah turned around.

"Something's punched a hole in the seatback." She pointed the snowbrush at a dark spot in the upholstery of the seat behind Dinah. "Looks like a bullet hole to me."

# Chapter Four

It was after midnight when Dinah got back to the apartment. Her hand shook as she unlocked the door and flipped on the light. She closed the door and leaned her back against it. Until a few hours ago, her life had been a bowl of cherries—a loving partner, a paying job doing work she enjoyed, and the unprecedented luxury of a beautiful apartment. She had read Nassim Taleb's theory of "black swans," impossible-to-predict events of extreme magnitude and monumental consequences. Now she had a flesh-and-blood Swan to contend with, and all the leading indicators suggested that her good luck was about to be swept away in a tsunami of black secrets.

She threw her purse on the foyer table and walked into the living room. Aphrodite had hawked up a hair ball on the new rug. Aphrodite was the semi-feral kitten that K.D., Cleon's seventeen-year-old daughter, had rescued from a dumpster in Greece, brought to Berlin, and foisted off on Dinah when she decided to return to Georgia. K.D. and her twin brother were co-beneficiaries of Cleon's money. If their mother could be trusted not to squander it all at once and arouse the feds' suspicion, Dinah would sign over control of the account to her with pleasure. At least that's what she'd told herself she'd do. Just now, it sounded like a lame excuse for doing nothing.

She cleaned up Aphrodite's mess, sat down at the kitchen table, took out her mobile and listened to her voice mail.

"*Hi, kjære.* I got your text. Hope your mother arrived safely. I'll try to finish my meetings early and be home on Saturday night. I'm looking forward to meeting her and your friend, Margaret. If your mother tells half as many funny stories as you do, I know I'll like her."

Oh, she's a regular riot, thought Dinah. The computer voice asked if she would like to replay, erase, or save the message in the archives. She erased it and powered off, wondering if there was an idiom in Norwegian that meant, "love me, love my dog." She couldn't expect Thor to understand or accept her dysfunctional, criminally minded clan. One night, flush with wine and in an expansive mood, she had tried to diagram her family tree for him, but he'd gotten lost in the multiple divorces and unorthodox alliances. Cleon Dobbs was at the center of the web. A folksy country lawyer with a brilliant mind and a wry sense of humor, he was still the most charismatic man she'd ever met.

From the day her father died when she was ten years old, Cleon had been like a surrogate father to her. He had been in love with her mother and seemed to love Dinah by extension. He'd showered her with books and trips and paid her way through college. Through the power of money and personal magnetism, he exerted control over his ex-wives and their children even after he took a new young wife and started a third family. He pulled strings and pushed buttons and manipulated them all shamelessly in order to get his way. Dinah had never known him to be deliberately cruel or evil. The truth crashed in on her four years ago when she found out that he had operated a drug-smuggling ring for more than two decades and that, with malice aforethought, he had caused the death of her father.

She had grilled Swan about her knowledge of Cleon's drug crimes, but she had never asked if Swan knew that Cleon killed Hart Pelerin in the hope of winning her back. The question haunted Dinah, but somehow she couldn't bring herself to ask. If Swan had known and done nothing, it would make her complicit and Dinah didn't think she could adapt to so stark a recasting of her mother's image. Willful ignorance didn't excuse

Swan, but it was a failing Dinah understood. She kicked herself every time she let the hard question slide, but she saw Swan rarely. Especially since she'd met Thor, she'd been preoccupied with happier thoughts and anyway, Cleon had done too much already to blight her life and undermine her sense of trust. Of course the final monkey wrench he had thrown into her life was the money.

He said she was the only one he trusted, the only one who had the common sense to know what to do with it. Ha! The fact that she'd done his bidding in the first place demonstrated a spectacular lack of common sense, and the fact that she'd failed to report it after four years, bordered on idiocy. Maybe the IRS would have granted her amnesty, awarded his children enough money to see them through college, even given her a reward. Well, it was too late now. She couldn't expect forgiveness from the government or from Thor. He had made allowances for a lot of her kinks. A hidden cache of drug money would be one kink too many for an officer in the Norwegian Criminal Investigative Service.

The cuckoo popped out of its house and hooted one o'clock. She'd gotten used to the ridiculous thing, but she didn't like it. Berlin wasn't the natural habitat of the cuckoo clock, but Thor had found it in a Christmas specialty store on the Kurfürstendamm and thought it would be a hilarious addition to their German love nest. Tonight, in particular, the humor didn't come through.

She poured herself a glass of wine and went into the spare bedroom. Since K.D. had changed her mind and gone home, she and Thor had converted it into an office with their desks placed against opposite walls. Thor's desk was neat and organized, Dinah's piled high with reference books and notes on tribal customs and the power of taboos. Her first class wasn't scheduled until next Tuesday, a week away. Today was just Tuesday…well, Wednesday at one a.m. She had six days to prepare, give or take. She didn't like to think what outlay of time and energy might be required to sort out Swan and Margaret, and getting the

Golf repaired would eat into her time, as well as her finances. Thor usually drove an Embassy loaner when he was in town. She hoped she could get the Golf hammered back into shape and repainted without him seeing the damage.

As it was a hit-and-run and she hadn't gotten the license plate number, there was nothing the police could do but file a report. The incident seemed to perplex them. Germany had its share of gun violence and shootings, but drive-bys were a rarity. The investigating officers had extracted the bullet and said they'd be in touch if additional information turned up, but they didn't sound optimistic. They could only speculate that he must have been *übergeschnappt*, a crazy Italian or a Turk driving under the influence of alcohol.

Dinah wasn't at all sure the driver was crazy or drunk. What if he had been aiming at Swan and Margaret? That story about the tax cheat they had come to find—had they contacted him? Did he know when and where they would arrive? What if he had followed them from the airport? Their trip made no sense unless they had some idea of his whereabouts. It occurred to her that there might be a connection between the man they were after and the powwow Swan had mentioned. She cleared off a spot to set her wineglass, sat down at her computer, and logged on.

The name Florian Farber, the man who collected Indian friends, had a Facebook page, but she couldn't access it. She expanded her search to "American Indians and Germany." The deluge of information astonished her. Evidently, Germans really were infatuated with American Indians. There were clubs, Wild West shows, books, magazines, study programs, dozens of powwows, and a profusion of Indian-inspired products for sale. Deerskin moccasins, turquoise jewelry, buffalo heads, sheets and towels printed with tribal symbols, and "authentic" hand-woven blankets. She put aside thoughts about the car attack and immersed herself in the Indian phenomenon.

It all began with a German writer named Karl May. Between 1865 and 1874, while serving time in prison for theft and fraud, May read a lot of travel books about the American West and fantasized about its wide-open spaces and untamed landscape. He read James Fenimore Cooper's *Leatherstocking Tales* and adopted a romantic view of the red man. After his release, May published a number of novels that portrayed Indians as wise and compassionate people, innately noble and courageous, yet constantly assailed by enemies and intruders intent upon stealing their land. He wore a necklace of bear teeth and claimed that he had lived among the Indians of the Western Plains. As it turned out, he was a prodigious liar or, as some believed, a victim of associative personality disorder. He didn't visit America until 1908, and never made it farther west than Massachusetts, but his books created the popular image of America in the minds of Germans and made "playing Indian" a deeply ingrained part of German culture.

Despite May's admitted fabrications, his novels sold over a hundred million copies and his fictional Apache Chief Winnetou became synonymous with virtue and heroism. In fact, he remained the quintessential German hero. According to what she was reading, this made-up Apache symbolized the very heart and soul of German identity. Over the years, his devotees had included Albert Einstein, Albert Schweitzer, Franz Kafka, and Adolph Hitler, who issued copies of May's books to his troops for moral guidance in spite of Winnetou's non-Aryan roots and pacifist leanings.

Dinah could see that she had a good deal of cultural boning-up to do. It crossed her mind that the offer to teach at Humboldt University might have had more to do with her Seminole cheekbones than Thor's connections or her sketchy credentials.

Aphrodite emitted a wild, direful yowl. Dinah remembered that she hadn't filled her food bowl this morning. She polished off her wine and scudded back through the living room. Aphrodite was lying on her side, pawing at something under the door. Dinah hoped it wasn't a spider. She had been extra skittish since last week when a local supermarket descried a venomous Brazilian arachnid crawling out of a crate of bananas. The free exchange of poisonous insects was an aspect of globalization she disliked.

"Quiet, cat. It's the wee hours."

In the kitchen pantry she found a can of tuna, peeled off the lid, and dumped it into the cat's bowl. "Here, kitty. Come and get it." She ticked her fingernails on the side of the bowl. "Come on, kitty, kitty." She fanned a hand over the tuna to spread the aroma.

Aphrodite didn't respond. She kept yowling and gnarring and pawing under the front door. Dinah set the bowl on the counter, folded a newspaper, and tried to shoo her toward the kitchen. If this were a normal cat, she would simply scoop her up and plop her down in front of her food. But Aphrodite had claws like needles and she didn't scruple at biting the hands that fed her.

What was she playing with anyway? It looked like...she took a step back...a lock of human hair.

She swatted Aphrodite with the newspaper. The cat sprang to her feet and streaked into the kitchen. Dinah bent close to look at the snarled strands of black. Aphrodite had raked them through the gap under the door, but couldn't pull them free. Dinah touched her fingers to the tangled hair, then pinched up a tuft and tugged. It was attached to something.

Was someone lying outside the door? Jesus, Joseph, and Mary. The hair was the same color as her mother's.

She fumbled with the lock and yanked open the door. Spread-eagled at her feet was a doll dressed in a ruffled cape and patchwork skirt, the traditional garb of Seminole women since the 1920s. Someone had jabbed a knife into its midsection.

She peered down the hall, which was empty, then knelt and picked up the doll. It wasn't like the palmetto dolls the Seminoles made and sold to tourists in Florida. The body was cloth, the head hard plastic with lifelike hair and the wide, fixed stare of a belladonna victim. It was an effigy of an Indian woman. Her mother?

She flung the door shut with a bang and ran to her phone. Hands trembling, she dialed her mother's cell.

On the fifth ring, a sleepy voice said, "Hey, baby. Is it time for breakfast already?"

# Chapter Five

"What have you gotten yourself into, Mom?"

"Don't scold so, honey. Here. Drink some of this delicious coffee and calm yourself." She poured a bit of fresh coffee into Dinah's cup, emptied half a pitcher of cream into her own, and reclined against a plump pink chair pillow. She wore a perfectly pressed white cotton blouse, smartly creased tan trousers, and an exasperating smile.

They were eating breakfast in the dining nook of the Gasthaus Wunderbar, which overlooked a tree-lined park equipped with children's slides and play tunnels. The sky was overcast, but young mothers pushed a caravan of baby strollers along the sidewalk and a steady stream of joggers passed by. They were probably training for the annual BMW Berlin Marathon at the end of the month. Thor had registered and planned to run unless the job interfered, which now seemed likely.

"How do you suppose they make their coffee taste so good?" Swan asked.

"It just tastes hot to me," said Margaret. Her clothes hung on her like a dipped flag and she looked as if she'd slept as poorly as Dinah. She seemed more interested in the newspaper than the food. "I see here that hunters in Texas killed an eight hundred-pound gator last week. Why is what happens in Texas news here?"

Swan knitted her brows. "I told you, the Germans love the Wild West, though I'd think they'd be more interested in rattlesnakes and Indian paint ponies than gators. However can you read that teeny-weeny print?"

Margaret pushed her glasses up her nose and folded the paper. "You could read it if you weren't too vain to wear glasses."

"I wear glasses when there's something worth my while to read about."

Their table was laden with *Schlackwurst, Bratwurst,* and *Weisswurst,* a variety of cheeses, boiled eggs, a basket of freshly baked bread from the bakery next door, and three jars of jam.

Swan sliced and buttered a roll. "What did our hostess call these little doohickeys? Is this the *Dinkelbrot* or the *Brotchen?* It smells divine."

"None of your beating about the bush, Mom. My apartment's just across the street, but I walked ten blocks out of my way looking over my shoulder to be sure I wasn't followed. Every time a man passes the window, I jump. I need answers."

Margaret thwacked an egg with the side of her fork and began to flake off the shell. "Tell her, Swan. If you don't, I will."

"Y'all sure are grouchy this mornin'."

Dinah took a breath and reined in her temper. "I get that way when I think somebody's trying to kill me. Or the people I care about. I get even grouchier when the people I care about are trying to pull the wool over my eyes." She pulled the doll out of her purse by one leg and slapped it down on the table. She had removed the knife and bagged it to preserve any possible fingerprints. "Somebody left this at my door with a knife stuck in it. What do you think the message is?"

"Why, that tacky thing looks nothing at all like a Seminole woman," said Swan. "The stuffing's not even palmetto."

"Stop being a manic digressive, Mom. Spit it out. Is the man that you're chasing…chasing you?"

"What makes you think one of those skinheads we're always hearing about didn't drop the thing at your door?"

"Because she's got a brain," said Margaret. "Tell her about Hess."

"Well." Swan steepled her fingers under her chin, a customary prelude to any explanation she found difficult. "Reiner Hess was one of Cleon's cronies, very high up the ladder, some sort of a lawyer like Cleon."

"And like Cleon, he was a lying sack of shit," added Margaret.

"I want to hear this from Mom, Margaret. Let her talk."

"It's kind of complicated," said Swan. "An employee of a Swiss bank sold the Germans a CD containing the names of people who own secret accounts, and Reiner Hess was one of them. The German authorities raided hundreds of houses belonging to the people on the list, but when they got to Reiner's, he'd flown the coop."

"How did you learn all this? Surely the Germans didn't publish the names before they had completed their investigation."

"Swan has a source," said Margaret. "One of the studs on her string of ponies."

Dinah glared. "Zip it, Margaret."

Swan flicked a crumb off the tablecloth and spoke only to Dinah. "You remember Lenzie, don't you, honey?"

"The one before Bill. Italian or Swiss."

"Swiss Italian. We're still on friendly terms and stay in touch. When Lenzie left Georgia, he moved back to Switzerland and socked his money away in a real safe bank in Bern where one of his buddies works. His buddy happened to mention he had another client, a German lawyer, who used to live in the U.S., in Georgia."

"Reiner Hess," said Dinah.

"Uh-huh. They gossiped a bit, like men do, you know. And this buddy told him that somebody at the bank told *him* that Reiner's name was *out there* as a tax dodger."

"So much for the myth of Swiss banking secrecy," said Dinah.

Margaret humphed. "I wouldn't be too sure about Panamanian secrecy. A hacker got into their database and exposed a slew of Germans with offshore accounts there. You'd best be on your toes, Dinah."

Swan nodded. "The Germans are just bearcats about taxes."

"Anyway," said Margaret, "I bet it was Lenzie's buddy who sold them that CD."

Swan continued. "Soon after I talked with Lenzie, Florian sent me a digital picture album of his last powwow. Lo and behold, who did I see got-up in a buffalo horn headdress and wavin' a tomahawk? Reiner Hess, big as life."

"I still don't understand," said Dinah. "Even if the man was in cahoots with Cleon, even if he cheated the Federal Republic of Germany, why do you think he owes you anything?" She bored deep into her mother's eyes. "You weren't part of Cleon's drug operation, were you?"

"I've answered that question before, Dinah. I was as shocked as you were. Margaret and I trusted Cleon just like you did. But that didn't stop the government from suspectin' us. IRS agents, DEA agents, FBI agents. Why, even today, every time I look out the front door, another one's on the porch with a briefcase and a list of questions. What's that old saying? The wife's the last to know? Well, it's true, but the feds have never believed me."

Dinah wanted to believe her. Swan had been a benign and indulgent parent, abstracted in a fuzzy, endearing way. Maybe she had been blissfully unaware of her first husband's crimes, but Dinah still had doubts. "Didn't you ever ask Cleon how a lawyer from Needmore, Georgia, wound up making such an obscene amount of money?"

"After he affiliated with that big Atlanta firm, his practice became international. All of his partners made scads of money and he made plenty of legitimate money, if you can call what lawyers do legitimate. Anyhow, Cleon handled our finances. I never asked for an accounting. How about you, Margaret?"

Margaret's left eyebrow spiked up. "I asked for one when he filed for a divorce to marry you. If he had money then, he kept it hidden from me and my attorney."

Swan made a sympathetic face. "He left you rather a lot in the end, Margaret."

"It took Dinah weeks to hunt it down in Panama and when I got it, I had to spend it all on defense lawyers."

"It would be drawin' interest today if you hadn't shot Cleon dead and got yourself arrested."

Margaret's jaws worked as if she were grinding rocks, but she held herself in.

Swan poured hot coffee all around and they sipped in silence for a minute. Dinah wished she'd taken notes. This Hess business sounded like an impossible muddle, and the news that a Panamanian bank had been hacked made her stomach roil.

The fire in Margaret's eyes cooled and Swan went on with her story. "I hate to be vulgar, but the fact is, Margaret and I need money. Poor Bill lost most of his retirement savings after the real estate market collapsed, and Margaret wants to get on with her life, do nice things for herself and her grandchildren. Reiner squirreled away millions, most of which he and Cleon made from their drug deals, which Margaret and I knew nothing about. How they made the money isn't important anymore. We want a share and Reiner's not going to scare us off."

"Why do you need money so desperately, Mom? Are you sick? Is Lucien or Bill sick? Does somebody need an organ transplant?"

"No, no. Nothing like that. Of course, your Aunt Shelly catches everything that goes around. The last was the shingles, I think. And Bill's mama is crippled up pretty bad with arthur-itis. But then, she's ninety-two. Other than that, we're hale and hearty."

So, then, this was about greed and some warped sense of entitlement. "Why haven't you hit me up for a cut of the money Cleon left me to dole out to his kids?"

"Because they need every dollar of help it will buy them," said Swan.

"No kidding," agreed Margaret. "Shrinks don't come cheap. The boy will probably wind up in the pen, but the girl, K.D., might yet be salvaged. She's probably got that PTSD syndrome. If I have any regret, it's that she had to go through the ordeal of her daddy being killed."

"Wasn't she tagging around Greece with you this summer?" asked Swan.

"Yes. Thor and I both became fond of K.D. She adored her father and she's wrestling with the knowledge that he wasn't what she thought he was. She's kind of a hard case, but since the summer she's been trending toward a healthier attitude. We invited her to live with us in Berlin for a few months, but she decided to go home and finish high school."

"Thor is either a saint or a fool," said Margaret, and sneezed into a handkerchief.

Swan patted Dinah's hand. "We know you wouldn't take a dime of the kids' money for yourself, honey. And neither would we. Goodness gracious, what kind of heartless monsters do you think we are?"

"Heart's got nothing to do with it," said Margaret. "That Panama money's radioactive. I wouldn't want the risk. Like Swan says, we still have feds nosing around our doors. It surprises me you haven't been caught, Dinah."

Swan dissected a boiled egg as tenderly as if it might hold a living chick. "Just out of curiosity, how much is in the account now?"

"Something over two million."

"That much." Her eyes went dreamy and crinkled at the corners.

Dinah forced a smile. Conversations with her mother had a tendency to leave her feeling seasick. She thought she could make out pieces of the truth bobbing here and there like flotsam, but it was hard to construct a narrative with all the froth foaming in between. "Did you warn Hess that you were coming to Berlin?"

"Not directly," said Swan. "We relied on Florian to tell him."

"You *wanted* Hess to know?"

"Can't negotiate with somebody if he's not around to negotiate," said Margaret.

Dinah massaged her temples. Why would Hess risk coming out of hiding to intimidate two elderly American women with no legal claim to his money? Why did they think he would part with a single Euro? She cut to the crux. "What possible reason would Hess have to shoot at you or try to scare you off?"

"One of those little computer doodads that store data," said Swan. "What did you call it, Margaret?"

"A thumb drive."

"Cleon called it an insurance policy," said Swan. "He said if I ever needed anything at all, I should show it to Hess and he'd be more than glad to help. I tucked it away in a box and forgot about it 'til I found out Reiner was sittin' on a pile of money."

"What's on this thumb drive?"

"Enough to have him extradited to the U.S. and charged with the murder of two federal agents."

"Jerusalem! Are you batshit crazy? Blackmail is a crime and even if it weren't, you can't threaten a double murderer."

Swan made a chastening little moue. "We're not gonna *threaten* him, honey. We'll negotiate a fair price for the thumb drive and be on our merry way."

Maybe she really was insane. She had made a career out of being fey and charmingly inscrutable, but insanity would explain her equally well. "Mother, you can't go through with this plan. It's cockeyed, it's criminal, and it's dangerous. You saw what happened last night. You have to pack your bags and hop the next plane home before you get yourselves killed."

"You needn't worry about us. What was that thing you said we had, Margaret?"

"A dead man's switch. If anything happens to us, the proof will automatically be sent to the Drug Enforcement Agency. We've got everything figured out, Dinah. All you have to do is put us on the right train. The subway map in our Frommer's guide looks confusing as a basket of two-headed snakes. God's sakes, how do people decide which direction to go?"

# Chapter Six

Dinah stuffed the doll back in her purse and, feeling slightly nauseated, went downstairs to the *toiletten*. The conversation she'd just had was an object lesson in the anthropology of lying. She felt fated, born into a cult where the only certainty was the knowledge that everyone lied, but inconsistently. Occasionally they told the truth so you could never know for sure. Margaret didn't give off any signals, but her mother transmitted a highly dubious vibe. The question was whether they were in imminent physical danger from this Hess character and, if so, what to do about it. The answer to all of her what-to-do's lately had been to call Thor. Her queasiness passed and she sat down in a rickety wicker chair in front of the basin, took out her cell, and dialed his number.

"Ramberg."

"Hey, Ramberg, I hope I didn't catch you in the middle of dismantling a bomb or foiling a plot for world domination."

He laughed. "I'm waiting for the Kenyan ambassador to get off the phone so I can take him to lunch."

The reassuring sound of his voice lifted her spirits immediately. "I miss you, Thor. I feel like I've fallen down the rabbit hole and you're my lifeline to reality."

"You sound miserable. What's wrong?"

"Me, my family, my whole life."

"Tell me."

And in that moment, she knew that she couldn't. Not yet. Not over the phone. Not the whole truth. She would give him an abbreviated version—the critical facts now and fill in the non-urgent ones later. "The thing is…" she cast about for a way to present "the thing" without emptying the entire bucket of worms. "The thing is, someone may be trying to kill my mother."

"*Kristus*! What happened?"

She described the hit-and-run and the mutilated Indian doll left outside the apartment door. "I've begged her to go home, but she has other…she says she won't."

"But you're all right? She and your friend Margaret are all right? No injuries?"

"Just to the Golf. It's drivable, but the left rear door is smushed and the right side is scratched and dented." She wavered. She didn't want him to overreact and fly home. "The driver of the other car fired a bullet into the Golf."

"*Sheisse!*"

"It didn't come close to anyone," she lied.

"Does your mother know anyone in Berlin? An ex-husband or jilted lover?"

Before they moved in together, Dinah had confided her mother's checkered marital history to Thor. She worried that she had inherited her mother's inability to sustain a long-term commitment, and felt he deserved fair warning. "Mom has a Facebook friend whose hobby is playing cowboys and Indians, and another man who attends the powwows was a business partner of one of her ex-husbands." The nature of Cleon's business was one of the non-urgent details she'd rather omit for the time being.

"Where is the ex-husband now?" asked Thor.

"Dead. He died four years ago."

"Was there a beef between the ex and this partner? Any reason why he'd try to take revenge on your mother?"

"No. I mean, I don't think so."

"I want you to call Jens Lohendorf. He's a detective working out of Directorate Three. I've worked with him once or twice.

He knows Berlin, underbelly and all, and he'll treat the situation seriously. Hold on. I'll give you his number." There was a pause.

Dinah fidgeted. How seriously did she want the situation treated?

"Here it is." He read off the number. "You're sure you're all right? Say the word and I'll come home this afternoon, *kjære*."

"No. The police are already involved. They think the driver was a drunk and the doll was probably some harmless initiation rite, put there by one of the Facebook Indians." Had she left the impression that she'd reported the doll? That the police thought it was harmless?

Thor wasn't buying it. "Whoever's responsible, the knife wasn't harmless. Give it to Lohendorf. He may be able to lift fingerprints."

"Yes, I will." Another lie. She would toss that knife and forget about it if she could persuade her mother to abandon her scheme and go home. To sic the police on Hess would only stir up questions about his connection to Cleon and, by declension, Cleon's connection to her. She said, "I think the safest thing is to get my mother and Margaret out of town pronto. I'll put them on a train to Paris this afternoon and maybe ballistics can turn up a lead."

"I thought you said they had refused to leave."

"They don't want me to feel slighted if they cut short their visit. They'll leave."

"Okay." His tone was skeptical. "But in the meantime, promise me you'll call Jens."

"I promise." She didn't know what she had expected him to say other than "go to the police." It was the only smart thing to do, for someone with nothing to hide.

He said, "The ambassador's walking out of his office. I'll call you later today."

They swapped a few quick intimacies and said good-bye. She pondered her reflection in the mirror above the basin. How many lies could she tell before she wouldn't be able to look at herself? Before she turned into a dyed-in-the-wool convert to the cult of

Cleon Dobbs? She despised herself for not coming clean with Thor at the start of their affair, but the more she felt for him, the harder it became. The fear of losing him had paralyzed her. But she couldn't carry this guilt any longer. She stood up and, in a determined voice, announced, "I will tell him about that damned dirty money the very next time we talk, so help me God."

The toilet flushed behind the stall door and she nearly jumped out of her skin. The anger she'd been holding back spilled over. She said, "You should be ashamed of yourself," and marched out of the room and up the stairs to have it out with her mother.

Margaret was alone at the table, dabbing at her eyes.

"Are you crying?"

"Damn cold makes my eyes water."

"Where's Mom?"

"She went back to the room. She wants to preen her feathers before we visit her friend, Florian."

Dinah sat down and tore off a piece of *Dinkelbrot*. "It's not like you to do something crazy like this, Margaret. You've always had more sense. More aplomb."

"Aplomb?" She crimped her mouth. "What the hell is that?"

"You know perfectly well what it is. Balance and self-control and—"

She snorted. "Sangfroid? That's what Cleon called it and he didn't mean it in a good way. He meant it literally. Cold blood. As it turned out, I was more cold-blooded than he imagined."

Dinah recalled every detail of that day. The glare of the sun, the roar of the gunshot, the smell of her own fear and Cleon's blood. She said, "He tried to kill himself, but he didn't have the *cojones*. You did him a favor, Margaret."

"The prosecutor said I did it for revenge."

"You had cause for revenge. But I think you did it to help him escape, to get away clean. I think you still loved him. I think you love him even now and that's why you resent my mother."

"Love. What a trap." Margaret covered her face and erupted into a series of violent sneezes. When the fit passed, she said, "At the trial, you testified that he would have shot you if I hadn't shot him first. I appreciated the lie, but you know he would never have hurt you. He loved Swan far too much to hurt one of her cygnets."

Dinah could only marvel that Cleon's sick obsession with Swan still galled Margaret. "I don't know what he'd have done. They say murder gets easier after the first one or two."

"Ya' think?" One corner of her mouth quirked up like a grapefruit knife. "Life is strange. I never thought I'd join forces with your mother to shake down one of Cleon's old gang."

"Are you broke, Margaret? Are things so bad you have to resort to extortion?"

"Bad enough. The benefits from thirty years of teaching school in Echols County, Georgia, are strikingly slim."

"If you're so gung-ho to become an outlaw, you can take control of the Panama money. I'll sign it over to you today. It's a curse, but it's yours if you'll take it. I know you'd be fair to the children. Help me convince my mother to forget this crackbrained idea to blackmail Reiner Hess and it's all yours. Is it a deal?"

"No. That money scares me more than Hess." She pressed a handkerchief to her nose and mopped her eyes. "Swan and I talked this over for a long time before we made up our minds. For every con I thought of, she came up with two pros. If you ask my opinion, I think she has more in mind than Reiner's money."

"What do you mean?"

"She never speaks Bill's name except in pity. Poor Bill this and poor Bill that. He's had some setbacks. I don't know anything about their finances or their marriage, but it wouldn't surprise me if your mama is on the prowl for a new man."

"Hess?" Dinah felt queasy all over again.

"Him, or maybe that Thunder Moon bird. Farber."

Dinah bit her tongue. Swan's track record with men might not comport with the Christian concept of family values, but she wasn't the tramp Margaret made her out to be. In fact, Dinah would bet that her mother had never once had extramarital sex. She was a stickler for marriage, even if the marriages didn't last.

The only reason she'd given for divorcing Cleon was his habit of leaving her alone so often while he traveled on business. Dinah suspected there was more to it than that, but Swan had married Hart Pelerin soon after the divorce. He undoubtedly had a hand in wooing her away from Cleon.

Margaret must have sensed her annoyance. She said, "I shouldn't dis Swan. She paid my way over here and she's trying to help me get back on my feet with a cut of Reiner's money. I'm sorry if I was out of line."

"Forget it." Dinah glanced at her watch. Swan ought to be finished with her primping by now. She dropped the ropes of uneaten *Dinkelbrot* onto her plate and wiped her hands. "Let's go up to your room and discuss some more pros and cons."

They took the elevator to the second floor. Margaret stuck the key card into the slot and opened the door. The curtains were open and the room dappled with splotches of tenuous sunlight. A vase of dahlias rested on the table between two queen beds and the hum of a hairdryer emanated from the bathroom.

"Come out and talk to us, Mom. You're spiffy enough."

She didn't answer and Dinah tapped on the door. "Mom?"

Still no answer.

She turned the knob and peeped inside. The hairdryer lay humming on the side of the basin, but Swan was gone.

# Chapter Seven

Dinah took out the number Thor had given her and opened her phone. She had no choice now. Her mother had been abducted. She said, "It must have been Hess. He had to have taken her out past the front desk. Go ask them, Margaret, while I talk to the police."

"Wait. She left a note. *Gone ahead to meet Florian at his art gallery and run some errands. Y'all don't have to come if you don't want to, but here's the address.*"

It didn't sound like it was written under duress, and Swan was notoriously absentminded. Maybe she just set down the dryer and walked away, negligent as a child. The address she gave was on the Kurfürstenstrasse near Breitscheidplatz, one of the busiest squares in the city.

Dinah stopped off briefly at her apartment, with Margaret on her coattails like a stick-tight. She hid the Indian doll in her bureau and took out the Smith & Wesson snub-nosed revolver that Thor had given her. She stowed it in the center pocket of her shoulder bag and tried again to dissuade Margaret. "You're sick. You should stay inside or you'll catch pneumonia."

"Bring it on. They don't call it the old person's friend for nothing."

"Good grief, Margaret. You should be on Prozac."

They walked to the U-bahn station at Hausvogteiplatz, around the corner from the apartment. At the station entrance,

Dinah reviewed her subway map. She jogged down the stairs to the trains, hoping to lose Margaret in the crowd milling around the tracks, but the woman proved remarkably spry for an old boiler with a head cold. Dinah stuffed a few coins in the ticket dispenser and hopped aboard the train at the last minute. Margaret squeaked through the closing doors in the nick of time, ticketless.

They found seats across from a young couple in soccer-flag T-shirts and cutoffs. They had matching leg tattoos from ankles to knees, stretched earlobes with silver flesh tunnels, and a bottle of beer, which they passed back and forth between them.

"If I'd known you could drink on the train, I'd have brought a traveler," muttered Margaret.

"You can't want a drink at this hour. It's not yet ten."

"I'm still on Georgia time."

As the train gusted through the tunnels beneath the city, Dinah worried the little piece of spray-painted concrete in her pocket, allegedly a chip off the Berlin Wall. Every souvenir shop in the city sold them by the gross. She knew it was fake, but it had a nice indentation for her thumb and she had rubbed it smooth. She rubbed it now and tried to assay how much of what Swan and Margaret had told her was true, and how much delusional nonsense. She thought about her mother striking out on her own in a huge foreign city where she didn't speak the language, to meet a man she'd only met on Facebook—a German who styled himself as Thunder Moon. Was this Thunder Moon a separate manifestation of Swan's insanity, or was he the go-between to Reiner Hess?

The train ground to a halt and the doors slid open. The couple with the beer got off and a platoon of Chinese tourists crammed inside. Margaret sneezed explosively and they covered their mouths and shrank away toward the rear of the car. The doors slid shut; the train gusted on and gathered speed.

Margaret said, "I've been watching how you are with Swan. You're tense as a wire, like you're afraid she'll blurt out something terrible. Maybe something you can't forgive."

"Such as?"

Margaret declined to go out on that particular limb, but ventured onto another. "Do you love her?"

It was a snide question. Backhanded and presumptuous, but painfully on target. Dinah wished she could come back with a resounding yes. The fact that she couldn't, made her feel like a traitor. How could she not love the woman who brought her into this world, who taught her to read and ride a bike, who played piano duets with her and filled her head with songs and *Mother Goose* rhymes and fairy tales? But there was a wall in her heart, love on one side, doubt and dread on the other. The doubts began with Cleon's admission that he had killed her father. Did Swan know and, if she did, when did she know? Dinah couldn't delete the question from her internal hard drive. She was afraid to hear the answer, yet she couldn't come to terms with the past until and unless she did. But however conflicted she might be, her feelings about Swan were none of Margaret's beeswax.

The train slowed as it approached the next station and she stood up. "She's my mother, Margaret. With all the *Sturm und Drang* that implies. And this is our stop."

The knot of Chinese passengers shoved their way out the door ahead of them. Dinah weaved her way through the mob onto the platform and followed the arrows to Kurfürstenstrasse. She heard Margaret huffing behind her, but she didn't look back. She jogged up the stairs to street level and headed toward the central shopping district.

There are almost no old buildings in Berlin. The Allies bombed the city to rubble during World War II and the new Berlin is a mosaic of uber-modern architecture and rampant development. Boom cranes sprout across the skyline like dandelions and the noise of construction is so constant that you cease to notice. One of the more curious sights is the jungle of gigantic pink, yellow, and blue pipes that parallel the streets, snake around corners, climb and loop overhead. At first, Dinah had thought it was some kind of art installation. In fact, it is plumbing. Berlin sits smack in the middle of a swamp and before a new building can be erected, water must be pumped from the foundation pit into the River Spree or one of the canals. Emerging onto Kurfürstenstrasse, they passed under and through a labyrinth of blue pipes.

Rows of shops selling everything from vinyl records and funky hats to designer fashions and elegant jewelry lined both sides of the street. The face of Chancellor Angela Merkel smiled serenely from a large political billboard. The country had trusted her to steer the ship of state for the last eight years and just this past weekend, voters reaffirmed that trust and re-elected her in a landslide. They called her *Mutti*, or mommy.

In the window of a second-hand bookshop, the lurid covers of pulp crime novels reminded Dinah of the gun inside her purse. She stopped and stared at the images of blood-drenched corpses, terrorists brandishing machine guns, and scantily clad babes with pouty lips and pistols. Feeling slightly absurd, she shifted the purse from one shoulder to the other. She ought to call that policeman Thor had mentioned, but there was no point until she knew whether her less-than-trustworthy *Mutti* had been snatched or gone off of her own volition.

"You won't get rid of me so easily," said Margaret, coming up alongside her. She wheezed and blew her nose. "Are we close?"

"It's somewhere in the middle of the next block, I think."

They walked on together until they came to a window that displayed a bronze sculpture of an Indian brave standing over a dead buffalo. The sign on the door read *die ewigen Jagdgründe*. She took out her smartphone and Googled it. The phrase translated to the Happy Hunting Ground.

"Geronimo," she said, and pushed open the door.

The air was thick with the incense of desert sage and piñon and the plaintive sounds of a flute wafted through the interior. Colorful canvases of Indians adorned the walls—Indians hunting, Indians dancing, Indians riding horses, Indians contemplating the mountains and the plains, and ghost Indians looking down from the sky. She felt momentarily disoriented, as if she'd been teleported to Santa Fe in the blink of an eye.

"*Guten Morgen!*"

"God's sake," said Margaret, as an Indian loomed from behind a stack of fur throws and pelts. His red-painted dome was bisected by a brownish mohawk and a necklace of mottled grizzly claws curved against his bare chest. A painted black hand cradled his chin and mouth, the thumb jutting up on his left cheek and the fingers extending up the right side of his face to his eye. A diagonal line of white dots extended from above his left eye to the tip of the black thumb.

Dinah didn't know whether to laugh or scream. Somehow, she managed to keep a straight face. "Good morning. We're here to see Herr Florian Farber."

His smile, in the context of all the war paint, appeared fierce, but his tone was friendly. "I am Florian Farber. Welcome to my gallery." He shook both of their hands. "Please do not be alarmed. I am dressed for an event later tonight. How may I help you?"

"I believe my mother had an appointment with you today. Mrs. William Calms. Is she here?"

He beamed. "You are Frau Pelerin, Swan's daughter? Yes, of course. I should have recognized you. She told me you had moved to Berlin and would be visiting the gallery. *Willkommen.* Come in. It is Dinah, *ja?* May I offer you a cup of tea?"

"Thanks, no." She ran her eyes around the place. Interspersed among the paintings were intricately painted masks, Hopi, she thought. They looked like those worn during religious ceremonies. A glass display case with an assortment of artifacts and jewelry cut through the center of the gallery. In the southeast corner was an ordinary business desk. In the southwest corner stood a stone statue, a fearsome combination of lion and bear and lizard that would have looked more at home in the Museum of Cairo.

"Is the lady here?" demanded Margaret.

"No. I don't anticipate that I will see Frau Calms until tonight at our powwow."

"When do you anticipate that Mr. Hess will arrive?"

"Reiner Hess?" The name seemed to rattle him. "Reiner has not been to a powwow since…a while."

Margaret scowled. "You mean since the police came after him for tax evasion?" She balled her fists on her hips as if she might clobber him if he didn't say what she wanted to hear.

The light of welcome dimmed in Florian's eyes, and the painted black hand that held his mouth, compressed. "I don't know anything about that. Reiner is an acquaintance. A member of *der Indianer* club for a long time, but not active in our meetings. I know nothing of his business or financial affairs."

Dinah laid a restraining hand on Margaret's arm and smiled—disarmingly, she hoped. "We don't know anything about Mr. Hess, either. We're just trying to locate my mother. She left a note that led us to believe she would be paying you a visit this morning. It's her first day in Berlin, she speaks no German, and I'm concerned that she'll get lost and won't be able to find her way back to her hotel. Do you have any idea where else she might have gone?"

The reference to Swan restored his obliging manner. "Yes, you would naturally be worried. I will of course be happy if she drops by the gallery today, but in her last communication to me, she said only that she looked forward to meeting me and the other club members at the powwow tonight."

"Here at the gallery?" Dinah couldn't picture a bunch of would-be Indians whooping it up in this crowded shop.

"No. It is held near the south shore of Müggelsee in the southeastern suburbs."

"Where exactly is that? And when?"

"Seven o'clock. Take the S-bahn to Friedrichshagen. There is a ferry across the lake and we will meet at the top of Kleiner Müggelberg."

Having so far not traveled much beyond the Mitte, Dinah had no idea where this Müggelsee might be. She racked her brain. Where could Swan have gone? Her note was vague as to time, but stated clearly that she was going to meet Farber. Had she taken the wrong train? What and where were the other "errands" on her itinerary? Or had she been kidnapped? Was she locked up somewhere in this gallery? In a secret chamber behind one of those paintings, perhaps? She scanned the walls and display cases.

Farber said, "You will of course be most welcome at the powwow tonight also."

"Thank you. Do you by any chance sell Indian dolls?"

"Dolls? No, I seldom see a doll worth acquiring, although I once had a very nice Inuit doll made in eighteen-twenty." He smiled. "While you are here, you must come into the courtyard and meet some of our other members." He gestured them toward the rear of the shop.

Margaret vented a succession of impressive sneezes. When she could speak, she said, "You go. I need to sit down and rest for a few minutes. If there's a chair."

"*Ja, ja. Durchaus!*" Florian fetched a folding chair from behind the desk and seated her. "Are you ill?"

"Just tired." She cut her eyes at Dinah. "My young friend sets a mean pace."

"I'd like to meet the other club members," said Dinah.

"Very good. Come."

She followed him past the desk, which was almost as cluttered as hers, and out the back door. A lanky man wearing long braids and a fringed buckskin shirt and leggings stood in front of a yellow tepee decorated with red zigzags and black buffalo heads. His face had been colored with tan makeup, but his hands were white. He wore a silver Indian head ring with a teal enamel headdress on one hand, and a Zuni ring with multicolor stone inlay on the other. A youngish blonde in a beaded deerskin dress squatted in front of a charcoal fire tending a tin kettle. She looked up at Dinah and smiled. "*Moin.*"

"Dinah, this is my assistant, Drumming Man, and his wife, Little Deer."

"A pleasure to meet you," said Dinah. Drumming Man shook hands with her, which was the usual manner of greeting strangers in Germany. His wife didn't offer.

"And I am Baer Eichen," said a silver-haired man sitting

cross-legged on the ground. He reached out and shook her hand. "Forgive me if I don't stand."

"He has an artificial foot," said Farber, which brought a look of frank displeasure to Eichen's face.

"I am not disabled," he said, and pushed himself to his feet. He wore a tan suit, blue shirt, and a braided leather bolo tie secured with a turquoise clasp the size of a duck egg. His blue eyes assessed her from behind avant-garde black wooden eyeglasses. He spoke perfect English with no discernible accent. "I'm in my banker's mufti, but tonight I will don leggings and a tattered ghost shirt and become Takoda. It is a Sioux name meaning Friend to All." His eyes twinkled. Flirtatiously, she thought.

She said, "You obviously take your hobby very seriously."

"It is more than a hobby," said Drumming Man. "It is our spiritual quest."

"Sorry. I didn't mean to make light."

"Don't apologize," said Eichen. "Drumming Man has a sensitive ear and is constantly on the defensive against mockery."

"As am I. I wouldn't like to think that your imitation of American Indians was a send-up." She softened the comeback with a smile.

The group apparently favored the dress of the Great Plains tribes, although it appeared to be a mix-and-match affair. Little Deer wore her blond hair in a perky mushroom bob with a plush scarf coiled around her neck like every other woman in Berlin.

"I assure you our admiration is sincere," said Eichen. "We Germans live pragmatic, prosperous lives, but we feel an absence. We have become alienated from nature and *der Indianer* club is an outlet for our nostalgia. One might say, a nostalgia for the forest."

"We dream a past that is innocent of the lust for conquest and the industry of murder," added Drumming Man, his face somber and spookily earnest. "We put on the simple garments that your Indian ancestors wore and harmonize our thoughts with the music of the drums, which is the heartbeat of life. In dreaming, we transcend this soulless time. In drumming, we are forgiven."

Little Deer giggled. She looked a lot younger than her husband and Dinah inferred that she wasn't entirely on board with his desire to transcend this soulless time.

Farber looked uncomfortable. It was an awkward moment between husband and wife, but Dinah got the feeling that Drumming Man's painful earnestness embarrassed Farber. He said, "Swan has told me that her Seminole ancestors are the only tribe that did not surrender to the United States Government. Is that true, Dinah?"

"The Florida Seminoles were never officially defeated. Like the rest of the Indian nations, they lost anyway."

Drumming Man said, "We are anxious to meet your mother. Her profile in the Native American registry says that her name was shortened from Suwannee, a river of wild black water and deep channels. She must be *geheimnisvoll.*"

"Mysterious," Eichen translated with a twinkle. "If she is anything like her daughter, she is a most attractive woman."

Not sure how to respond, she said, "Tell me about Chief Winnetou. I understand he's practically deified in Germany."

"Not deified," said Farber. "The stories of Winnetou are fairy tales, good against evil. It was Buffalo Bill Cody's Wild West Show in Munich in eighteen-ninety that gave rise to clubs like ours."

"The Indians are a tragic people," said Drumming Man, sounding tragic. "They were vanquished from their land and murdered, just as Winnetou was murdered by the Yankees who lusted for Indian gold."

"And what a *fine* time we had last year searching for the burial mound of the great chief," said Little Deer, the bite of sarcasm unmistakable. "In Wyoming I understood what it feels like to be buried."

Eichen clapped an arm around Drumming Man's shoulders. "Karl May made many mistakes in his books about the Indians, but with Winnetou and his German blood brother Old Shatterhand, he evoked a spirit of loyalty and comradeship. Like the knights of legend, they rode through the wilderness, fighting off enemies and righting wrongs."

The kettle whistled and Little Deer lifted it off the fire and stood up. She was as tall as her husband, with an athletic body and a goading smirk. She smirked at Dinah and asked, "Did the Seminoles take the scalps of white people as trophies?"

"In rare cases," said Dinah, staring pointedly at her blond bob.

Drumming Man looked as if he might strike his wife, but Eichen intervened. "We each have our view of the Indians and their history. It is not required that we believe the same things in order to enjoy a shared general interest."

Dinah didn't perceive an excess of congeniality among these Indians, but she hadn't seen or heard anything to suggest they might have shanghaied her mother. If what Farber had said about Hess was true and he hadn't participated in the club's powwows for a long time, it was possible that Swan's interest in this group was incidental to her dealings with Hess. In any case, Dinah was back to square *eins*. "It was a pleasure to meet you all, but I need to check on my friend Margaret and find my mother."

"We look forward to seeing the three of you this evening at the powwow," said Eichen, shaking her hand again.

She said good-bye, shook hands again all around, even with Little Deer, and Florian Farber ushered her back through the shop. The chair where Margaret had been resting was empty.

"She must have gone out for a breath of air," said Farber.

Suckered again, thought Dinah. Another of Cleon Dobbs' *geheimnisvoll* ex-wives was in the wind. She wondered if Margaret knew all along where Swan had gone and was on her way to meet her, or if she'd had a brainstorm. Either way, Dinah ruled out abduction. She almost felt sorry for Reiner Hess.

# Chapter Eight

Dinah stormed out of the Happy Hunting Ground and collided with a woman encumbered with too many shopping bags.

"*Pardon*," said Dinah.

"*Ist nicht*," said the woman, summing matters up better than she knew. "Nothing," as in nothing good. As in, nothing but clouds.

The first fat drops of rain splashed onto the pavement and umbrellas began to go up. Dinah ducked under a construction scaffold and considered her options. She could A, stake out the gallery and hope that her mother eventually turned up; B, call the friendly cop she had promised to call and report her missing; C, hang around with the Indians and try to cajole some information about Hess out of them; or D, go home and prepare for her class next Tuesday.

Arguing against Option A, there was no guarantee Swan would turn up ahead of her heralded appearance at the powwow tonight. In light of the note she'd left, Option B seemed premature. Why would the police waste manpower scouring the city for a ditzy American tourist who'd been missing for only a couple of hours? There were factors that might galvanize them into action. She could show them the mutilated Indian doll. Germany had laws against hate crimes based on ethnicity or national identity. But something about that doll, or Swan's reaction to it, smelled fishy.

As for Option C, Florian Farber had seemed none too eager to discuss Hess, and if he did tell her where to find him, what could she do? Telephone for an appointment? Ask him if he'd taken a potshot at the Golf? Demand money—Swan's and Margaret's just desserts for time they spent married to Cleon? The more she thought about that scheme, the nuttier it sounded. No, Option D was the only one that made sense. D as in delay. D as in don't make matters worse. D as in denial, which had always been her strong suit. Like mother, like daughter.

She climbed the stairs to the apartment just as her across-the-hall neighbor Geert poked his head out the door to retrieve the *Berliner Morgenpost*. He worked from midnight to six or seven as a bartender at the White Noise Club on Schönhauser Allee. His stubble of yellow beard was always the same length and his gaunt face was perpetually wreathed in cigarette smoke. It was impossible to tell if he'd been to bed yet, or if he ever went to bed.

He took the cigarette out of his mouth. "*Moin*, Dinah."

"*Moin*, Geert. Did you notice anyone suspicious in the hall last night as you left for work?"

"Only myself. Why?"

"Someone left an effigy of a dead Indian in front of my door."

"*Saublöd.*" His eyes pinched tight as paper cuts and he blew a mare's tail of smoke down the hall. "Bloody stupid. No fascist punks around here. The *faules* in boots and donkey jackets live in Lichtenberg and Marzahn. Where is Thor?"

"Oslo. On business. I'm spending the week with my mother and a friend."

"Don't worry. I will test the downstairs lock. And I will kill this *Dummkopf* if he comes back. I will rip out his eyes."

"Thanks, Geert. Will you get his name first?"

"No problem." He put the cigarette back in his mouth and vanished like a fume into his apartment.

Dinah confirmed that her apartment door was locked before inserting her key and pushing inside. Everything appeared normal. Aphrodite had ignored the scratching post and continued to shred one end of the new sofa. Dinah fed her, fixed herself a grilled cheese sandwich, and sat down to sort out her feelings. Anger, fear, aggravation, guilt, and a feeling of ambivalence about the make-believe Indians. The romanticization of the "noble savage," uncorrupted by civilization, had been a common theme since the sixteenth century. It was simplistic and patronizing, although preferable to attitudes of racial and cultural superiority. But what was that slam about scalpings? Maybe Little Deer had been thinking about an episode in one of Karl May's books.

As a matter of fact, American tribes weren't the only practitioners of scalping. The Germanic tribes of yore were enthusiastic scalpers. In the ninth century, the Visigoths scalped their victims, as did the Franks and the Angles and the Saxons. During the Crusades, lopping off the entire head was all the rage. But during the colonial and French Indian wars in North America, the British and European colonists offered bounties for Indian scalps, including those of women and children, and conducted scalp-hunting expeditions.

The subject was not one to dwell on. She finished her sandwich and rummaged in the freezer for the tub of Mövenpick Swiss chocolate ice cream. She had gained five pounds since moving to Berlin, but so far she hadn't opened the pack of Pall Mall filters stashed away in the pantry for emergencies. In fact, cigarettes were losing their psychological appeal. Back in the States, smoking had a subversive, outlaw cachet. In Berlin, it was commonplace. Although it was verboten to light up in public buildings, the streets reeked of smoke and when Geert was at home, smoke leaked from under his door and invaded this apartment. The odor lingered in spite of regular applications of Febreze.

She grabbed a spoon and dug into the ice cream. She ought to call the Wunderbar to see if either Swan or Margaret had returned. She ought to call her mother's cell again, or Margaret's, or Farber's gallery. She ought to take the Golf to the repair shop. She ought to compartmentalize this Hess farrago and concentrate on her class prep. She ought…

The buzzer sounded. Terrific. The wanderers had returned. She stuck the lid back on the ice cream and chucked it into the freezer. What kind of a story could she concoct, or what kind of threat, that would motivate them to get the hell out of Dodge? If she told them she had it from a reliable source that Hess had moved to Argentina, would they believe her?

She walked into the living room and stopped short. What if it wasn't her mother and Margaret at the door? What if it was the shooter or the phantom who'd left the doll? She eyed her purse with the Smith & Wesson still inside.

The caller buzzed again, longer and more insistently. She pushed the button on the intercom. "Yes?"

"Reiner Hess. I am here to speak with Frau Calms."

She caught her breath. Now what?

"Hello? Is this the apartment of Dinah Pelerin?"

"Yes. Wait, please."

She went out into the hall and pounded on Geert's door.

After a minute, he materialized in a cloud of smoke.

"Geert, I have company downstairs. I don't know what he wants and I don't want to meet him alone. Will you come over and stay for a few minutes? Just in case?"

"*Ja*, sure. If you don't like, I will bounce him." He stubbed out his cigarette and followed her across the hall.

She spoke into the intercom. "Come up now, Mr. Hess." She buzzed him in and held her apartment door open.

Geert slouched onto the sofa and hitched his pipe-stem arms across the back.

Hess took the steps to the second floor two at a time. He had chiseled features, arrogant blue eyes, and a bristly head of pale hair that reminded her of a hedgehog. Geert would be no match for this well-muscled hunk if he became threatening.

"You are Frau Pelerin?"

"Yes. Won't you step inside?"

"*Danke*." He projected a brash sexuality and looked too young to have been one of Cleon's contemporaries. Then again, the drug business was an equal opportunity employer and Cleon had probably recruited plenty of muscle from Generation X. As he entered the room, he slung a sidelong glance at Geert. "Who are you?"

Geert didn't rise or offer to shake hands. "I am Geert Hendrik. Do not try nothing funny, I am warning you."

Hess frowned. So did Dinah. She had expected a touch more discretion from Geert.

Hess leveled his blue eyes on Dinah. "Is Frau Calms here?"

"No, she isn't."

"Hendrik, I would like to speak with Frau Pelerin in private."

"I am not going noplace." Geert unhitched his skinny arms from behind the sofa and rocked forward. "I have seen you before. At one of the *massagesalon* brothels in Oranienburger Strasse, *nicht wahr?*"

The veins in Hess' neck bulged.

Dinah reconsidered the wisdom of inviting Geert's help. "Will you have a seat, Herr Hess?" She moved away from the foyer table and motioned him toward a chair. "Would you care for coffee, or a glass of iced tea?"

"I've come to bargain with your mother. She said she would be here."

"She's on her way home to Georgia, actually. I took her to the airport this morning."

"You are lying. She came to Berlin to bargain. She will not leave until she has what she came for."

"You're wrong. Someone tried to kill her and she left."

"You can't fool me. She is like Cleon Dobbs, greedy and cunning. She will have what she wants."

It was one thing for Dinah privately to question her mother's integrity, quite another to hear this gorilla insult her. "My mother said you were a lawyer, but you don't act like one. You act like a thug. What exactly did you do for Cleon Dobbs?"

"Ask your mother, why don't you?"

"I will, if and when she returns to Germany."

His lip curled. "I have no time for games. She has something I want and I am willing to pay. Four hundred thousand Euros, no more. This is not the Orient. In Germany, we don't haggle. Tell her to be at the Müggelturm tonight at nine o'clock and bring the item she wishes to sell." He lobbed a menacing look over his shoulder at Geert and stalked out the door, slamming it behind him.

"*Das Arschloch*," said Geert, pushing himself off the sofa.

If it meant what Dinah thought it did, she couldn't agree more. "What's the Müggelterm?"

"An old, falling-down tower in the hills above Müggelsee, a lake east of the city."

Müggelsee was where the powwow had been scheduled. So there was a connection after all.

In her mind's eye, Dinah saw Hess lurking in the dark behind a dilapidated tower. He had killed two federal agents and God only knew how many others while he was running drugs for Cleon. How likely was it that he would meekly turn over a suitcase full of cash to Swan and let her walk away? He'd never be sure she hadn't made copies of the incriminating material and try to bleed him again. Where was Swan now?

Her stomach growled and she was beset by a gnawing hunger. It was as if that cheese sandwich and ice cream never happened. She couldn't think straight until she got something else to eat. "Would you like a sandwich, Geert? I'm starving."

"You have now the *Kummerspeck*."

"The what?"

"When you feel trouble in your gut, it is like hunger. In German, we call it *Kummerspeck*. Grief bacon."

# Chapter Nine

It wasn't dark yet, but the lights were winking on along Bölsches-
trasse, the main drag in the village of Friedrichshagen. A few
blocks ahead, the street dead-ended at the lake. The sky had
cleared and a horned moon hovered low over the water. Dinah
rolled down the car window and breathed in the mingled smells
of sausages, brewer's yeast and, if her nose wasn't mistaken, rotting mulberries.

Her driver said, "My sergeant will meet us on the trail to
Kleiner Müggelberg. If Hess is here, we will arrest him. Besides
threatening you and your mother, he is the subject of a large
tax evasion probe."

"Really?" Hours of unanswered calls to her mother's and
Margaret's phones and to Farber's gallery had stoked her anxiety to the point of desperation and she had broken down and
called Thor's friend, Inspector Jens Lohendorf. She had spieled
off some malarkey about Hess being a former boyfriend of her
mother's who learned about her trip to Berlin through a mutual
acquaintance in *der Indianer* club. But the more she thought
about it, the more panicky she became. Lohendorf didn't know
he was going after a double murderer and Dinah couldn't think
of a way to warn him without embroiling her mother in an
international police investigation.

She said, "I don't think you should assume that he's just a
non-violent tax evader. He may have fired a gun into my car

as I drove my mother from the airport. I couldn't get a license plate number, but I filed a report."

"Yes, I've read it."

"You have?"

"Thor called me. He wasn't sure you would follow up."

The news that Thor had gone behind her back threw her off balance. She knew he'd done it out of concern for her safety, but he'd put her in a precarious situation with Lohendorf. He would have told the inspector about the doll with the knife in its chest, which she hadn't mentioned. And Lohendorf would have told Thor about the tax-dodging former boyfriend. When the two men got together to compare notes, she would no doubt be asked to account for the holes and disparities in her story.

They had reached the landing dock. Lohendorf parked the car and walked around to open the door for her. "We're in time to catch the last ferry. Sergeant Vogel and his men have cars in Rahnsdorf at the other end of the lake."

She squared her shoulders and snugged her shoulder bag close under her arm. If needed, she had her gun. She had shot it many times at the shooting range. Thor had insisted she take lessons. But designated lanes and paper targets hadn't prepared her for a real-life encounter.

They stepped aboard a flat-bottomed, open-air foot ferry with rows of benches occupied mostly by young couples taking advantage of what would probably be one of the last mild evenings before winter set in. They cuddled and necked in the gathering dusk. Lohendorf made his way toward the stern and she followed. They sat down together on a vacant bench and he reached inside his jacket. "Care for a cigarette?"

"No, thanks. I'm trying to quit."

He lit one for himself. "Smoking is banned on public transport, but in the open air, I don't think it will offend." He had a clean-cut, angular face with a sharp nose and a Dick Tracy chin. His physiognomy telegraphed his occupation in spite of his plain, but obviously expensive, clothes. He exhaled a brume of smoke across the slate-colored water. "How long have you known the woman who is traveling with your mother?"

"Margaret?" She'd been so wrought up about her mother that she'd almost forgotten about Margaret. "I've known her since I was a child. She and my mother were married to the same man, at different times, of course. Cleon Dobbs. He left Margaret to marry my mother and a few years later, my mother left Cleon to marry my father."

"Like an American soap opera."

"You've got that right. Lots of intersecting storylines, bare-fisted discord, and sexual dramas."

He laughed. "Not a boring family."

"I used to pray for boring. We all lived in the same small town, shopped at the same stores, went to the same beaches, attended the same football games, socialized on holidays." She was babbling. If she didn't shut up, she'd start running on about the pet rabbit she got when she was ten, the same year Cleon murdered her father hoping to get Swan back. Shit, and she shouldn't have mentioned Cleon by name, although he obviously knew. He probably had a dossier on the old devil. She said, "I've changed my mind about that cigarette."

He reached into his pocket, shook out a Lucky Strike, and lit it with his BIC.

She took a drag and quieted down.

"Mr. Dobbs must have been a remarkable man."

"You could say that."

"Margaret Dobbs killed him in two thousand and ten in Australia. Do have any concern that she might also wish to harm your mother?"

Dinah flinched. He really did have a dossier. "Margaret was tried and acquitted. She poses no danger to my mother or anyone else."

"I mean no disrespect. As I'm sure Thor has told you, the police have a duty to be aware of persons with reckless pasts."

She offered no reply.

The ferry lurched away from the dock and she braced one hand against the rail. Somebody at the other end turned on a boom box and a pulsating electro beat drowned out conversation. She was glad for the interruption. All she could think about was her mother, who could broaden Lohendorf's definition of recklessness by an order of magnitude. That she would try to blackmail a man like Hess defied all reason. Dinah prayed that she could latch onto her at the powwow before Hess found her. She ground out her cigarette and focused on the fringe of trees in the distance.

Lohendorf pulled a photograph out of his pocket. "Do you recognize this man?"

It was a bland, middle-aged face, nothing unusual or out of proportion except for a rather narrow, ridge-like nose. His mouth was set in a grim line—the mouth of a man who didn't laugh much. "No. Who is he?"

"A person of interest. I thought you might have seen him in your neighborhood."

Perhaps he was a known racist and Lohendorf suspected him of planting the doll. She was up to her eyeballs in "persons of interest." She couldn't worry about another just now.

The wind had picked up. It rippled the darkening waters of Müggelsee and sent small wavelets toward the shore. She knew that *see* was the German word for lake, but what was Müggel? In the Harry Potter books, a muggle referred to someone who had no magical powers. But surely Müggelsee was named long before J.K. Rowling began writing about wizards. There was a hiatus in the music and she asked Lohendorf, "What does Müggel mean in English? Müggel lake?"

"I've read that it derives from the Slavic word for grave. And *Berg* is hill. Müggelberg is grave hill."

Not everything is an omen, she told herself. "Is someone famous buried there?"

"Not that I know."

The music blasted again and she brooded until the ferry bumped stern-first into tire fenders on the dock and the ferryman opened the gate. She had assumed they would be the first ones off, but they were elbowed aside. Berliners had many fine qualities, but they did not queue. They disembarked en mass and dispersed along the shore to picnic tables and a row of bars and eateries.

When she and Lohendorf made it off the boat, he pointed her toward a sign: Müggelberg Spur. "That is the trail to the area where the powwow has been authorized. It is a short climb. A little muddy, perhaps, but not strenuous." He drew two flashlights out of a shoulder pack and handed her one. "It will be dark in another hour."

She took her light and walked ahead of him through the forest. The trail was wide and smooth, groomed like a suburban park, but to her, it felt creepy and ominous. Even if she weren't en route to save her mother from a murderer, the name Grave Hill wouldn't have lightened her step. She looked back to make sure Lohendorf was there. He walked five or six feet behind, his phone to his ear. Without attracting his notice, she lifted the flap on her purse and touched the gun inside.

The smell of wet leaves and wood smoke permeated the air. After they'd gone about three quarters of a mile, the modern music the young people were playing on the beach below faded, replaced by the percussive, primitive beat of Indian drums and chanting. She wondered if Hess would dress up in Indian garb and paint his face. He couldn't disguise himself completely. His looks were too distinctive.

The drumming and chanting grew louder. Ahead, she could see a clearing in the trees and the spectral glow of a fire. She quickened her pace. Five minutes more of walking and she entered a scene she could only describe as surreal. A dozen Indians decked out in a motley of tribal clothing assembled around a fake bonfire. White silk streamers had been attached to glow logs and as a small fan caused them to flutter, orange and yellow and blue lights created the illusion of flickering flames. A barbecue grill seemed to be the source of the wood smoke. An Apache sporting a red cloth headband and an ammunition belt fed wood chips into the bowl of the grill. Several men sat around a table chanting and a circle of drummers, including Drumming Man in his braids and buckskin, beat out the rhythm on a large drum.

A man in a yellow tunic and porcupine hair roach was selling *das feuerwasser*. Dinah's German was minimal, but she knew the words for fire and water. The liquid being siphoned from a keg into the clear plastic cups appeared to be ordinary beer, but it seemed to be amping up the party mood.

She scrutinized the faces and builds of the revelers. She didn't see Hess. The only familiar figure was Drumming Man.

Lohendorf joined her at the edge of the clearing. "Do you see your mother?"

"No." She scanned the clearing. "She's not here."

"Are you sure? There are women sitting in the shadows by the grill."

She looked them over and recognized Little Deer, who wore the same buckskin dress accessorized by a pair of glittering diamond shoulder-dusters. "My mother's not one of them. I'd know her hide in a tannery." It was an old Southern saying, a cliché that tumbled out without thought. Suddenly, the gruesome image made her shudder.

Lohendorf said, "Wait here. I'll make inquiries."

He moved off and spoke with a man in an eagle-feather war bonnet that dangled all the way to his moccasins. She wondered when and how he had acquired it. Eagles had been a protected species in the States since the early sixties and anyone who bought or sold their feathers faced a stiff fine, perhaps even prison.

It was after seven. Hess' message had been for Swan to meet him at nine, but she should be here, charming the loincloths off these Indian braves. Farber and the others were expecting her. Had Hess found her already? Had he thrown her and her incriminating thumb drive into Grave Lake? That foolishness about a "dead man's switch" and the evidence going to the Drug Enforcement Agency if anything happened to the blackmailers would make a man like Hess laugh.

"*Willkommen.*"

She spun around to see a bare-chested Baer Eichen staring at her over the tops of his wooden glasses. His was strung with multiple tiers of beads and a small stuffed bird peeked out of his long, black wig. "Herr Eichen, what a transformation."

"Tonight, you may call me Takoda. It's a delight to see you." He initiated another handshake.

She couldn't help but notice that his Indian name, which he had said was taken from the Siouan language, clashed with his Crow costume. Looking around at the others, she marveled at the casual blending of native cultures.

"Did you come with your mother?"

"No. She isn't here. I'm trying to find her."

"You seem always to be searching for her."

If Dinah weren't so worried, the observation would have irked her. She surveyed the clearing again. Lohendorf was now talking with Little Deer and three other women clustered around a camp stove.

Eichen's eyes followed hers to where Lohendorf stood. "Who is your friend?"

"Inspector Lohendorf of the Berlin Police. He's trying to help me find my mother."

"Police?" He appeared taken aback. "Is there a reason for you to be so concerned?"

"No."

If he was stung by her curt response, he didn't show it. He smiled. "It's early yet. The S-bahn doesn't run as often as the U-bahn, and if she missed the seven o'clock ferry, she would have to take a taxi to Rahnsdorf and follow the trail through the forest from there. May I get you a beer or a curry wurst? I believe there's also schnapps."

"Maybe later." She saw that Lohendorf was now talking on his cell.

"I shall look forward to it." Eichen nodded and moved off toward the keg.

She spotted Florian Farber, alias Thunder Moon, with his black hand war paint, which she thought was an Iowan symbol of victory in combat. She crossed the clearing and touched his arm. "Herr Farber, have you seen or heard from my mother today?"

"Hallo, Dinah. No, not yet." The corners of his mouth curved upward as if pushed by the painted hand. "We are expecting her very soon. I plan to make a formal introduction to the club and grant her honorary membership."

She looked back to where Lohendorf had been standing, but he had disappeared. Had he found Swan? Had that phone call brought news? She hurried across to the barbecue grill to ask Little Deer.

"How," said the twerp, and threw up her hand.

Dinah resisted the temptation to swat her. "Did you overhear if that call to Inspector Lohendorf was about my mother?"

"No."

"Have you seen her tonight?"

"Yes. I showed this to the policeman." She held up her camera phone with a photo of Swan next to the ferry dock.

"When was this?"

"About five o'clock."

More than two hours ago. "Did you see where she went?"

"No."

"Was she with anyone?"

"An old woman with *der spitzer Haaransatz*." With her two index fingers, she mimed a widow's peak. "She and the squaw made a big noise with their arguing."

Dinah didn't have time to retort. She had an ominous feeling, like the smell of ozone before lightning. "Which is the trail to the tower?"

She pointed to a wooden sign saying Müggelturm, and Dinah dashed off like a halfback. She shoved a Sioux warrior out of her way and sideswiped a Hopi woman beating a small water drum. She didn't stop to beg anyone's pardon. The trail was rougher than it had been below and the forest more dense. She aimed her flashlight on the ground to keep from tripping on a rock or a root. Her thoughts churned with fear and misgivings. Margaret had obviously caught up with Swan, but what had they argued about? Did Margaret think Swan was angling to cut her out of the deal?

Her heart beat faster as she climbed and she wasn't sure if the pounding in her ears came from the drums or her pulse. Up ahead, she heard shouts. She began to sprint, feeling for her gun as she ran. She crested the hill and saw the tower, floodlit and surrounded by uniformed police. Two of them were stringing crime scene tape.

She willed herself forward, too filled with dread to pray. Shafts of white light crisscrossed the darkness and delved into the gaps between the trees. What were they shouting? Had someone said the word *mord?*

A uniformed officer stooped and planted a white evidence flag. She edged closer and trained her flashlight on the object next to the flag. What...? Oh. Oh, God, no.

Her thoughts reeled. She turned blindly and collided with Lohendorf. She steadied herself and anchored her gaze on his face. "Is that...hair?"

"Yes." He took the gun out of her hand and slipped it into his pocket.

The only person that bristly blond mat could belong to was Hess. "Is he alive?"

"No. The body was discovered a half hour ago by a hiker. The Rahnsdorf police are investigating."

"And my mother?"

"We are searching." He called out to one of the uniforms. "Please escort Frau Pelerin to a safe area and make her comfortable until I've finished here. I will speak with her shortly."

# Chapter Ten

"This club has been meeting for ten years. Nothing like this has ever happened." Florian Farber sat at the table previously occupied by the chanters, scrubbing off his war paint with a wet towel. "It's not something a German would do."

The first part of that assertion had to be the understatement of the decade, thought Dinah. But given Germany's record of war-making, atrocities, and genocide, the second part showed a breathtaking lapse of memory.

Inspector Jens Lohendorf and his sergeant, a dour-faced man with ears that stuck out like satellite dishes, had divided the "Indians" into seemingly random groups of two for questioning. The method struck Dinah as flawed, but she was a stranger in a strange land and the balance of her mind was seriously disturbed. She was still coming to grips with the fact that Reiner Hess had been killed and scalped, and her mother had apparently hightailed it.

Farber and the man with the porcupine roach were the third pair that Lohendorf had summoned for questioning. He had parked Dinah at the end of the table and ordered her to wait for someone named Wegener to show up and drive her home. While she waited, she listened and watched. The colloquy had been in German until Farber sliced in that zinger in English. His insinuation was unmistakable, but not all that shocking given the inspector's frequent allusions to "Frau Calms."

Little Deer had seen Swan and Margaret together at the ferry landing at five. They had separated and no one had seen either of them leave. Lohendorf was kind enough to tell her that much, or wily enough. He looked at her as if he knew she was withholding information, and if he jollied her along with an occasional translation, she would start to cooperate. She had given him Swan's and Margaret's cell numbers, but they weren't answering. Lohendorf was right to think that leaving the scene was hinky. And if they were alive and not tied to a tree, not answering their phones was hinky in the extreme. Being female and "of a certain age" didn't eliminate the women from consideration as suspects. Dinah would never forget the statue she'd seen in Boscawen, New Hampshire, honoring Hannah Dustin, a colonial woman who, in 1697, took ten Indian scalps single-handed and cashed them in for the bounty.

But what if the reason Swan didn't answer her phone was because she had been killed by the same person or persons who killed Hess? Her body might be lying undiscovered under a pile of rotting leaves.

Dinah hugged her arms and shivered. She couldn't shake the mental picture of that ragged strip of hair tossed in the dirt like garbage. The savagery of the murder seemed calculated to incriminate *der Indianer*, but some things were unthinkable—her mother killing a man and ripping off the top of his head being one. She didn't care how many years this club had gone without a murder, there was no doubt in her mind that this particular murder was as German as apple streudel.

She didn't understand much of the language, but she knew her numbers. *Eins, zwei, drei*, and from the snippets she picked up, the victim had been shot *zweimal*—twice, in *die Brust,* which sounded like "breast." The porcupine roach man, Herr Amsel, who seemed to have imbibed too much of his own firewater, banged his fist against his chest and gesticulated broadly. He answered Lohendorf's questions in rapid-fire guttural bursts. Was he really that drunk, or was he putting on a show?

She wished she could pose a few questions to the witnesses. Had anyone seen or spoken with Hess? When did he arrive? The time of death would have to be determined by a medical examiner, but Lohendorf would already know the parameters. What time did the earlier ferry arrive with Swan? He should interview Little Deer and the club members who came to build the phony bonfire and set up the bar. Her fingers itched to try Swan's cell again. Where had she gone after arguing with Margaret? Had she set off in the direction of the powwow and gotten lost? Had she gone to the tower to meet Hess four hours early? Or had she hied off back to the hotel?

A brisk woman in uniform appeared at Lohendorf's side and handed him a piece of paper. He read it and folded it in his pocket. "Thank you, Sergeant Wegener. Frau Pelerin, the sergeant will walk you to her car in Rahnsdorf and drive you home. After she has delivered you to your door, she will stop in at the *Gasthaus* where your mother and Frau Dobbs are staying to see if they made it home safely." He turned to Wegener. "If the ladies are present, please take their statements, Sergeant, and advise them that I wish to interview them first thing in the morning. Nine-thirty."

"Yes, sir." Her eyes fairly sparkled with zeal.

In a cautioning tone, he added, "Be clear, but don't antagonize."

"No, sir. I will not add fuel to the fire." She seemed to know her way around American idioms. Dinah wondered if he had assigned her as chaperone for precisely that reason. "What shall I do if they have not returned to the hotel, sir?"

"Call me and I will notify the BKA and issue an alert." To Dinah, he said, "I will come to your apartment tomorrow at eleven o'clock. If that is convenient."

"Certainly." She took his meaning. *If that is convenient* was entirely rhetorical. He would interrogate her like any other witness, and she would have to decide whether to divulge her mother's plot to blackmail Hess, or lie. She felt weighed down by internal contradictions and the overriding fear for Swan's safety. She said, "I want to go with Sergeant Wegener to check on my mother, Inspector. Please."

"I regret that I must ask you to wait until tomorrow."

She opened her mouth to object, but he waved her off.

"Will you at least call me and let me know if my mother is still missing?"

"We will keep you informed." He removed her gun from his pocket and handed it to her. "Weapons ownership does not entitle you to carry a loaded weapon on public premises in Germany. We will forget your carelessness tonight, but I recommend that you put it away and rely upon the police." He accorded her a rueful smile. "And will you please remain in your apartment? I don't need any more crises tonight."

You and me, both, she thought, and trudged off behind the sergeant. As they passed the bonfire, she noticed Little Deer and Drumming Man huddled in conversation. Little Deer appeared agitated. Drumming Man held her by the shoulders, but her arms jerked about like one of those air dancer balloons. Dinah wanted to talk with her at the earliest opportunity to find out if she'd overheard what Margaret and Swan had argued about and who else she might have seen nearby, but she didn't know her real name.

She moved up to walk side-by-side with Wegener. "What is that girl's name?"

"Lena Bischoff."

"And her husband?"

"Viktor Bischoff."

Dinah matched her stride with Wegener's and the beams from their flashlights bounced along the path in sync. The sergeant probably wouldn't volunteer much information without the approval of her boss, but nothing ventured, nothing gained.

"How many people attended the powwow, Sergeant?"

"Twenty-six. The full membership, but one."

"Who?"

"The dead man."

"No one saw him arrive?"

"We have not yet completed the interviews."

"Has the medical examiner stated an opinion as to the time of death?"

"Before you and the Inspector arrived."

They passed by the tower where the police were still working. Dinah's eyes strayed to the flag where she'd seen Hess' hair. She wasn't Catholic, but she crossed herself anyway and held her breath until the tower was behind them. The moon was still visible, but smudgy and ringed with clouds. Ring around the moon, rain coming soon. She felt the suggestion of a mist already and wished she had worn a warmer jacket. She ached to be with Thor, to take in his warmth and pour out her fears. Her vow to tell him the truth seemed, at one and the same time, more urgent and more difficult.

"Inspector Lohendorf has briefed me," said Wegener. "Your mother's companion is *die Scharfschütze.*"

"What?"

Wegener made a finger pistol. "A sharpshooter. Like Annie Oakley."

"What are you suggesting?"

"Do you know if she owns a gun?"

"No."

"Does your mother own a gun?"

"If she does, she keeps it at home in Georgia." This line of questioning fed Dinah's fears and sharpened her focus. "Have you found the murder weapon?"

Wegener dummied up and Dinah mulled the chronology of events in silence. Hess had obviously skipped the meet-and-greet at the bonfire and gone straight to the tower. Had he gotten in touch with Swan and arranged to meet early? If so, they could have closed their transaction and split up before the murderer arrived, or perhaps Hess had another transaction on his docket. The murderer could easily have sneaked away from the powwow, killed Hess, and rejoined the party without arousing anyone's attention. With all the drumming and chanting, the gunshots wouldn't have been heard.

The woods thinned and they strode out onto a lighted city sidewalk. She followed Wegener to her unmarked car and the sergeant motioned her into the front passenger seat. As they were leaving the outskirts of Rahnsdorf, Wegener became curious again. "Does your mother know anyone in Berlin besides Herr Hess?"

"Florian Farber, but I don't think they've actually met. They met virtually, on Facebook."

"Anyone else in *der Indianer* club?"

"Not to my knowledge. Look, if you'll let me go with you to their hotel, I can explain things. My mother and Mrs. Dobbs will be more cooperative if you let me speak with them first. They probably don't know there's been a murder and I should be there in case the news upsets them."

"My orders are to speak to them alone. If they are available."

Dinah's head began to throb with conditional clauses and questions and the more she stressed, the more headachy and hungry she grew. It was the *Kummerspeck*. She thought about asking Wegener to stop at Konnopke's for an order of currywurst and fries to go, but the sergeant didn't seem like a person who suffered from grief bacon, or would sympathize with one who did.

They turned onto Niederwallstrasse. Dinah had been so lost in thought that she'd blanked out on the drive back through the city.

"Which building is yours?" asked Wegener.

"Past the park, third on the right."

Wegener parked a few feet from the front entrance.

"Thanks," said Dinah, and got out of the car.

Wegener got out, too. "I will see you to your door."

"That's not necessary."

"To make sure you are safe." She had the implacable stare of a warden.

"Right." Dinah punched in her key code. The door buzzed and she pushed it open and stepped inside the entryway. Over Wegener's shoulder, she saw a white and green *polizei* car cruise past. She supposed Lohendorf had ordered a stakeout of her apartment and the *Gasthaus* down the block on the theory that sooner or later, Swan and Margaret would show up at one place or the other. "Am I under house arrest?"

"You are detained temporarily for your protection."

"What's the difference, Sergeant? You said so yourself. The murder was committed before I got anywhere near the damned powwow. I have an airtight alibi and you have no right to detain me, in my home or anywhere else. I'm an American citizen." With that, she turned on her heels and stomped up the stairs.

Wegener didn't follow.

On the landing, Dinah glared back at her and dialed her mother's cell. Still no answer. Ditto Margaret's phone. "Hell and damnation!" She jammed her key in the lock, kicked open the door, and steamed into the apartment.

K.D. sprawled on the sofa with Aphrodite curled on her stomach like an orange Slinky.

"What the bloody hell are you doing here?"

The cat flattened her ears, vaulted onto the floor, and vamoosed into the bedroom. K.D. swung her legs off the sofa and sat up. "Whoa. What's got your panties in a wad?"

"Not what, who. I put you on a plane to Atlanta ten days ago. You can't just come skying back like a boomerang."

"That's kind of cold. I mean, you invited me to live with you."

"And you chose to go home."

"I tried, Dinah. Really, I did. I just couldn't bear those dweebs in my high school. They are so-ooh immature." She stood to her full six feet, flipped her long auburn hair, and unfurled her arms as if laying fresh claim to ceded territory. "I saw you'd moved my bed, but don't worry. I'll crash in Thor's sleeping bag here in the living room until we can set up my room again."

# Chapter Eleven

Dinah went to the refrigerator, opened the freezer, and reached for the ice cream. It was gone. She spied the empty carton in the waste bin with a discarded boarding pass and a bottle of Sparkle Purple Nail Lacquer inside.

K.D. traipsed into the kitchen. "Where's Thor?"

"Oslo."

"Is that what's eating you? Did you break up?"

"Not yet." It was pointless to ask her where she got the money for a ticket to Berlin or how she bypassed two locked doors. Housebreaking was her specialty and her habit of barging into Dinah's life at the worst possible time was uncanny. "You chose to go home, K.D. You have to live with your decision. Things around here have changed and I can't rearrange my life every time you get a whim."

"But you promised I could stay for a year if I behaved myself. It's not fair to send me back to Georgia. My mother is a total crayzoid. Everything has to be about her. She's like, 'I sacrifice myself for my children and what do *I* get in return? A daughter who treats me like gum under her shoe and a son who wishes I was dead.'"

"Don't exaggerate," said Dinah.

"You know it's true. And my brother Thad is like a character out of *Doctor Octopus' Masters of Evil*. He's like, one dose of Adderall away from a homicide."

"Has he threatened you or your mother?"

"He eyeballs vodka. Does that tell you something?"

"No. I don't know what you're saying."

"Duh? He pours Stoli into his eyes, which makes them go fireball red, which is totally gross, and then he passes out in the basement with his pet boa constrictor. Don't you see? You're my only refuge!"

Dinah sank into a chair and rubbed her head. "Did you get in trouble with the police again?"

"No-oh." She brought off a more or less believable catch in her throat. "You made me understand that I had to own up to my mistakes and trust the system. I did what you said and everything was like, totally resolved."

When Dinah had invited K.D. to live with her, she had thought that giving the kid some time away from her troubled home life and her problems with the DeKalb County juvenile court would help her through her rebellious phase and give her a fresh perspective. They had spent a lot of time together over the summer and Dinah had come almost, *almost* to trust her. But it wouldn't do to have her back now. Not with Margaret in town. K.D. was still grieving over her father's death, trying to reconcile her memory of the man she loved with the scumbag he turned out to be. A reunion with the woman who killed him would be too dramatic.

"Going home was the...the mature thing to do. Tough it out 'til the spring, graduate with decent grades, and we can work to get you into a good college. Someplace far away from your mother and your wacko brother. Maybe here in Berlin if you want."

"Fine. Go ahead. Sign my death warrant. Everyone will be thrilled to have me dead in my grave and out of their way."

"Don't overplay the scene, kid. I've been manipulated by better liars than you."

K.D. pouted and opened the fridge. Behind the door, she said, "While you were out, I noticed a sticky on your computer. Eight-fifteen, Air France eighteen thirty-four, Atlanta to Berlin. Is *your* mother here? Is that why you're so bummed out and gritchy?"

"You *noticed* the sticky?"

"It was in plain view, okay? On the desk where my bed used to be." She took out a carton of yogurt and a spoon and flopped into a chair. "So is she here?"

"Yes, she's here. And when I'm not working, I'll be busy entertaining her and showing her the sights. I can't ride herd on you both."

"Oh, please. You know what my Daddy would say? He'd say, that 'showing her the sights crap' sounds like a bunch of who-shot-John."

It was an unfortunate turn of phrase, but Dinah had lost patience. "Margaret is with her, K.D."

The girl's face went taut.

Dinah reached across the table and touched her hand. "I'm sorry for dredging up sad memories, but that's how it is. You don't want to be here."

"I thought Margaret and Swan were arch enemies."

"They've patched up their differences."

She sneered. "They didn't kiss and make up with *my* mother. I suppose they think they're too superior to associate with her because Daddy threw her under the bus."

Harboring contradictory feelings toward one's mother was a syndrome Dinah understood only too well. "Your daddy threw everyone under the bus, K.D.—you, me, and Margaret's only child included. I wish Margaret hadn't done what she did, but I can't judge her. She was, still is, as conflicted about Cleon as the rest of us. And I'm sure that neither Swan nor Margaret thinks herself superior to your mother."

Dinah's phone rang and she pounced. "Hello."

"Inspector Lohendorf speaking. Frau Pelerin?"

"Yes, yes. Have you found her, Inspector?"

"Both ladies are safe in their rooms at the Wunderbar."

Dinah breathed a sigh of qualified relief. They were alive. And neither was on the lam. "Thank you for letting me know."

"They profess to have had a disagreement over whether to remain on the beach and wait for one of the club members to escort them through the forest to the powwow, or go ahead by themselves. Mrs. Dobbs insisted that they wait. Mrs. Calms preferred to go ahead and she did, but took the wrong trail and ended up lost in Rahnsdorf."

His tone was matter-of-fact, but his choice of the word "profess" sent a chill down her spine. "Do you have some reason to doubt their story, Inspector?"

"Actually, it is your story that causes me doubt."

She stiffened. "How so?"

"Could you have misunderstood the name of the man who came to your apartment and demanded that your mother meet him at the tower?"

She looked up into K.D.'s avid green eyes and took the conversation into the living room. Swan wouldn't have backed her story about Hess being an old flame, but surely she would have acknowledged that she knew him. She waffled. "It was a tense encounter. He sounded threatening and I thought he might have been the one who ran my car into the bridge abutment and shot at us."

Lohendorf said, "Mrs. Calms admits that she is familiar with the name Reiner Hess. He worked for her first husband many years ago. But she denies having had any contact with him, romantic or otherwise. So you see, it is a mystery how he knew where her daughter could be found or why he would come looking for her."

Dinah tried to think of a response that didn't compromise Swan or herself any further. Nothing plausible came to mind. "People do strange things," she said.

K.D. drifted into the room and perched one hip on the arm of the sofa.

Dinah turned her back and asked Lohendorf, "Did you find the murder weapon?"

"No. We will continue our search in the morning when it's light, but I am not optimistic. A clever killer would have thrown the gun and knife into the lake. Still, it is a popular area. Eyes and phone cameras everywhere. The murderer might have taken the weapons away to dispose of them later." He let a nervous few seconds pass. "I regret to add to your distress, but it will be necessary for you and your mother to view the body."

"But he's a wanted tax dodger. You must have photographs. Besides, he's been a member of the Indian club for years. Florian Farber or one of the other members should confirm his identity."

"They have confirmed it."

"Then if you know—"

"The body is not that of Reiner Hess."

"Not..." she stumbled. "Not Hess?"

"His name is Alwin Pohl, the newest member of the club. I need you to tell me if he is the same person who called on you earlier today."

Her thoughts scattered. Why would anyone impersonate a wanted man? Did Hess send this Alwin Pohl to meet her mother? Did he fail to obtain the thumb drive and Hess killed him? Or did he make the deal with Swan, and Hess killed him to make sure he left no witnesses? She wilted onto the sofa beside K.D. "Sergeant Wegener said that the only member of the club who didn't attend the powwow was the dead man. Does that mean that Hess was there?"

"It means that six months ago, Hess was drummed out of the club. If you'll forgive the pun. Your mother didn't recognize the name Pohl, but she may recognize him when she sees him. Again, do not go out again tonight. I have borrowed the ladies' phones to run a check on the numbers called and messages left. If there is nothing relevant to my investigation, I will return them tomorrow."

"But I need, I want, to speak with my mother tonight."

"It will be best to wait. I'll pick you up in the morning at eleven."

"Are you ordering me not to communicate with my mother?"

He expelled an audible breath, like a tire going flat. "Because you are Inspector Ramberg's friend, and because he is a trusted liaison to the Berlin police, I have accommodated your concerns. But there are rules and I must ask you to abide by them."

He ended the call, leaving Dinah in a quandary. If the dead man wasn't Hess, or a henchman of Hess, then Swan and Margaret were in the clear as far as the murder investigation. As for the rest, they needed to get their stories straight before tomorrow or Lohendorf could arrest them all on a charge of obstruction. She said, "We may as well be back to the stone age and sending smoke signals."

K.D.'s eyes glinted in a devilish way that put Dinah in mind of Cleon. She said, "Nobody knows I'm here, if you need somebody to deliver messages behind enemy lines."

# Chapter Twelve

Dinah's phone was almost out of juice. She plugged it into the outlet above the kitchen table to recharge and helped herself to the last two inches of red wine to steady her nerves. Just as she inserted the cord, the phone began plinking. Thor's name appeared on the display.

"Hi."

"Hi, *kjære*. Sorry for calling so late. I've been in 'round-the-clock meetings. Maybe you've seen the news. A Norwegian citizen was involved in that terrorist attack on the shopping mall in Kenya."

"No. I hadn't heard."

"It's been crazy here and I don't know when I'll be able to break away and get home. Did you call Jens Lohendorf?"

"Just as promised. I understand you beat me to the punch."

"I hope you're not angry. I wanted to make sure you stayed safe."

"Listen, Thor, I need to…"

"Dinah, we haven't used the word love, but you must know how I feel. Do you?"

"I think so."

"Well, let me remove any doubt. I love you. We haven't been together long, and there's still unmapped territory, things we haven't told each other. Important things. It's easy to let the time slide and wait for the right moment, but we need to talk. We need to know that we can trust each other."

"I understand."

"I hope you do. Sometimes you're so impulsive. You make snap decisions and don't think how they can sabotage our whole future."

"I said I understand, Thor. I don't want there to be secrets between us." Whatever he knew or suspected, he seemed to be issuing an ultimatum. She drank half the wine and nerved herself. This was where her rubbery conscience met the Get-Real Road. "I would rather have this conversation in person, Thor, but..."

"Me, too. This damned Kenya crisis has me pinned down, waiting for orders from on high. Believe me, I will get there as soon as I can."

"Okay." For once, she didn't want a reprieve and she was getting one anyway. He probably wanted to let the news of the murder soak in for a few hours before he quizzed her about her mother's involvement. She asked, "What did Lohendorf tell you about what happened tonight?"

"I haven't spoken with him. Is there something that I need to know?"

"Not really. Just that the danger is past. The man who threatened my mother won't be bothering us again."

"That's great. I told you Jens was good, didn't I?"

"Yes, you did. And as soon as you get home, we'll have a heart-to-heart about all that unmapped territory."

"Dinah?"

"Mmm?"

"I will do everything I can to get back to Berlin ahead of schedule. But if something should happen before I arrive, something that makes you feel you have to run away or take some drastic action, please don't."

If he hadn't talked with Lohendorf, then what the hell was he hinting at? Maybe N.C.I.S. had looked into the doings of their agent's girlfriend and the cat was out of the bag about the Panama account. Maybe Thor thought she would cut and run rather than face him. If that's what he believed, he was wrong. This was a reckoning she couldn't run away from. Whatever happened, she would tell him the unvarnished truth and hope that he could find it in his heart to forgive her. She said, "I promise I won't do anything rash or impulsive."

"Thank you. Now I can go back to worrying about the murders in Kenya."

She finished the wine. It was going to be a rude homecoming. "Don't let the bad guys blow up the world, Double-0 Seven. I'll be here when you get home and..." she faltered. If it wasn't in Thor's nature to gush, it was even less in hers. She took a deep breath and a big first step toward honesty. "And I love you, too."

# Chapter Thirteen

*They have no business prying into our affairs. Confiscating our phones, taking our clothes and shoes, and carting us off to the morgue in the morning. Goodness' sake, they're acting like Nazis, which they were just a few short years ago. It's not your fault sending them after us. Margaret said you were real worried when you couldn't find me. We'll just have to mind our p's and q's when they ask their bullying questions. Margaret and I are very much let down that Reiner got himself murdered, but we haven't given up on the money. We hope he left a trail of breadcrumbs that will lead us to it. We'd all better put on our thinking caps.*

*Hugs and xxxx*

*P.S. You'd better burn this when you're done reading.*

The courier who delivered this extraordinary missive rolled her eyes. "They don't know that the dead dude isn't Hess."

"You read it?"

"You knew I would." K.D. hurled herself into the corner armchair and draped her long, blue-jeaned legs across the arm. "I read yours, too. Why didn't you enlighten them?"

"I don't want to confuse matters more than they are already. I assume the dead man was a messenger sent by Hess." She wished there was such a thing as a thinking cap, or a Vulcan mind meld, or a spaceship waiting to whisk her to a galaxy far, far away. She kneaded her head and paced. Why hadn't Wegener told Swan that the victim was Alwin Pohl? Insofar as Dinah knew, Reiner

Hess and Florian Farber were the only two people Swan knew in Berlin. Never having seen or heard of this Pohl guy would be exculpatory. She could have no motive for killing a stranger.

"So." K.D. stuck a foot out to block Dinah's pacing. "What's the story with the money?"

Holding K.D. at bay was a fool's game. She would ferret out the sordid details regardless of any effort to conceal them, and Dinah saw no reason to try. Theaters let seventeen-year-olds in to *House of 1000 Corpses*. "Margaret and Swan feel that Cleon shortchanged them in their divorces. They think Hess has some of your father's ill-gotten gains, or a share of them, and they thought they could waltz into the country and hold him up for a bundle."

"How funny. Away over here in Berlin and we're still talking about Daddy."

"It seems that all roads, particularly the one to perdition, lead back to your daddy."

"What's perdition?"

"Eternal punishment."

K.D. pursed her lips and examined her purple fingernails. "Did Hess mule for Daddy?"

"Probably not. He was a lawyer of some kind. Did your father ever mention a German partner, or did a German visit him?"

"No. I think I'd remember if a German came to the house, but Daddy didn't talk business much at home except for law stuff."

Dinah resumed her pacing. "It's easy to forget he had a parallel career as a lawyer."

"How does Swan know Hess?" asked K.D.

"I'm not sure. She says Cleon left evidence that Hess killed a couple of federal agents in the U.S."

"And she wants to sell it to him?"

"That was the plan."

"Whoa, that's hardcore crazy."

No screaming shit, thought Dinah. She had assumed the dead man was Hess, but why did Swan jump to that conclusion? It must have been the way Wegener asked the questions, the repetition of his name. But if Lohendorf related Swan's lies and evasions to Pohl's murder, he wouldn't rest until he'd wrung the truth out of her. "Did Margaret say anything to Swan while she was writing this note?"

"The old puss took one look at me and scuttled off to the toilet. Hashtag guilty conscience."

"Hashtag drop it, K.D. It's almost midnight. Go to bed."

"I'm going to take a shower first. Is Thor's army sleeping bag in my bedroom closet?"

"The office closet, yes."

"There isn't enough space in the *office* with the two desks and the TV. Until he comes back, is it okay if I sleep in your bedroom?"

Dinah smothered a groan. How many hours ago had she woken up in Thor's arms and congratulated herself on being happy? It already felt like a distant memory. "Sure. I stored your pillows in my closet on the top shelf."

The cuckoo lunged out and began its infernal HOO-hooing. K.D. stopped her ears and bugged off to the shower. Dinah stopped her ears and returned to the kitchen to open another bottle of red wine. If she was going to sleep, she needed a soporific. She had just dug the angel wings into the cork when the buzzer blatted.

What fresh hell…?

Or could it be Thor? Had he dropped everything and rushed home? Couldn't be. He was in Oslo less than an hour ago and he wouldn't buzz his own apartment. Swan? Margaret? Lohendorf? She left the angel wings sticking up in the cork and went back to the living room and the intercom.

"Yes?"

"It's Lena Bischoff."

"Little Deer?"

"Yes, all right. I have come to see your red bitch mother."

Like Pohl, Lena apparently believed that Swan was camped in this apartment. What had prompted her to come name-calling at this hour and why, if the cops still had the place under surveillance, did they let her? "Is your husband with you?"

"No. I am alone. Let me in."

Dinah blew out a breath. You wanted to talk with her and here she is, like the mountain to Mohammed. "Okay, come up." She buzzed her in, closed the sliding door to the bedrooms and bath, and stepped out the front door into the hall to meet her.

Lena blitzed up the stairs, shouldered Dinah out of her way, and charged through the door into the apartment. She had changed into jeans, a red leather jacket with a cashmere scarf around her neck, and black high-heel boots. "Where is she?"

"My mother isn't here."

"Where is she? Where is she hiding?"

"Little Deer…Lena, what is it you have to say to her?"

"She murdered Alwin. Now I will kill her."

"You're wrong. She didn't even know the man. She had no reason to kill him."

"It *was* her." She craned her neck around as if she expected Swan to swoop down on her like a witch on a broomstick. "It had to be her."

"Why do say that?"

"She knew him. Oh, yes. It was arranged. For sure, she knew him." She looked toward the sliding door that led to the bedrooms and took a step.

Dinah moved around the sofa and blocked her way. Lena was a big girl. If she wanted past, the only way to stop her was to knock her feet out from under her. "Tell me how my mother knew Alwin. Had they met?"

Lena's expression turned wary. Was she present at this alleged meeting or, holy moly, had she placed Swan at the crime scene?

Dinah's heart was in her throat. "Did you see what happened at the tower? Was my mother there?"

"No."

"No, she wasn't there or no, you didn't see what happened?"

"Because I didn't see doesn't mean she didn't kill him. Only a savage would do such a thing." Tears welled in her eyes.

"Alwin must have been a very special friend. Was he your lover?"

She let out a sob and simultaneously, K.D. appeared in the door, encased in Thor's outsized robe with a towel turbaned around her head.

"You!" Lena ran at her.

Dinah tackled her with an outthrust shoulder and tried to trip her, but couldn't bring her down. She grabbed Lena around her middle and pinned her arms. "Use your eyes, damn it. Does this girl look like my mother?"

"*Nein.*" Her body slackened and she began to sob. "I loved him and now he is dead."

Dinah let go of her and she sagged onto the sofa.

K.D. sat down and put her arm around her. "Aw, that's terrible. Is it Lena? I'm K.D., Lena, and I know what it feels like when someone you love is murdered. It's the worst feeling in the world." She loosened Lena's scarf and fussed with the cushions behind her back. "My Daddy was shot in the heart by one of his ex-wives, and even though he had done some bad things and hurt some people, it was shattering. I know he loved me way more than my mother ever has. Anyway, it happened like, four years ago and I still have nightmares."

Dinah watched K.D. stroke and coddle and empathize and thought again how much emotional trauma the girl had undergone in her short life and how resilient and perceptive she was in spite of her foibles. She and K.D. were similar, if not in personality, in experience. They both lived with the pain of murdered fathers and the deep-down insecurity of unreliable mothers.

K.D. pulled a tissue out of her pocket and handed it to Lena. "I was in counseling for a while, but I just hate the way those people talk. Like, all the king's horses and all the king's men can never put you back together again? And you wouldn't believe all the drugs they give out. They make you feel spaced out, like a science experiment. But you'll be okay eventually, Lena. You will."

Dinah didn't think Lena was absorbing much of what K.D. said, but the stroking and the soft words seemed to settle her down. She lifted her face and K.D. took out another tissue and blotted her smeared mascara. "How long had you and Alwin been together? Not that the length of time makes any difference. If you'd known each other only a few days, it would still be shattering."

Dinah remembered Lena's arms flailing at her husband and grasped at the possibility of another suspect. "Does your husband know about you and Alwin? Did he know before tonight?"

"You cannot confuse me. Swan Calms is a fatal woman." She shrugged off K.D.'s arm and stood up, red-faced and angry. "Because she is American and rich, she thinks she can get away with it. Tell her that I will see her dead first."

Dinah's temper flared. "You're hysterical, so I'm going to let that threat pass for now. But come near my mother, and I will make sure you're locked up, either in jail or in the loony bin."

"*Zur Hölle fahren.*"

"Whatever. I'm sure you've provided the police with a full statement of what you know, or claim to know. There's nothing more you can do now but wait until they've gathered all the evidence."

K.D. said, "The killer probably left behind DNA evidence, Lena. There's always DNA."

"*Ja*, like the Phantom of Heilbronn." She swished her scarf around her neck and stormed out the door.

"Who do you suppose the Phantom of Heilbronn is?" asked K.D.

"I don't know. But Lena just supplied her husband with an excellent motive for murder."

"I know where you're coming from. You want to convince yourself that Swan's innocent." She got up and fished for something behind the cushions. "You'd like to believe that one member of the family isn't pathological, especially the one whose DNA you share."

"You're quite the little psychologist," said Dinah. "But I can't think about this anymore tonight or I'll go crackers. All I want is to wash my face, brush my teeth, and fall unconscious." She locked and chained the door and turned off the overhead light. "Let's call it a day."

"Whoa, not yet. Turn the light back on."

"You can stay up if you want, but I'm beat."

"You'll cheer up when you see this."

Dinah switched on the light and K.D. held up an elongated, periwinkle blue wallet.

"You swiped her purse?"

"It must have fallen out of her little clutch."

Dinah had seen K.D.'s sleight of hand before. She was a criminal prodigy, and in the circumstances, far too useful to discourage. "What's inside?"

K.D. opened the wallet and took out a Lufthansa ticket jacket. "Alwin and Lena were scheduled to leave for BCN tonight. Where's BCN?"

"Barcelona," said Dinah, taking the tickets out of her hand. It was one-way, first-class, and stamped *handgepaeck*, which was one of the few German words Dinah knew. It indicated that they would be traveling with hand luggage only.

"I count a thousand Euros here," said K.D. "There's also a bank card, an identity card, what looks like a German driver's license and, I don't know, maybe a health card."

"Don't get sticky fingers with the cash," warned Dinah.

"Do you think she'll come back for it tonight?"

"I don't know, but I've buzzed in my last visitor for one day. I'll give it to Inspector Lohendorf tomorrow, and he can return it. Did you find anything else of interest?"

"See for yourself." She handed the wallet to Dinah, leaned back with a smug little smile, and folded her arms behind her turban. "Maybe Lena did the dirty. Maybe Alwin backed out of their trip to Spain, they fought, and she canceled his ticket permanently. That could explain why she's so hot to pin the blame on Swan."

Dinah filed that hypothetical under the heading Unlikely, but Lena's accusations about Swan had unnerved her. An extended roster of suspects would get her through the night. She gave K.D. an affectionate fist bump and headed off to bed.

# Chapter Fourteen

Dinah woke up from a dream about a funeral where she could see the body inside the coffin, but not the face. No morning that entails a trip to the morgue can be called pleasant, but she had a feeling that this day would only get worse. She rolled over and buried her face in Thor's pillow, breathing in the lingering pheromones and feeling sorry for herself. It would be easy to lie here all day and wallow in misery. But she had a date with Inspector Lohendorf, who asked that she abide by the rules, and her mother, who assumed that she would break them.

She wondered what the penalty for obstruction of justice was in Germany. Stiff, she imagined. But she'd read somewhere that most prisoners are eligible for parole after fifteen years. Maybe Thor would wait for her.

She sat up and rallied. Aphrodite was boxing with the curtains, which billowed in the airflow from the furnace grate. Her claws snagged in the fabric and she jigged about furiously and made gnarly jungle noises. Dinah wished K.D. hadn't made such an eloquent case against having the creature declawed.

She left K.D. asleep on the floor in Thor's sleeping bag and went to the kitchen. The rain spatted against the window and the furnace roared without generating any heat. She should tell Geert, but it was almost nine o'clock. He had probably just gotten home from his bartending job and she hated to disturb him. She cinched her robe tighter and turned on the oven. Only in jest did she consider sticking her head inside. A snatch of *Mother Goose* doggerel floated into her mind. *It's like a lion at the door, and when the door begins to crack, it's like a stick across your back, and when your heart begins to smart, it's like a penknife in your heart, and when your heart begins to bleed...*

Eat something. She filled the coffeepot, fixed herself a bowl of granola, and sat down to mope. The unthinkable had wormed its way into her head. *It was arranged. She knew him.* Was it true? Did Swan know Pohl? Did she know that it was he and not Hess they'd be viewing on a morgue table this morning?

Aphrodite came in, growling and grumbling. Dinah scraped a can of tuna into her bowl and then the cuckoo started in. She snapped. She grabbed a roll of duct tape out of the cupboard, stuffed the obnoxious pest back into his box, and taped him in. The clock still made a noise, something like the suppressed moan of a torture victim. It matched her mood. She went back to the kitchen and dumped the granola, which tasted like bird pellets.

The coffeepot gurgled. She poured herself a cup and went into the office. Last night's mention of the Phantom of Heilbronn nagged at her. It sounded macabre, probably a German opera or movie or something. She sat down at the computer, typed in the phrase, and Google came back with the answer immediately. The Phantom was the name the German police had assigned to an unknown female serial killer of Eastern European extraction whose DNA had turned up at a half-dozen murder scenes in France, Austria, and Heilbronn, Germany. They had searched for this "woman without a face" for sixteen years only to discover her working in the factory that manufactured the cotton swabs used by the police to collect DNA. Somehow, her DNA had been transferred to the swabs. Dinah made a mental note that German efficiency was not infallible. If, for example, they were to find her mother's DNA at the scene of the crime, there might be an innocent explanation. Or if not innocent, an explanation that didn't prove murder. Swan had her defects, but she simply could not do what was done to Pohl.

Dinah took a break from conjuring up worst-case scenarios involving her mother and conjured worst-case scenarios about Thor. What was that phone call about? Did he expect something to happen that would drive her to "drastic action"? The stress was giving her a sour stomach and the granola definitely hadn't agreed with her. She squelched her forebodings about Thor and went to shower and dress.

At ten o'clock she was pacing up and down the living room like a nervous sentry. When K.D. dawdled in, yawning, at ten-thirty, Dinah unloaded the last two hours of needles and pins on her. "I'll be gone for most of the day and I swear, if you give me one ounce of grief, one ounce, I will ship you back to Georgia in a heartbeat."

K.D. flumped onto the sofa and sprawled like a seal. "Let me know if there's anything else I can do to help."

Dinah laughed, which deserved its own thank you. "You did help, K.D. You always do, although I could be prosecuted for encouraging you. Thank you, and I apologize for taking my surly mood out on you."

"You're welcome."

Dinah checked her watch. "Inspector Lohendorf will be here in a few minutes. I don't know if he'll have Swan and Margaret in tow, but I need you to be discreet and speak only if spoken to. Please."

"Got it."

"However you feel about Margaret or your father or the police, just suck it up, K.D. I mean it. Let me tell Lohendorf about Lena and her lover."

"Too bad you have to throw a grenade into her marriage."

"Lena's marriage was defunct the day she decided to abscond with her lover. Anyway, the police will already have questioned her and if she didn't fess up to her extramarital shenanigans, that air ticket will tell the tale." Dinah browsed through the wallet for the umpteenth time. Lena had sounded as if she knew a lot more than she was willing to say about Pohl, but there was nothing informative in the wallet.

K.D. said, "She acted all emo, like 'boo-hoo, my poor heart's breaking.' But underneath, I think she's afraid that maybe she said or did something that got Alwin killed. Maybe she bragged that he was better in bed or something, and in her heart of hearts, she believes her husband offed the dude."

In addition to her talents for breaking and entering, picking pockets, and spycraft, K.D. had developed a knack for psychoanalysis. Maybe it stemmed from all the expensive counseling she'd had. Dinah said, "The Bischoffs do seem to have the most credible motives."

"Sex rules."

"I guess. By the way, the police may have seen you leave and come back last night. If they ask, don't deny it."

"If anyone saw me, they'll think I'm Geert's live-in."

"You've met Geert?"

"Yeah, I was having a smoke in the hall when he got home this morning around five. He's kind of cool and swaggy, and his German accent slays me. He's going to take me clubbing one night."

"I don't think that's such a..." Dinah looked at the set of K.D.'s mouth. It was futile to preach caution to her. It would make her all the more determined.

"Such a what?"

"Never mind."

The buzzer signaled the start of the main event. Dinah took a breath and went to answer. "Yes?"

"Inspector Lohendorf."

"Shall I come down?"

"No. I'd like to come up and meet your new houseguest."

Dinah buzzed him in and shot K.D. a look.

She shrugged. "No biggie."

Dinah opened the door and Lohendorf walked into the apartment with Swan at his side. She was dressed in a teal turtleneck, tailored brown trousers, and her blue kitten heels. The powdery fragrance of Chanel clung to her and she carried off a semblance of serene self-assurance. "K.D., what a surprise! I thought you'd gone home to Georgia."

Dinah saw Lohendorf's eyebrows lift.

"Hi, Swan." K.D. executed a deft double-cheek kiss, as if she'd just blown in from France. "You haven't aged at all."

"Bless your heart. You have. You look all grownup and sophisticated."

The charade embarrassed Dinah. Lohendorf had to know that K.D. had been to see Swan at the *Gasthaus* last night. She said, "Where's Margaret?"

"With Sergeant Wegener. They will meet us at the morgue." Lohendorf held out his hand to K.D. "I am Inspector Jens Lohendorf. You are a family friend of Frau Pelerin?"

"Oh, hi." She shook his hand. "I'm K.D. Dobbs, Cleon Dobbs' daughter. Dinah was with my father when he died and, afterward, we sort of bonded. She's like my adopted big sister."

Dinah grabbed Lena's wallet off the table and handed it to Lohendorf. "Lena Bischoff was here last night. She seems to have had an intimate relationship with the deceased. She left in a hurry and forgot this."

Lohendorf opened it and read the ticket. "Thank you. I'll see that it's returned." If it altered his view of the case, he covered it well. "We should be going now."

"Don't worry if I'm not here when you get home," said K.D. "I think I'll rent a bike and go for a ride around the Tiergarten."

"*Bis später*," said Lohendorf, and shepherded Swan and Dinah into the hall. Dinah flashed K.D. a slit-eyed look and followed her mother down the stairs.

The Leichenhaus was no different from the morgues Dinah had seen on American TV shows except this one engaged her sense of smell. She tried to convince herself that the whiff of death was only in her imagination and the antiseptic odors were the same as those in a hospital. It was hard. She had an overwhelming sense of whiteness—the walls, the floor, the ceiling. Backless white benches had been distributed along the hall at intervals, she supposed in case a visitor was overcome by grief. Or guilt. She kept her eyes on her mother. Lohendorf had walked on ahead and the closer they got to the room where Alwin Pohl lay, the farther behind Swan lagged.

Orderlies in light blue scrubs hastened past in silent hospital clogs, as if they were on their way to an emergency. They left a backwash of bleach in the air as they passed. At a T in the hallway, Lohendorf turned right. On a bench across from a swinging metal door, Margaret slumped with her head between her knees.

Wegener stood over her holding a bottle of water. She said to Lohendorf, "We have viewed the body already."

Dinah swallowed hard. It must have been horrific to get to Margaret like that.

"Was she distressed by the viewing or is she ill?" Lohendorf asked.

"She has the grippe," said Swan. She joggled Margaret's arm. "You all right, honey?"

Margaret looked up, gimlet-eyed. Her skin had a greenish cast and her lips quivered. "I need a drink."

Swan jostled Wegener out of her way and reached into Margaret's bag on the seat beside her. She took out her flask, unscrewed the cap, and put it in Margaret's hand. "Have yourself a good long swig."

She had two.

Lohendorf exchanged a look with Wegener. "Were you acquainted with the deceased, Mrs. Dobbs?"

"He didn't look familiar," said Margaret.

"I see." He turned to Swan. "I'm sure you want to get this difficult business over with as quickly as possible, Mrs. Calms."

She smiled. "By all means. I know I can count on you to catch me if I faint, Inspector."

Her put-on charm rankled Dinah, but she couldn't help but wonder if there was a trace of sadism behind Lohendorf's determination to bring them face-to-face with the dead man.

"This way, please." Lohendorf pushed open the metal doors and motioned them inside.

*And when your heart begins to bleed, you're dead and dead and dead, indeed.* Dinah linked arms with Swan, not sure who was supporting whom.

A row of shiny metal gurneys stretched from one end of the room to the other. On the one nearest the door, a white sheet covered a human shape. Swan did a little stutter-step and let go of Dinah's arm.

"Mom?"

"I'm fine. I've seen dead bodies before."

"Embalmed and in a casket," Dinah clarified for Lohendorf's benefit, but if he heard, he gave no sign.

Dinah had boycotted funerals since she was ten and forced to look at her father embalmed in a casket, but she had seen other dead men. She had witnessed Cleon's murder and last year in Greece, she and Thor happened on the body of a man who'd been shot to death. Those sights were seared into her memory. Now she was being compelled to look at corpse that had been scalped.

A pasty-faced man stepped forward to meet them. He had small, sad eyes and a chin that receded like a terrapin's. The coroner, she presumed. Lohendorf spoke to him in German and he beckoned them to come and stand beside the covered gurney. At a signal from Lohendorf, he drew back the sheet to reveal Alwin Pohl.

"His hair…" Dinah was flummoxed. "I thought he'd been scalped."

"I asked the doctor to cover his head wound for the purpose of this viewing. Do you recognize him?"

Even with the platinum blond hairpiece, his face was unforgettable. "It's the same man who came to my apartment and identified himself as Reiner Hess."

"How about you, Mrs. Calms?"

"I don't know the man from Adam's off ox."

Lohendorf frowned.

"She means," said Dinah, "that she's never seen him before."

"Would it help you to remember him if we removed the wig?"

"No. He's a complete stranger."

"Why would a stranger seek you out, Mrs. Calms?"

"I haven't the foggiest idea."

"And you still maintain that you've never met Reiner Hess, or anyone calling himself Reiner Hess?"

"That's right. I've told you all the people I know in Germany." She turned away from the gurney. "May we leave now?"

Lohendorf nodded and the coroner drew the sheet back over the deceased.

Dinah avoided Lohendorf's eyes and trailed her mother out into the hall. She had prepared herself for something grisly and it wasn't. She couldn't understand why Margaret had been so shaken unless—

"Mrs. Dobbs and Mrs. Calms, you will please provide Sergeant Wegener with a DNA sample and we will speak again tomorrow." Lohendorf sounded annoyed and he didn't seem to care who knew. "Sergeant, when you have their samples, drive them back to their lodgings and be certain that they surrender their passports."

"Are we under arrest?" asked Swan.

"When I have made that decision, you will not be in any doubt." He gave them a slashing look and walked away.

"Snippety when he's thwarted," said Swan. "Can he take our passports, just like that? I swear I don't know how some people live with themselves."

Margaret's eyes smoldered. "You've turned not knowing into an art, Swan."

"If wishes were horses, Margaret. But you're too chewed up with envy and bitterness to see straight."

Sergeant Wegener's eyes widened expectantly, but the heat passed without shedding any light. After the cheek swabs had been collected, the two women retreated into a frigid silence. Nobody said a word in the police car on the way home. But today, Margaret commandeered the front seat. Dinah sat in the back with Swan.

*If wishes were horses, beggars would ride.* Was there a message in the rhyme? Did she wish she didn't know? Know what? Dinah finished the rhyme in her head. *If turnips were swords, I'd wear one at my side.* Other than a growing fear that it would take a sword to prize the truth out of her mother, she was at a loss. But she had a sinking feeling that Margaret had recognized the dead man, and so had Swan.

# Chapter Fifteen

Wegener pulled up in front of the Wunderbar and Swan reached for the door handle. Wegener reached an arm over the seat. "Your passport, please."

Swan rooted it out of her bag and handed it over without protest. She seemed less defiant than she had been at the morgue, although it was impossible for Dinah to intuit what was going on in her mind.

"Thank you," said Wegener.

Swan didn't hear. She was already out of the car and making a beeline for the hotel door. Margaret handed over her passport and clambered out, coughing.

"You can let me out here, too," said Dinah. "Assuming it's no longer *verboten* for me to communicate with my mother."

"Do as you wish."

"*Dankeshön.*" She got out and followed Swan and Margaret into the lift. They rode up in silence and walked single file to the room. Swan unlocked the door and went directly to the toilet.

Margaret went to the minibar. She said, "I did some shopping yesterday afternoon at that KaDeWe store. Amazing place." She brought out a bottle of gin and a jar of olives. "These come all the way from Morocco. Care for a martini?"

"You recognized him, didn't you?"

She blew her nose and poured four fingers of gin into a water glass. "He was Cleon's driver and bagman for at least a dozen years. Always had a smartass remark about something or somebody."

"Why didn't you tell Lohendorf that you knew him?"

"Did you see the way he and that female storm trooper look at me? They're thinking hey, she's already killed one man. They probably think I killed Pohl and Swan went native and took his hair." She plunked two olives into her gin and downed half of it in one gulp. "Anyhow, chump that I am, I thought Swan might have stepped up and ID'd the bastard instead of playing dumb and pretending to be outraged."

"Mom knew him, too?"

"Cleon hired him shortly after Swan took over the title of Mrs. Dobbs. She dubbed him Polly. Polly Wolly Doodle. What a piece of work."

It wasn't clear if the "piece of work" referred to was Pohl or Swan. "You could have stepped up and told the truth, Margaret, instead of acting all weak-kneed and wussy, sniveling for your little flask of courage."

She laughed a mirthless laugh, which triggered a hacking cough. "Before I spill my guts," she wheezed at last, "and get us in still deeper with these Germans, I'd like your mother to tell me if she whacked the bastard. I'd like her to tell me why she gulled me into making this trip."

"Gulled you how? Is that what you and she argued about on the beach before the powwow began?"

"We had some back and forth about lies." She discharged a snort of palpable disdain. "In short, how many are too god-damned many."

Swan walked into the room, fluffing her hair. "I must look a sight."

Dinah could have slapped her. "Why did you say you didn't know Alwin Pohl?"

"It's irrelevant that I knew him. It wouldn't help the police find his murderer."

"We'll come back to that in a minute. How did you gull Margaret?"

"Let me count the ways," said Margaret. "She lied about Reiner Hess meeting us at that Indian art place yesterday. She lied about him even being in Berlin. She lied about having something he wanted to buy. I should have checked out the 'doodad' that was going to make us rich before we left Georgia." She plucked a thumb drive out of her jacket pocket and dropped it in Dinah's hand. "There it is, the insurance policy she says Cleon gave her. I read it yesterday on the hotel's computer. It's empty as a bubble."

Swan actually managed to look indignant. "Reiner wouldn't know that right off."

Margaret gave a derisive hoot. "Only an idiot would take for granted that it contained what you said it did. An idiot like me. Serves me right for imagining that I would ever come out ahead in this rat-infested world."

"Mom?" Dinah labored to keep up. "You were going to try to bluff Hess into giving you money?"

"Not exactly bluff. I thought the incriminating thingummy might add a little extra incentive, presented in a nice way. Reiner and I are old friends. It's kind of a ticklish situation."

"Ticklish doesn't begin to cover it," said Dinah. "You came here intending—in a nice way—to blackmail your old friend, the double murderer?"

Margaret scoffed. "It was all bullshit. Turns out, they're pen pals. I smelled a rat when she pulled that disappearing act yesterday. Hanging around waiting for you in that bizarro gallery, I got to thinking maybe she'd kept something back from me. So I returned to the room and rifled her suitcase. Besides the empty thumb drive, I found a letter from Hess, postmarked Cyprus. '*My dear Swan, I wish I could lend you the money you need, but at this time…*'"

Swan said, "I don't believe those are his final words, Margaret. And I don't believe he's still in Cyprus. His daughter Elke's expecting a baby any day now and I'm sure he'll want to be here in Berlin for the birth. If we can find him, I'm sure he'll help us out with the money."

"Why are you so almighty desperate for money?"

"It's not a matter of desperation. It's only fair. I'm the one who has to fend off the government agents still looking for Cleon's money. I'm the one who has my bank account examined and my poor husband's accounts questioned, while Reiner gets to enjoy all that money and he doesn't even pay taxes on it."

"Screw Hess!" Dinah was close to her wit's end. "Can't you get it through your head that money is the least of your problems? A man you know, a man you've lied about knowing, was brutally murdered. You're a suspect. The police have your shoes and your DNA and your passport and they won't give up until they find out the truth."

"If I thought you'd brought me along to set me up as a scapegoat," said Margaret, "I'd strangle you with one of your Frederick's of Hollywood brassieres."

"Y'all are ganging up on me. I didn't kill that man. And the police would never have known we were anywhere near that Müggel-de-doo place if Dinah hadn't gotten so het up and called 'em in. Not that you're to blame, baby. You did what you thought was right. As for you, Margaret, I've been trying to help you. If there was any money to be had, I'd have given it to you. I would still. Don't forget, I bought your ticket and I'm the one paying for the hotel."

"Thanks for the room and board, Swan, and oh, yes, for putting me in the crosshairs of the German police. All I need is another murder rap. You are *too* generous."

"I'm suffering, too, Margaret. In ways you'll never know and trust me, that's a blessing."

"Oh, for the love of God. I've had more than enough of your forked tongue and your wild-eyed fantasies. I plan to get roaring drunk this afternoon, and quite possibly violent. It would be safer if you found yourself a different place to sleep tonight."

Dinah felt ambushed, duped six ways from Sunday by a mother whose veil of lies she couldn't pierce and whose love she couldn't trust. She permitted herself a brief moment of self-pity, then gritted her teeth and hardened her heart. Either Swan had come to the end of her lies, or her daughter had come to the end of the umbilical tether. She said, "Take a nap, Margaret. I'm going to give Mom a little walking tour of the city. If you feel the same way when we get back, I'll help her pack."

# Chapter Sixteen

An anemic sun shone through the clouds as Dinah nudged Swan out onto the street and pointed her in the direction of the Gendarmenmarkt. Gendarmenmarkt was Dinah's favorite square in Berlin, perhaps because its architecture reflected the past in a city whose skyline was jagged with modernity. The bomb damage to the Konzerthaus and the graceful eighteenth-century French cathedral had been repaired, and the German Cathedral, burned to the ground in 1945, had been painstakingly reconstructed to the last detail. It was a short walk and Dinah felt the need for open space and a view of the sky.

At the corner of Niederwallstrasse and Jerusalemstrasse, her eye was drawn, as it always was, to the quotation by Albert Einstein stenciled in large red letters on the windowless wall of an apartment building. Thor had translated the German for her, which went something like, "When concerning oneself with matters of truth and justice, there's no difference between small and big problems." She didn't like to quibble with a man of Einstein's intellect, but in her humble opinion, concerning oneself with the truth about murder dwarfed the small shit. She said, "We're going to have to discuss Alwin Pohl. Why did he come to my apartment to see you and why did he use the name Hess?"

Swan could usually deflect an unwelcome question by veering off on a whimsical tangent, but for once she stayed quiet. Dinah left the subject of Polly Wolly Doodle until they reached the square. She guided Swan to a bench midway between the two cathedrals. "Let's sit, Mom. The bench isn't wet."

Swan sat and pointed to a statue of Friedrich von Schiller. "Who's that?"

"A German poet and philosopher. Schiller."

"And what did he make of this cruel ol' world?"

"He believed that mankind was doomed to suffer."

"Doomed." Her smile was uncharacteristically sardonic. "Like Higgledy-Piggledy. Picked and plucked and put in a pie."

"You said that you were suffering, Mom. Do you want to tell me about it? The truth's going to come out sooner or later and I would appreciate being the first in line to hear it."

"If a woman can't trust her own daughter with the truth…" She broke off and steepled her fingers under her chin. It was a familiar sign. This was not going to be easy for her.

Dinah was seized by that old seasick feeling, not knowing which way the waves would break. Margaret had nailed her dead to rights. She *was* afraid that Swan would say something she couldn't forgive. If you loved someone, you should be able to forgive anything. But "should" was a highly aspirational word. Doubts could be staved off, rationalized, managed. Knowing would require so much more—judgment, perhaps action. Hallmark sentiments aside, love had its boundaries. While the logical part of her brain struggled to chart them, her subconscious took over. "I love you, Mom."

"I love you, too, baby. I wish there weren't this wall between us." But even that admission was too much for her. Her eyes darted as suddenly as a dragonfly. "I'm so hungry I could eat a buttered rock. Could we go somewhere and have ourselves a bite of lunch?"

"You can't wriggle out of this situation with a smile and a digression. I need to hear the truth now. Love has its limits."

"I hope you're wrong about love, Dinah. I'd hate to see you end up like poor Margaret. But I'll tell you about Mr. Alwin Pohl if we could please go inside someplace where it's warm."

Dinah saw that she was shivering. They were only a few steps from the Café Aigner where she and Thor often ate. "Okay, come on." She helped her to her feet and they crossed the square, arm in arm. She tried not to think of it as a perp walk.

The headwaiter, or *Oberkellner*, remembered Dinah from previous visits and seated them right away.

"Do y'all have bourbon over here in Germany?" asked Swan.

"Jim Beam, Wild Turkey, Four Roses, Maker's Mark…" The waiter seemed prepared to go on.

"That's fantastic. My husband Bill just loves Eagle Rare. Do y'all have that?"

"I will ask the bartender."

"No." Dinah scrunched her eyes. "One of the ones you named will do."

Swan hesitated for a split second, then smiled up at the waiter. "I'll have a double bourbon Presbyterian with Maker's Mark."

"I'll have a glass of the house red wine," said Dinah. She waited until he was out of earshot. "I've never known you to drink anything but chardonnay. It must be bad if you need to buck up your courage with the hard stuff."

She did the steepling thing.

Dinah steeled herself. "Let's have it."

"What's that thing Cleon used to say? Overtaken by events. Somebody was always being overtaken by events. Well, I was overtaken by Polly's murder."

"Did you kill him?"

"I did not. I wished he was dead, or gone off somewhere so I'd never hear from him again. He was a slimy toad and if somebody had killed him while I was in another country, I'd be singin' hosannas."

"Why? What did he do to you?"

She glanced around as if to make sure Lohendorf wasn't skulking about with a portable mike. "Pretty much everything I told you is the truth, only backwards and with the name changed."

"Backwards how? Did you intend to blackmail Pohl instead of Hess?"

"Truth to tell, Alwin was blackmailing me."

Dinah's thoughts cornered hard. "What in the name of all that's holy could Alwin Pohl have to hold over *your* head?"

"Did you know they've got a law back in the States that says, even if you had no idea in the world that the person you were with meant to kill somebody, you're just as guilty as he is?"

"Sure. I used to work for lawyers. If somebody dies during the commission of a felony, even if it's accidental, all of the participants can be charged."

"That's what Alwin had on me. It's as unfair as a tumor, but there you are."

A different waiter brought their drinks. This one was young and blond with a gold hoop in his left ear.

"Thank you kindly." Swan smiled up at him. "If you don't mind my saying, you look just like the attractive young lieutenant in that movie about the plot to assassinate Hitler. What was it called?"

"*Valkyrie*. It was a good film. Germans are always the bad guys in American films, but there were some good ones in *Valkyrie*. Matthias Schweighöfer played the lieutenant. You are not the first to say that I resemble him. He lives here in Berlin."

"Well, isn't *that* a coincidence."

"I see him sometimes at the clubs. He is a good guy. Not at all arrogant."

Dinah glowered at Matthias' doppelgänger. He seemed to get the message and beat it back to the kitchen.

Swan tasted her drink. "I wouldn't have guessed you could get bourbon in Berlin. And everybody I've met speaks perfect English."

"But only you can use it to say nothing. Are you telling me that you were present when somebody committed a murder?"

"Nearby. Believe me, Dinah, I didn't know it was going to happen."

"Just tell me."

"Ten years ago, Cleon asked me to ride along to Brunswick with him. He said he had to stop off on the way to town to serve a subpoena. Polly drove. We got to this witness' house and he and Polly went inside. I waited in the car. When they got back, Cleon had blood on his shirt and jacket. He said, 'It was a bleeping trap,' and when I asked about the blood, he said he had shot a couple of drug cops."

"Weeping Jesus. Cleon killed federal agents and you knew about it?"

"I was scared to death of him from that day on."

"Let me get this straight. It was Cleon who killed these people and not Reiner Hess?"

"That's right. I never told a soul for fear of what Cleon might do. I didn't know until a month ago that Polly had recorded what we said in the car."

Dinah took a long drink of her wine, mostly to give herself time to process the rolling revelations. Ten years ago, 2003. Swan had been divorced from Cleon for twenty-five years. She had been married to Hart Pelerin and widowed, and she had remarried three times since then. "What were you doing palling around with Cleon? Were you planning to go back to him?"

"No. It was supposed to be a friendly drive to Brunswick, that's all. If I'd known he was going to shoot somebody, I'd never have gone."

If Swan didn't know what Cleon intended, if she just happened to be sitting in his car, she wasn't liable under the felony murder rule. Of course, she could be prosecuted by a district attorney who didn't believe her. How could she prove she didn't know? And if she'd helped Cleon escape, she was guilty of aiding and abetting. With Cleon dead and the other felon blackmailing her, Dinah could understand how she would feel she had no choice but to accede to Pohl's demands. Still, there were too many loose threads to weave into a coherent whole. "How does Hess fit into this disaster?"

"I wrote him and asked if he could reason with Polly. Buy him off or scare him off, do *something* to help me out of this pickle. But that tax scandal has forced the man to go to ground like a hunted fox."

"You expected Hess to pay the ransom to Pohl for the recording?"

"Why not? I thought he would take care of Polly and share some of his money with Margaret and me, for all our trouble. I've never given his name to any of that plague of agents who've pestered me since Cleon's death." She drank a few sips of bourbon. "Anyhow, Reiner was never the villain that Margaret imagines. Cleon may have hidden money from her, but it wasn't Reiner's doing. Cleon was the devil incarnate. If it hadn't been for him—"

"Oh, stop it. You stayed close to him after your divorce. You stayed close the whole time you were married to my father and long after he died."

"I told you I was afraid of Cleon."

"Since when, Mom? Ten years? Twenty? When were you first afraid of him?" Dinah felt the old compulsion to ask her straight up if she knew that Cleon had killed Hart Pelerin, but she chickened out again. "You could have been smart and told the feds that Cleon had killed two of their own. They would have locked him away where he couldn't hurt anyone else."

"Smart?" Her eyes glistened with tears. "I had three years of high school on the Big Cypress Reservation. I dropped out after my father hanged himself and I married Cleon the day I turned eighteen. He was already a lawyer, working for Highbrow, Uppity and Snob up in Atlanta. Smart for me has always been to say as little as possible and let other people believe whatever suits them. You don't have to tell me that I've been stupid, that I've put myself and Margaret in jeopardy. I just hope it doesn't suit my daughter to believe that I'm a murderess."

Dinah thought of all the times she'd faulted her mother for being glib and superficial, hiding behind her smiles and her charm. It had never occurred to her that the studied nonchalance covered feelings of inferiority.

The Matthias lookalike returned to take their order and Swan turned on the charm automatically. "Would you recommend something for me? A specialty of Berlin?"

He recommended the Brandenberger Landente, stuffed duck with red cabbage and potato dumplings. That reminded Swan of a numbered duck she'd had in Paris once, which reminded the waiter of duck-hunting on a private estate on the Baltic last year.

Dinah hardly heard. Her thoughts were in ferment. She supposed Pohl had recorded Cleon to use as leverage in case they were caught and Cleon tried to lay the blame off on him, but why had he waited until now to threaten Swan? He must have seen her picture among Farber's Facebook Indians, remembered the recording, and decided to dig it out to fatten his kitty for Barcelona and a new life with Lena.

"What will you have?"

"Dinah? The young man asked you a question."

"Oh. Just another glass of wine, please."

Swan patted his sleeve. "Bring us an extra plate, Kurt. We'll share the duck." She ordered another bourbon Presbyterian and sent him away with a grin on his face.

When they were alone, Dinah said, "How much money did Pohl want from you?"

"Four hundred thousand Euros. That's more than a half million dollars. I told him I didn't have that kind of money, but he didn't believe me. He said he knew I had the wampum, which I took as a very disparaging word. He said he knew about Panama. He said Cleon told him that's where he parked his cash."

"Why would Cleon entrust a goon like Pohl with his banking info? And why would Pohl think that you inherited it?"

"I don't know. I told him you were the only one who could dip into that money."

Dinah rubbed her temples. Her mother had thrown her to the wolf. Did Pohl tell anyone else? She would have to think about that later. She could juggle only so many hot potatoes at a time. "If Pohl believed you were going to pay him, why would he run our car off the road and shoot at you before he got the money?"

"I said you wouldn't give it to me unless you thought my life was in danger. That's what that doll was about."

A minute went by while Dinah digested yet another lie. She felt as if she were swimming underwater in one of those deep, murky channels of the Suwannee. How could she believe anything Swan said? An old brain twister sprang to mind, something about a lost traveler on an island with two tribes, the Truthful Whitefeet and the Lying Blackfeet. They all wore moccasins so that the traveler couldn't tell them apart. The only way to ascertain the right directions was to ask a question that both the truth-tellers and the liars would answer in the same way. Dinah couldn't think of a single question that would produce a straight answer. Anger boiled out of her. "You've played us all for fools, haven't you? Margaret, Pohl, me. And you're still fooling Margaret, letting her think you need money when you don't. Your money problem is lying dead in the morgue. Now all you have to do is fool the police."

Swan aimed a moist, contrite look over the rim of her glass. "I lied to y'all, I sure did. I don't know if the truth would've worked out any better. Maybe, though it didn't seem like it would at the time. There's nothing I can do now but say I'm sorry. I truly am. I hope you won't be stingy meting out grace, baby. You may need a smidgen of forgiveness yourself someday."

Dinah had underestimated her mother's instinct for the emotional jugular. She thought about her upcoming confession to Thor. A smidgen of forgiveness from him would be a godsend. Anyhow, she didn't believe that Swan had killed Pohl. Call it filial devotion or hereditary insanity, it amounted to the same thing. Now her first priority was to get her crossed off Lohendorf's suspect list.

"Did you meet Pohl last night?"

"Yes. He called and told me to meet him at six. I went to the tower like he said, but when I got there he was already dead. I took a gun, but I didn't fire it."

"Jerusalem! How did you smuggle a gun into the country?"

Kurt returned with the duck and the second round of drinks. Swan smiled absently, but made no attempt to restart the banter. He offloaded the food and departed.

Swan cupped her hands around the bourbon. "About the gun…"

"As easy as smuggling kudzu honey, I'm sure. Someday you can regale me with the story of how you bamboozled airport security on two continents. Right now, I need to know if you touched Pohl's body, or took anything away with you."

"I felt inside his coat to try and find the tape. I couldn't keep from seeing his face." Her voice quavered. "It was hideous. I can see it still." She pressed her palms against her cheeks. "Do you think the police will let me go home?"

"Maybe. But you need to admit that you *did* know Pohl. It's your lies that have put their hackles up. You can be sure Lohendorf knows that Pohl spent time in the States. He may even know that he worked for Cleon. Play the 'old lady' card. Tell him that Pohl was intimidating you, demanding money. You don't have to say for what. Having a secret isn't a crime. Tell him you discovered Pohl's body, you checked to see if he was still alive, and when you saw blood, you were frightened and ran away."

"What if they found the tape? They'll play it and turn me over to the feds as an accessory to the murders."

"We'll see. You didn't know what had happened until it was all over and Cleon said what he did. You were probably in shock. But Lohendorf will want an explanation of why Pohl pretended to be Hess."

"I had to keep Margaret thinking it was Reiner we were dealin' with or she wouldn't have gone along. And Polly agreed it would be best not to use his real name."

Dinah was past surprise or anger. She said, "Here's what we'll do. We'll hand over your gun. Lohendorf will see it hasn't been fired. He'll probably reprimand you for touching the body, but if you stick to the story about checking to see if the man was still alive, that will explain any trace of DNA you may have left behind. You could be deported for misleading the police and smuggling a weapon into the country, but at least you'll be out from under suspicion of murder."

"It's a little more complicated than that."

"I know, I know. We'll have to get around the tie-in with Hess, but…" The look on Swan's face stopped her. "What complication were *you* thinking of?"

"The gun's gone missing."

# Chapter Seventeen

*On his way to Japan in 1492, Christopher Columbus bumped into the Bahama Islands and, thinking they were the East Indies, he labeled...he mislabeled the inhabitants Indians.*

Dinah crossed out the sentence and began again.

*Indigenous peoples of North America were called Indians because of a nautical miscalculation that Columbus never acknowledged.*

She x'd that out and scrolled through her notes on the computer. Troubles and misunderstandings had abounded from the first meeting between Europeans and Indians and they persisted like anthrax spores. The Indian problem in Berlin played havoc with her thoughts and once again, the forecast of things to come didn't bode well for the Indians. She had hoped that a temporary shift in focus would give her yeasty thoughts time to take shape and some simple, obvious solution would rise out of her subconscious. It hadn't. The only thing on the rise was her angst. She gave up and drifted into the kitchen.

If Swan could be believed, the gun she took to her rendezvous with Pohl was a Taurus .22 semi-automatic with gold accents and a rosewood grip. It had entered the country legally, shipped unloaded and properly documented by a licensed gun dealer in Georgia to her, care of the Hotel Adlon where she had reserved a room. The Adlon is where she'd gone when she disappeared after breakfast on the morning of the murder. She had taken possession of the package containing the gun, checked in, and phoned

Pohl. He provided her with the number of his bank account and instructed her to make *eine Geldüberweisung*, a transfer of funds. Since the money was supposed to come from Dinah's account, and Germany is six hours ahead of Panama, it wouldn't show up in Pohl's account until the next day. Notwithstanding this delay, Swan had conned him into giving her the tape at the powwow, ahead of the transfer. At least, she assumed that she had conned him. It was possible. In his haste to jet off to Barcelona the next day, Pohl might have given her the benefit of the doubt. They'd never know now.

Absentmindedly, Dinah opened the freezer. A new tub of chocolate ice cream greeted her eyes. A yellow sticky glued to the carton read, *Borrowed yr coral shirt Hope u don't mind, ciao, kd.* That blouse was Dupioni silk from the KaDeWe and it had cost Dinah most of what she earned working on the dig in Turkey. Nervy brat. What good would it do if she did mind?

She grabbed the ice cream and a spoon and sat down for some heavy brain bashing. Who could have taken the gun from Swan's hotel room at the Adlon? Who knew she had a room there? Swan said that she had told only Pohl, but Pohl must have told Lena. She was privy to his extortion of Swan. Was she his co-extortionist? Lena had fixated on Swan as the murderer, but she might not be the only one of Pohl's acquaintances with a dangerous secret. What if he had other victims? Blackmailers didn't stick to a limit, like fishermen.

Whether the motive was blackmail or sexual jealousy, Lena was the key. Lohendorf and Wegener would already have interrogated her about her relationship with Pohl. They were undoubtedly good cops, but they didn't have a mother in the suspect pool and Lena had had time to polish her story since her wild visit on the night of the murder. Had they asked her about blackmail? She was hiding something. Dinah wondered if she could find out what while keeping under the radar of the police.

The cuckoo moaned five times. Late, but if she hurried, Florian Farber's gallery might still be open and he could tell her where the Bischoffs lived. She had no idea where K.D. had gone, but there was no sense worrying. She was nothing if not self-reliant and she wouldn't go out without a few bills in her pocket. Dinah tossed the ice cream back in the freezer and, on a hunch, counted the cash that Thor kept in a sugar canister in the pantry. She was pleasantly surprised to find it all there. Maybe K.D.'s delinquent phase was winding down. Dinah scribbled a note reminding her to feed Aphrodite and clean the litter box. She added a P.S., *I'll be home by nine if you want to have a late dinner.*

She found one of Berlin's ubiquitous taxis idling in front of the Presse & Tabac in Hausvogteiplatz. The driver didn't understand her when she gave him the address so she jotted it down on a scrap of paper. He nodded, like how-could-you-not-pronounce-something-that-simple, and motioned her into the backseat. As he zipped in and out of traffic, she listened to retro American pop songs on the radio and rehearsed her opening gambit with Farber. He had seemed enamored of Swan yesterday morning, but his attitude changed following the discovery of Pohl's body last night. Could he seriously believe she had something to do with the murder?

The driver navigated around the Gendarmenmarkt onto Behrenstrasse and swung onto Ebertstrasse past the Holocaust Memorial. Drifts of yellow leaves swirled across the field of gray, tomblike slabs dedicated to the memory of the Jews killed by the Nazis between 1933 and 1945. The enormity of the crime, the systematic extermination of six million souls, never failed to astound her. It was humanity's moral nadir, an indelible stain on the German State and the German psyche. Several times she had walked through the maze of stone blocks. She hadn't yet mustered the courage to visit the subterranean "Room of Names," where the lives of individual victims were recounted by a disembodied voice.

Opposite the Holocaust Memorial, invisible from the street, stood the concrete cube commemorating the homosexuals persecuted and killed by the Nazis. Its location had sparked controversy when it was first erected. Some believed that it encroached too close to the Jewish Memorial. Others believed that the homosexual victims of the Third Reich had been slighted when their memorial was placed out of sight in the bushes. Dinah saw nothing irreverent in the proximity. Germany had a multitude of victims to remember and in Berlin, monuments to the dead were thick on the ground.

As the taxi turned onto Tiergartenstrasse, she wrested her thoughts back to Florian Farber and those Indian masks that ornamented his gallery. She'd read an article just recently about a contested auction of sacred Native American masks in Paris. The Hopi tribe had filed a lawsuit alleging that some of the items had been stolen, but their attorney was unable to halt the sale. Had Farber acquired his masks legally? Could he have been another of Pohl's blackmail victims?

The taxi rounded the corner onto Klingelhöferstrasse and her eyes were drawn reflexively to the Norwegian Embassy with its green, modernistic louvered siding. She had made Thor a promise that she wouldn't do anything impulsive and already she was breaking it.

The taxi driver let her out on Kurfürstenstrasse in front of the gallery. She handed him a ten Euro note and went inside. The ambience of desert sage had changed to juniper and the flute music had been replaced by the eerie whine of a primitive fiddle. Today, the Indians staring down from the walls looked glum and aggrieved, as if they'd been falsely accused and were counting on her to uphold the honor of all the tribes.

Florian Farber, sans war paint and dressed in ordinary business attire, donned wire-rim eyeglasses and scowled at her from behind his desk. His mohawk had been moussed flat and when he spoke, his voice was as blunt as a bat. "What do you want?"

"Hello, Herr Farber." She affected an appeasing smile. "I've come to ask for your help."

He walked to the front of the shop. Without the painted black hand and the white dots, his nose and cheeks appeared red and chapped, with a filigree of broken capillaries. His gray eyes appraised her with the shrewdness of a croupier. "Do you wish to make a purchase?"

"Not today. Please tell me why you sounded so accusing last night. It seemed almost as if you had some reason to suspect my mother of the murder."

"Our club has been meeting for ten years. The only new person was Frau Calms. I feel responsible. I invited her. She is a *hexenspruch*. A jinx."

"Please. You're far too intelligent and practical to believe in jinxes. My mother is innocent and no one could possibly hold *you* responsible for what happened."

He said, "No one knows what to think."

"Tell me about Herr Pohl. I understand that he was new to the club."

"Alwin came only a few months ago. He had lived for some years in America. He had visited several reservations in your Dakotas and in Arizona."

"And what about Reiner Hess? You said that he was a long-time member."

"Yes. Like me, one of the original founders."

"Why was he expelled?"

"His legal situation made it impossible to attend meetings. Also, some members did not wish to associate with an individual who avoided his duty as a citizen to pay taxes."

"When did you see him last?"

"Six months, perhaps seven. I don't understand your interest."

She upped the wattage of her smile. "He and my mother are old friends from his days in America. Do you have any idea where he is now or how I could get in touch with him?"

"If I knew where he was, it would be my duty to tell the police."

She took a different tack. "I'm intrigued by your mask collection. Did Alwin Pohl acquire them for you when he was in Arizona?"

Before he could answer, she wandered over to look at one of the masks up close. Crafted from wood, leather, and horsehair, the blue and yellow face imparted an almost spectral aura. She was no expert, but it looked like an authentic *katsinam*, which the Hopi people regarded as living souls. To sell one would be a sacrilege. "What's the provenance of this one?" she asked, reaching her hand out.

"Don't touch!" He started forward.

She withdrew her hand. "Sorry."

"As someone versed in Native American cultures, I'm sure you know it is from the Hopi, a one-of-a-kind mask and quite fragile. I would be happy to sell it if you are interested."

"I'm sure I couldn't afford it," she said, and moved on to study a red gourd mask replete with turquoise, wood, and horn beads. But by not volunteering a single detail about the chain of ownership, he had ignited her suspicions. She could feel his eyes drilling into her back. She couldn't tell whether his wariness was because of her questions about the masks or Reiner Hess. She returned to him with a smile. "Is your assistant, Herr Bischoff, here today?"

"No."

"His wife Lena seemed especially upset by Herr Pohl's death. Did you know that she had planned to travel to Barcelona with him today."

"It is not my business."

"But you knew?"

"It was obvious that they were involved. Lena is too young for Viktor. She would rather spend her time in the nightclubs than listening to him drum and talk about his spiritual journey."

"Do you think he knew about the affair?"

"He has been depressed over the last weeks. He looked sad in the photographs from last night."

"You took photographs at the powwow?"

"Yes. I showed them to Inspector Lohendorf and he downloaded them onto his computer."

"Will you show them to me?"

"If you wish."

Surprised but grateful, she followed him to his desk. He sat down, opened his laptop, and set up a slideshow. She leaned over his shoulder, careful not to get too close to his spider-veined cheek.

The first few slides showed Viktor Bischoff in his Drumming Man wig as he arranged the glow logs for the faux bonfire. He appeared not so much sad as stoic. Lena stood with her back to the camera tying the silk streamers.

"Does your camera time-stamp the photos?"

"No. It shows only the date."

That would have made it too easy, she thought. The show continued. She pointed to a group gathered next to the makeshift bar. "Who are these people?"

"The man with the brown trade blanket around his shoulders is Kicking Horse."

"What's his name in the real world?"

"Hans Oostrum. Next to him is Luther Wurttemberg, whose Indian name is Quidel, which means Burning Torch. He brought the schnapps. And behind him—"

"Herr Amsel," she said. "Inspector Lohendorf questioned him at the same time as you last night."

"Yes. Stefan Amsel. He calls himself Doba, which is from the Navajo. He is a senior executive at the Adlon Hotel."

Dinah's ears pricked up. "Did he arrive at the same time you did?"

"Within a few minutes, yes. Baer Eichen, the Bischoffs, and I came early to set up the barbecue grill, build the bonfire, and place the LED lanterns. There are rules about fire in the park and we can't be as faithful to the old ways as we would like."

"What time did the four of you arrive?"

"Between four-thirty and a quarter to five. Stefan and Luther arrived just after with the beer keg and the schnapps. The others arrived together at about half-past six. There, that is Baer in the ghost shirt with the bird in his hair. We were all assembled except for Alwin when you and the Inspector arrived."

"Seven-thirty," she said, thinking out loud.

It was odd that Baer had chosen a shirt that symbolized so much disillusionment and death. The Ghost Dance religion was the brainchild of a Paiute medicine man named Wovoka who claimed that Jesus Christ had returned to earth as an Indian to reunite the spirits of the dead. Wearing what he called a "ghost shirt," Wovoka performed a magic trick whereby he appeared to "catch" a bullet fired at him by a shotgun. Believing their shirts could repel bullets, the Lakota Sioux rebelled against the white settlers at Wounded Knee Creek on the Pine Ridge Reservation in South Dakota in 1890 and the U.S. Cavalry mowed them down. The ghost shirt had become emblematic of the massacre, which any student of Indian culture would know.

Farber went through the rest of his slideshow. She couldn't keep the names or their Indian get-ups straight. They merged in a hodgepodge of feathers and painted faces, indistinguishable, like the homogenized Indians in old Western movies. With each slide, her hopes of spotting a telltale clue dwindled. Wegener had said that there were twenty-six attendees packing God only knew what lethal weapons under their tunics and buckskins. And with all the drumming and dancing and chanting, nobody would have noticed if one of them had slipped off into the forest to answer a call of nature, or shoot and scalp Alwin Pohl. Adding to the confusion, there was Hess, who lurked "off camera," like a figment of everyone's imagination.

What was the actual time of the murder? Swan said she had gotten to the ferry dock at about five-thirty, later than Lena claimed to have taken her photo. Margaret was already there, waiting for Swan. They argued for a few minutes, then Swan walked to the tower, which would have taken her a good half-hour. When she reached the tower, she found Pohl already dead so the murder must have occurred before six, while it was still daylight and before the dancing and the drumming revved up. The hiker who reported the body must have come along shortly after Swan left, and the Rahnsdorf police arrived before Lohendorf and Dinah got to the tower a little past seven-thirty.

It dawned on her that the prime suspects were the early birds—Florian Farber, Viktor and Lena Bischoff, Luther Wurttemberg, Stefan Amsel, and Baer Eichen. In spite of his seeming intoxication last night, Amsel warranted special scrutiny because of his connection to the Adlon. "Did you or any of the others hear gunshots?"

"No. Luther thought he heard fireworks down by the lake around six."

Nobody expects gunfire, she thought—at least not in Germany, and it isn't always clear where the sound has come from, depending on the distance and caliber and the physical terrain. It was possible that the murderer used a silencer and what Luther heard was, in fact, fireworks.

"Other than Viktor, did any of the other club members have a bone to pick with Pohl?"

"I don't know what you mean."

"A grudge. Some reason to hate him or fear him?"

Farber's forehead puckered and he closed the laptop. "I am not a priest. I do not take confession." He closed his laptop and stood up. "It is past my closing hour now."

"I won't keep you. Thanks so much for showing me the photographs. If you'll be so kind as to give me the Bischoffs' address, I'll be on my way."

He looked doubtful.

She smiled. "Lena popped by my apartment last night. She was all torn up and I want to check on her. To make sure she's all right."

"You had better be careful, Frau Pelerin. Lena is a volatile woman and she thinks your mother killed Alwin."

"I intend to convince her she's wrong."

"Then I wish you good luck." He took a business card from a holder on the desk, wrote an address on the back, and put the card in her hand. "She and Viktor quarreled last night after the police questioned them. I doubt you will find them at home together."

# Chapter Eighteen

Kurfürstenstrasse swarmed with evening shoppers, making their way west to the retail mecca of the Ku'damm or maybe the vast and luxurious KaDeWe, short for Kaufhaus des Westens—the department store of the West. Dinah glimpsed the KaDeWe sign a block away over the roofs of other buildings. She thought about the array of fantastic desserts in its seventh-floor café and her mouth watered. The tiramisu törtchen with the chocolate frosting seemed to cry out to her. She held out against temptation, afraid that if she stopped even briefly, she would talk herself out of a visit with Viktor and Lena.

She waited on the corner for the red traffic light man to change to green. The jaunty little man in the hat had been a popular icon in East Germany and, despite efforts to replace the *Ampelmännchen* with standardized traffic signals, he remained as a sentimental relic. He was by far and away the most innocent reminder of the German Democratic Republic's oppressive communist regime.

Green Ampelmann appeared and she crossed to Budapester-Strasse and hailed a taxi. She showed the driver the address on the card and he assured her he could get her there in twenty minutes. For some reason, she had a feeling of urgency and a raft of second thoughts about blackmail as the motive for murder. More often than not, the simplest explanation was the correct one and sex was as simple as it got. Viktor fit a profile common in the States—depressed man, unable to cope with his wife's infidelity, flips out, buys a gun and kills his rival. Some head cases went on to kill the wife, the children, and the in-laws before killing themselves. It occurred to her that Lena might be in danger. This line of thinking led her to recall stories of third parties caught in the line of fire between feuding couples. She envisioned her obituary.

*Dinah Pelerin, 34, long known for her habit of being in the wrong place at the wrong time, was shot dead in the Berlin suburbs by a make-believe Kiowa brave named Drumming Man. Her mother, exonerated of murder, wore kitten heels to the funeral.*

The taxi cut through the Tiergarten to the intersection of Strasse des 17 Juni, the former Nazi triumphal boulevard renamed in 1953 in tribute of the East Berlin protesters gunned down on that day by the Red Army and the East German Volkspolizei. Straight ahead, on a small traffic island at the hub of six avenues through the park, stood the memorial column commemorating the Prussian victory over the French in 1870. The Soviet troops who captured Berlin in 1945 referred to the golden angel who sat atop the column as "the tall woman." Berliners called her Golden Lizzy. Geert called her the chick on a stick. The chick had looked down on a lot of history in her time. Some thought her pedestal was a place where angels congregate. Some thought ghosts. Keeping her secrets, she glimmered noncommittally as a light rain began to fall. The taxi skirted around her island and headed toward the River Spree.

This driver liked classical music. The radio played a soothing serenade by Brahms and her thoughts reverted to Thor. He would think of something sensible and incisive that would never have occurred to her. But Thor was tied up with an international crisis and how could she possibly explain her mother's situation?

They crossed the River Spree and after a couple of miles, the driver turned right onto Otto-Dix-Strasse. She recognized the name. She had seen a few of his paintings exhibited in the New National Gallery. The Nazis had deemed him a degenerate and burned some of his work. Two of his canvases had been recently discovered among a trove of masterpieces stolen by the Nazis and hoarded in the home of an elderly art dealer's son in Munich. Come to think of it, those paintings remained in legal limbo because the art dealer, like Reiner Hess, was under investigation for tax evasion.

The taxi slowed and came to a stop in front of a row of modest townhomes, each painted a different color. The driver consulted Farber's card and pointed. "That one. The house with the blue door."

She pushed a fifty Euro note into his hand. "Will you wait please? I shouldn't be more than a few minutes."

He pocketed the note. "Take your time."

She pushed open a low gate and followed a brick path through a well-tended small garden. In the rainy dusk, it was hard to see what the Bischoffs grew other than cauliflower and kohlrabi. A sensor light came on when she stepped up onto the stoop. The doorknocker was the bronze head of an Indian chief. No question this was the right place. She rapped the knocker against the door with force several times. No one answered. She looked back at the taxi driver, who lolled against the seat enjoying his music.

She rapped again.

"*Wer ist da?*" answered a sullen male voice.

"Dinah Pelerin."

The door swung open and Viktor appeared, disheveled and unsteady on his feet, but dressed in normal Western clothes and without his braids. "*Was willst du?*"

She assumed it was the same question that had greeted her when she strolled into Farber's gallery. "I'd like to speak with your wife."

"*Geh zur Hölle.*"

"I don't speak German, Herr Bischoff."

"Go to hell." He turned and staggered down the hall, thumping a drumstick against the wall as he went.

She caught the door and held it open. A wave of heat rolled over her. The house was like an oven. "Lena? Are you in there?"

Leaving the door ajar, she tiptoed inside and followed Viktor down the hall into a scorching-hot wreck of a room. Cowhide armchairs had been overturned; shards of Hopi, Zuni, and Navajo pottery littered the floor; a large oil painting of a warrior astride a galloping horse had been slashed and thrown against a wall; and the hilt of a knife stuck out of a large rawhide drumhead.

A fire blazed and crackled in the fireplace. There was no screen, and cinders spat out onto the stone hearth. Viktor appeared immune to the heat. He sank down cross-legged in front of the fire and tipped a bottle of Magic Horse Scotch to his mouth.

"Did you and Lena have a fight?"

He didn't answer.

"She's not injured, is she?"

"I am the one who is injured."

Something crunched under Dinah's foot. She picked up a clay fragment of a frog, a Zuni motif. A dustpan containing black-on-orange fragments, probably Hopi, had been set on a tray table. She picked up the frog's severed head and a piece of a reddish-brown bowl. The bowl looked antique. "You must feel awful losing so many beautiful pots. They look valuable."

"They were. But not to my wife."

Dinah wondered if these treasures had come from Farber's Happy Hunting Ground. Maybe Viktor received an employee's discount. She said, "Lena visited me last night. She was extremely emotional over the death of Alwin Pohl."

"He was *die Viper*. Nature and the sacredness of life that we value, he treated with contempt."

"Did you know that Lena planned to go away with him?"

"Water seeks its level. In the nightclubs they met in secret. The Berghain, the White Noise, Cookies. I am not a fool."

"You must have hated him."

"*Ja, sicher.* I hated him." He turned the bottle up to his mouth. He wiped his lips and glared, daring her to ask the obvious question.

She dashed a drop of salty sweat out of her eye, judged the distance to the door, and asked it. "Did you kill him?"

"I hate killing." He maundered something else in German and seemed to lose his train of thought. "My wife says I am not man enough to kill."

Under the windows opposite the fire stood an undamaged étagère with a few framed photos and a collection of books sandwiched between a pair of antique binoculars and what looked like a gas mask and canister. She walked over and looked at the books. Several were by Karl May, but a few carried English titles like *Native American Spirituality, Listen to the Drum*, and *The Wind Is My Mother*. She picked up a black-and-white photo of a man in uniform posed in front of a swastika. "Did your father fight in the war?"

"That is my grandfather. He was a Nazi. A war criminal and a coward. He killed himself to avoid capture, but my father revered his memory. He remained a Nazi until he died. I hated them both."

"If you feel that way, why do you keep the photograph?"

"It is *das Büßerhemd*. My hair shirt." He picked up a shard of pottery and scratched a swastika on the wood floor. "Did you know that was a symbol of peace for the Hopi? It is a symbol of healing in Navajo rugs and baskets." He pulled a baggie out of his pocket and began to roll a joint. Sweat trickled out of his hair and ran down his long face as he licked the paper and lit up. "I should have been born a pagan in another century."

"Some of your pottery looks as if it came from another century. Do you and your partner import from dealers in the U.S.?"

"That is not my responsibility. I write histories and take pictures and present the pieces to our clients."

She wondered again about the provenance of some of the items for sale in the Happy Hunting Ground, and the idea of blackmail reasserted itself. "Do your histories include information about where and how the pieces were acquired?"

He stared at her. She wasn't sure how much the alcohol had dulled his thinking, but his eyes appeared sharp.

She took a chance. "I think Pohl was blackmailing someone in *der Indianer* club. Do you have any idea who? Or why?"

"*Erpressung?*"

"*Press* sounds right. Was Pohl pressuring anyone? Demanding money for his silence?"

"Blackmail." The word seemed to have a profound effect. Either he was a great pretender or the possibility genuinely startled him. He grimaced and waved her away. "Who are you to come into my house and ask these questions?"

"I'm the daughter of a Native American woman who was invited to your Indian show and got a very nasty surprise. I know that Lena thinks Swan murdered Alwin, but she didn't. I'm hoping to prevent the German police from charging her with a crime she didn't commit."

He took a deep drag and exhaled a cloud of pungent smoke. "Reiner Hess came to the gallery with Pohl six months ago. At the next meeting, Florian presented Pohl as a new member. It is possible that Pohl knew of an American law Hess broke."

"When did you last see Hess?"

"The first time I saw Pohl was the last time I saw Hess."

Dinah cranked this detail through the mill. Had Hess put Pohl up to blackmailing Swan? As Cleon's lawyer, he would have been more likely than Pohl to know about Cleon's various bank accounts. Maybe he thought he could glom onto the Panama money by threatening Cleon's favorite ex-wife. But surely he would have demanded more than a half million dollars. "Where is Lena, Viktor? I'd like to talk with her."

"On her way to hell. I don't care."

Dinah cared. Viktor might hate killing in general, but he made Lena sound like a special case. She couldn't decide if "on her way to hell" was hyperbole or confession. Before she left, she had to make sure that Lena's body wasn't decomposing in a back room. Viktor stared into the fire, seemingly absorbed by his private sorrows. Dinah latched her hands behind her back, affected an air of aimless curiosity, and moseyed into the rear hallway.

There were two bedrooms, lights left on. She slipped into the larger one and looked inside the closet, which was two-thirds empty. The only clothes on hangers were men's shirts and suits and a man's overcoat. She reconnoitered the dresser drawers, but all she saw were Viktor's socks and skivvies. She peeked under the bed and scoped out the adjacent bathroom. There were no cosmetics on the double vanity, no perfumes, no jewelry. And no blood. A woman could be murdered bloodlessly and her belongings deep-sixed, but Dinah's provisional assessment suggested the Lena had packed up and decamped under her own steam.

She gave the smaller bedroom a look-see. There was nothing suspicious and she ambled back into the living room. Sweat streamed down her sides and she felt as if her bones were melting. She had to get out of here or she'd dissolve into a puddle. "Do you have any idea where Lena has gone, Viktor? Does she have family in Berlin, or a best friend?"

He staggered to his feet and pulled the knife out of the rawhide drumhead. "Baer was lucky his wife died young. A man is lucky who never knows the falseness of his Frau."

She would have asked if he owned a gun, but the time didn't feel right. She bid him *Auf Wiedersehen* and hurried out into the rain.

# Chapter Nineteen

On the ride home, the orchestral music didn't soothe Dinah's nerves. Viktor was drunk, stoned, and in a misogynistic frame of mind. The more he drank, the more likely he was to take out his hatred on Lena or some other poor frau who knocked on his door. Belatedly, she thought how easily he could have gone to work carving her up with that knife. She should phone Lohendorf to give him a heads-up, but he would probably read her the riot act for meddling in his investigation or, worse, place her under house arrest. For the time being, Lena was out of range of Viktor's knife and, after her rampage, she probably wouldn't risk an encore appearance any time soon.

Dinah hunched her shoulders and buried her hands deep in her pockets. After being half-roasted, the dash to the car in the cold rain had chilled her. Her hair and jacket were damp and the smell of wet wool made her nose wrinkle. She wished she could curl up in her bed, pull the covers over her head, and sleep until Thor got home. If he were here, she wouldn't feel so vulnerable and alone. If he had spoken with Lohendorf, he would know already that her mother was a suspect in a murder case.

Her head seethed with questions. Was Hess behind the blackmailing scheme? Were they all in it together? Pohl? Farber? Stefan Amsel? It was a bit much to believe that Swan just happened to book a room at the hotel where Amsel was the senior executive. Had Hess hatched the plot and directed it from afar? Now that his name had cropped up in connection with Pohl's murder, the police had probably intensified their search for him. He was the ghost in the machination. He might be the mastermind, or he might be moldering at the bottom of Müggelsee, as dead as Pohl.

"We are here," announced the driver.

She snapped out of her reverie, tipped him an extra ten Euros, and hurried to her door. She entered her security code and slipped inside, shaking the water out of her hair. More than anything, she yearned for a hot shower and a hot toddy. She felt the onset of a sore throat. Either she had breathed too much wood smoke or she was coming down with Margaret's cold.

She climbed the stairs, turned the key in the door and walked in on a little boy, eight or nine years old, lying on the floor on his stomach playing with a fleet of model cars. There was something disconcertingly familiar about him. His wide-set brown eyes regarded her with a penetrating frankness.

"Hi," she managed after a minute. "I'm Dinah. Who are you?"

"I'm Jack."

"Is K.D...?" she started to say babysitting, but Jack didn't impress her as the kind of kid who thought of himself as needing a sitter. "Is K.D. here?"

"Here I am." She sashayed into the room and pushed a letter into Dinah's hand. "Dinah Pelerin, meet Jack Ramberg."

Dinah stared, speechless.

"Thor's my dad," said Jack. "He told me all about you. You're his new girlfriend."

"His mother had a medical emergency," explained K.D. "Her dad is about to undergo heart surgery in California, where she's from, and her boyfriend works on an oil rig somewhere miles out in the North Sea."

"Erik's a mud man," said Jack. "He monitors the drilling fluid as the hole gets deeper."

"Ah," said Dinah.

"Did Dad tell you a lot about me?"

"Not, not nearly as much as I'd like to hear."

K.D. was flush with information. "Erik can't get off the rig to look after Jack and Jennifer doesn't have any relatives in Norway to leave him with. She said it would be Thor's turn to have Jack at Christmas and this way, he'll get him for a couple of extra months. She left his school records and says Thor will have to find him a private school so he doesn't fall behind."

Jack said, "I speak English and Norwegian, but not German. Anyway, I don't think it would be so bad to miss two months of school. I can catch up when I go back after the Christmas holiday."

Dinah wasn't ready to wade into the practicalities of school. "How long have your mother and Thor been divorced, Jack?"

"I don't think they got married." He spun the wheels on his toy car. "If they did, they never told me."

"Well," said Dinah. "What a very great, fine surprise it is to have you here. I'm sure your dad will be over the moon. I guess your mom let him know that she'd be dropping you off here in Berlin?"

"Yes. She wanted to leave me with him in Oslo, but he was meeting with some undercover guys from E-Fourteen and couldn't break away. He's told her all about you, but she was sorry she missed seeing you. She says you sound like a good listener for all of Dad's stories."

Oh, I'm a first-rate listener when the man talks to me, thought Dinah. It seemed however that Jennifer was his primary audience for the important stories. At least he kept her informed as to what was going on in his life. "Have you had supper, Jack?"

"Just a snack. K.D. said you'd be home for dinner so we waited."

"Do you like pizza?"

"Sure. I eat a lot of frozen pizza at home."

"Let's do a fresh-baked one tonight. K.D., will you call Joey's and place the order? They speak English and they deliver. The number's in the napkin holder on the kitchen table. You and Jack choose the toppings you like. I'm going to take a hot shower before hypothermia sets in."

She held her face under the steaming water and reached deep inside herself for an adult response. It wasn't there.

Thor was thirty-eight. She knew he had had lovers. But a child? How could he have failed to mention a child? Were there others? Did Jack have siblings or half-siblings? It was no secret that Scandinavians had a different outlook from Americans about marriage. Many disregarded the formality of a ceremony, and having a child or several children out of wedlock carried no stigma. But the failure to disclose a child? How could Thor not share that biographical tidbit with the woman he claimed to love?

It felt as if she had lived her whole life engulfed in lies and deceit. Thor was the rock she'd grabbed onto, the solid, unbudging granite of truth and reliability. Now that rock had been dislodged.

She pressed the heels of her hands against her eyes. What a crock of...irony. She had been beating herself up for not telling him about a secret bank account, which was a crime and an embarrassment, while he didn't have the courage to tell her about his son, who seemed like a peach of a kid. That phone call about trusting each other, imploring her not to make any snap decisions if something should happen that made her want to run away. Ha!

K.D.'s voice cut through the steam. "You've been in here a really long time."

"The bathroom is occupied. Go away."

"Don't you want to know what she looked like?"

"Okay."

"Taller than you, long sandy blond hair, good figure."

"Thanks."

"She was kind of a sad sack, if that makes you feel any better."

"Her father's facing major surgery. She could hardly feel jolly." Dinah shut off the water. "Hand me a towel."

K.D. tossed it over the top of the shower. "What are you going to do?"

"Dry my hair. Eat pizza."

"About Thor, I mean. It's pretty obvious he didn't tell you about Jack. Your face out there was like, boom! Epic burn."

Dinah wrapped the towel around herself and stepped out onto the mat. "I appreciate your sympathy, K.D., but it's none of your concern. It's not Jack's concern, either. This has nothing to do with him. He doesn't need to worry that he's caused a problem, so don't roll your eyes and make this into a drama. Just leave me alone for a few minutes. Knock on the door when the pizza gets here."

"'Tis not mine to reason why," K.D. said, and flounced out of the room.

Dinah dried her hair, pulled on jeans and a sweatshirt, and dusted off her suit of armor. If she'd let down her guard and taken a hit, it was her own fault. The one constant in her thirty-four years on this earth was that everybody lies. No exceptions. No Truthful Whitefeet. Just liars like her, with an agenda to push. She applied a touch of concealer to her red eyes and walked out of the bathroom. Fortified. Hungry.

The smell of warm pizza pervaded the apartment. Jack and K.D. had already helped themselves. Dinah sliced off a triangle piled with sausage and pepperoni, slid it onto a plate, and sat down at the table. Jack seemed unfazed at being dropped off in the care of strangers. She wondered how many of Thor's girlfriends he'd been fobbed off on in the course of his short life.

"How old are you, Jack?"

"Nine-and-a-half."

"Do you see your dad often?"

"Mom and Dad usually trade off every six months, but that was before the Service transferred him to Berlin. It'll probably be just at the holidays now unless I learn to speak German."

"You certainly speak English very well."

"That's what I speak at home. Mom hasn't ever really learned Norwegian. She says it's too sing-songy and there are too many dialects. Erik and I speak it sometimes. Dad would mostly rather speak English."

Dinah's phone rang and she flinched when Thor's name appeared. "Speak of the devil. Jack, why don't you answer and tell your dad that you arrived safely and we're feeding you and looking after you until he gets home? Talk as long as you like."

He picked up the phone and Dinah poured herself a glass of wine and repaired to the living room. K.D. followed. She set her plate on the coffee table and ensconced herself on the sofa, tucking her long legs under her like a yogi.

"Are you going to talk to him?"

"Yes, of course. But I can't think of anything he needs to hear from me tonight."

"You're going to screw it up, aren't you, Dinah? You'll be like, all lofty and holier-than-thou and in ten years you'll end up the crazy old-maid aunt who only goes out on bingo night and carpet bombs the relatives with Claxton fruitcakes at Christmas."

"You're a bright girl, K.D., and I've grown fond of you over the last year. But we are not gal pals and my love life is not open to discussion. And my closet isn't your personal shopping mall. If you get grease on that shirt, I will..." she broke off. What disciplinary options did she have? She wasn't cut out for minding children. Thor had never said he wanted any, and she certainly didn't. She would be a terrible mother, or step-girlfriend. Less suited to the job than even her own mother.

"You'll what?" taunted K.D.

"I will padlock the closet," she finished, feeling incompetent.

"He says he wants to speak to you," said Jack, walking into the room and holding out the phone to her.

She eked out a weak smile. Not taking it would only confuse Jack and provoke more psychologizing from K.D. Better to get it over with. She took the phone and went into the bedroom. "I'm here."

"Dinah, I'm sorry to spring the news on you this way. I thought I could be back with you in Berlin before Jen had to leave for America, but her father's condition worsened. Her parents are divorced, she has no siblings, and I'm in a bind here in Oslo."

"You've had a year to break the news to me, Thor."

"I wanted to tell you, but there never seemed to be a right time. You've said you don't want children of your own. I wasn't sure how you'd take the idea of being a part-time mother to somebody else's child, although you've been great with K.D."

"Did you arrange your custodial visits, or whatever you call them, when I went back to Hawaii after we met in Norway? And later, when I was finishing my dig in Turkey?"

"That's how the timing worked out, yes. I thought you and I could settle in, get comfortable with each other and by Christmas, when I was scheduled to have Jack again, you'd be prepared and excited to meet him."

"It's late September, Thor. We're settled in. At least, I thought we were. Now I'm not so sure."

"Don't be childish. We love each other."

"That makes everything hunky-dory."

"And don't be flippant. We didn't find each other brand new. Both of us had lives before Longyearbyen. What did you expect?"

"Honesty."

"The way you're honest with me?"

"You don't have to tell me I'm a hypocrite. I detour around the truth sometimes. I leave out things that are hard to say. I thought you were the exception to the rule."

"What rule is that?"

"The Everybody Lies rule. I could understand you not getting down into the weeds, providing an inventory of your exgirlfriends and ex-roommates and ex-wives."

"I don't have an ex-wife."

"You should have, but be that as it may. I could rationalize an ex-wife. An undisclosed child is beyond the pale."

"Well, he's disclosed now and I love him very much." His voice carried a rare charge of anger.

She self-censored. She was punishing him because she was hurt, but what was done was done and hurting him wouldn't make her feel any better. She remembered her mother's admonition to show a little grace. "He seems like a very lovable kid. Smart and sociable and independent. I know you must be proud of him."

"I am."

"The thing is," she said, "I've been steeped in secrets all my life. Granted, I have some I should have disclosed, but I'm not in a mood to be fair right now. The situation is going to take some time to put into perspective."

"I know that. Dinah, listen—"

"I'm sure Jack told you about K.D. She's back in Berlin and between the two of us, we'll take good care of him, so please don't worry. Would you like to speak to him again?"

"No. The reason I called was to warn you. You need to start looking for an attorney."

"What?"

"Forensics found your mother's DNA on the body of that murder victim you forgot to tell me about, and the vic's blood on her clothes."

She drew in a choppy breath. "Is Lohendorf going to arrest her?"

"If no other leads are found, he'll have no choice. He didn't go exactly by the book when he passed the information on to me. It was his roundabout way of giving you notice of what's to come."

She wanted to pour out her heart to him, tell him to come home and take charge, but pride and punctured expectations stuck in her throat like gravel. All she could say was, "She didn't do it."

"I hope not, for your sake. Go to the American Embassy if you'd feel more comfortable, or there's a directory of Berlin criminal lawyers in my bottom left desk drawer. Several of them speak English. Better to bring in somebody early, before charges are filed."

# Chapter Twenty

Jack got the sleeping bag, K.D. got half the bed, and Dinah got a crick in her back clinging to the outer edge while trying to keep her sprawling, bumptious bedmate from pushing her off onto the floor. When the cuckoo moaned at six, she was already wide-awake, sitting at the kitchen table poring over Thor's list of English-speaking criminal attorneys and mentally composing a to-do list. She sank her second cup of Einstein and copied down the telephone number of Winheller und Busse, located on a street off the Gendarmenmarkt. She should have realized what her mother's misstatements would lead to and advised her not to speak to the police until she had obtained counsel.

The law office wouldn't open for another two hours, but the first item on her list was to call and make an appointment for the earliest possible time. After that, she would visit her mother in her new room at the Adlon and find out what, if anything, she knew about Stefan Amsel—the senior exec and ersatz Navajo who appeared to have partaken too freely of the schnapps on the night of the murder. If she could wangle a tête-à-tête with him, she could narrow down the timing of the comings and goings at the powwow and compare his version of events to Farber's. Amsel had appeared blotto, but her new motto in life was to take all appearances with a grain of salt.

She nibbled a bite of cold pizza and added a trip to the market to her list. What did nine-year-olds eat besides pizza? Milk, eggs, bread, bacon, and cheese seemed sufficient for the first half of the day and she assumed that a few *Pfannkuchen*, the city's signature jelly-filled donuts, wouldn't rot his teeth during the short time he would be in her custody. Should she be reminding him to brush? Floss? Put the toilet seat down? She hoped that K.D. could be bullied or bribed into babysitting. Dinah couldn't see dragging Jack along on this day's business.

Margaret was just across the street in the Wunderbar. If she weren't contagious, she could take care of Jack for a few hours. Dinah rubbed her sore throat. She couldn't quiet a twinge of resentment. It was more than the gift of a virus. It was the needling suspicion that Margaret had lied. She was a keen observer and a cynic from way back. Cleon had fooled her, but she'd had the bad luck to love him. Love made people susceptible to believing all sorts of ackamaracka. But Margaret despised Swan. How likely was it that she would have been taken in by her far-fetched scheme? How likely that she would neglect to preview that thumb drive? Dinah scrawled her name at the bottom of her list with a question mark.

"Is there any muesli?" asked Jack, walking into the kitchen already dressed with his hair neatly combed.

"There will be." She added muesli to her list. "Start with a slice of cold pizza. I'll run out to the store and get us some breakfast." She grabbed her coat and shoulder bag off the back of the chair. Should she lay out some ground rules? She said, "Don't buzz anyone in while I'm gone or fall out the window or anything."

He took a knife out of the knife box and deftly sliced a wedge of pizza. "Where's the TV?"

"In the office. In the cabinet next to your dad's...next to the clean desk on the right. You'll have to figure out the remote by yourself. I don't know the cartoon station."

"I don't watch cartoons. I watch car races. Today is the last day of the Coronado Speed Festival. There's a nineteen seventy-two Ferrari three-twelve P entered."

"Be careful with the knife," she said, and left him to his own devices.

A gray drizzle was falling and she pulled the hood of her jacket close around her face. Legally, Berlin's shops and stores could be open twenty-four hours a day except Sundays. But in this neighborhood, the shops didn't open until ten. The nearest early-opening food store was the Refugium auf dem Gendarmenmarkt. It was the anti-supermarket experience, a combination restaurant and food boutique. Any other time, it would be a pleasure to shop there. Today, her thoughts revolved around Thor's deception, the murder of Alwin Pohl, and Swan's impending arrest.

She stopped in the middle of the street and added another note to her list, "White Noise." That was the club where Geert worked. She would have to ask him if he knew Lena Bischoff. Maybe Lena had other lovers who didn't fancy the idea of losing her to a jerk like Alwin. And with a temper like hers, she couldn't be discounted as a suspect.

The Refugium offered not one, but three brands of muesli. She chose the one that listed the most vitamins. She bought milk, peanut butter, jelly, bread, and cheese. As she plied her cart through the aisles of the Refugium, she was startled when a man with wooden eyeglasses stepped in front of her.

"Frau Pelerin. We meet again."

It took her a second to place him. "Herr Eichen. Hello."

He wore a natty tweed jacket and a fleecy scarf twined around his neck. He lowered his glasses on his nose and fixed her with blue, analytical eyes, as if she were the offshoot of a phylum he couldn't categorize. "I've been thinking about you since that terrible night. I trust you found your mother and she is all right?"

"Yes, thank you."

"By getting lost, at least she didn't have to endure the horror you did."

"Right." She smiled weakly and reached a box of crackers off the shelf.

He said, "You seem pressed."

"I have a lot of fires to put out."

"I won't keep you, but if you and your mother would do me the honor of having dinner with me this evening, I would be very pleased. I live quite nearby. I don't have time to prepare a gourmet dinner for you today, but we could have cocktails at my house and go to a restaurant afterward."

The invitation seemed like pure serendipity, a prime suspect volunteering to be interviewed. Sort of. "That's kind of you. I don't think my mother will be able to get away, but I'm free."

"Then you must come." He whipped a card out of his wallet. "This is my address. I shall expect you at seven." He put the card in her hand, smiled, and pushed his cart off in the direction of the cheese counter.

She put the card in her pocket and finished her shopping. This day was turning into a marathon.

The TV was blaring when she got back to the apartment. Engines thundered and tires screeched. She walked through to the kitchen where K.D. was scrambling eggs. She wore the peach silk negligee Thor had given Dinah for her birthday.

Dinah felt a stab of anger at K.D., at Thor, at herself. Had those sporadic undercover missions Thor enjoyed so much predisposed him to stealth and secrecy? And why would a man with a dependent child risk his life playing spy games if he didn't have to? She had a host of such questions to puzzle over, but they would have to wait until her mother crisis was resolved. Maybe someday she'd write a book. *How Keeping Mom From Going Down For Murder Makes Breaking Up A Breeze.* She relegated Thor Ramberg to the back of her mind and began putting the groceries away.

"I need you to watch Jack for me today, K.D."

"As long as you're home early. I have a date tonight."

"What kind of a date?"

"Geert's taking me to his club."

Dinah didn't distrust Geert exactly. He was less standoffish than the Germans she'd met on the Humboldt faculty, always willing to lend a helping hand or rip out someone's eyes if asked. And he was a whiz with anything mechanical. Even so, she didn't see him as a suitable playmate for K.D. "Hanging out in a nightclub with a thirty-year-old man in a strange city isn't a good idea. Anyway, I need you to stay with Jack tonight, too. It's important."

K.D. took a truculent tone. "For your information, the age of consent in Germany is fourteen so long as the older person doesn't take advantage of the younger person."

Dinah was stunned, not as much by German mores as by the idea that K.D. saw Geert as a possible sexual partner. "Has he come on to you?"

"A little."

There was a good chance she was just being provocative, and Dinah had already given her the contraceptive lecture. But if she was serious, arguing would only egg her on. "Geert doesn't go to the club until eleven or twelve, so it won't inconvenience you to stick around until then. I should be home by the time you leave."

"Shizz, Dinah. What could happen if he was left by himself for a few hours?"

"I don't want to find out," she said, and went to call Jack in for his muesli.

While her accidental new family ate breakfast, she called and scheduled a meeting between Swan and Herr Winheller at five o'clock. She then phoned Swan and arranged to meet her in the Lobby Lounge at the Adlon at eleven to catch her up on Lohendorf's discovery and the need for an attorney. In spite of the fact that Cleon had been an attorney, Dinah didn't think Swan had much understanding of the attorney-client privilege. Dinah wanted to remind her to tell him the truth.

She changed into an oversized maroon sweater, black wool slacks, and her Italian ankle boots, only slightly water-stained from their last outing in the rain. The ensemble should take her from the lobby of the Adlon to the offices of Winheller und Busse to an expensive restaurant in the Gendarmenmarkt without embarrassment. Berlin chic was luxe, but casual.

Reasonably confident of K.D.'s cooperation, she programmed Jack's cell number into her phone, made sure that he had hers, and hurried out the door at nine-thirty, half a *Pfannkuchen* clamped between her teeth. The rain had stopped, but a dense ground fog spread over the street like a flannel blanket. She stared through the fog at the curtained second-story window of Margaret's room at the Gasthaus Wunderbar across the street and debated with herself. On the one hand, she liked Margaret, commiserated for all the pain and hardships she'd lived through. On the other hand, there was something not quite kosher about her story. She finished her *Pfannkuchen,* licked her fingers, and hoped she'd find Margaret sober and in a conciliatory mood.

The receptionist at the front desk hailed her with a sunny, "*Guten Morgen, Frau.*"

"Good morning. I'm here to see Frau Dobbs."

"*Ja,* I will announce you. Your name please?"

"Just say Dinah."

She rang the room and Margaret was apparently awake and well enough to receive visitors. Dinah took the stairs—Margaret's line about how many lies are too goddamn many, reverberating in her head.

At the first knock, she opened up and motioned Dinah inside. One corner of her mouth quirked up in what Dinah construed as a smile. "The cold has broken. I guess I'll live."

Dinah sat down on what had been her mother's bed and regarded the suitcase lying open on Margaret's. "Did the Inspector return your passport?"

"I talked with him this morning. He promised he'd return it this afternoon. Or rather, that bossy sergeant of his will drop it off at the front desk." A rumbling cough ratcheted into a harsh laugh. "I won't be continuing my European Grand Tour. I'm flying home tomorrow."

"Had you planned a grand tour?"

"Maybe. If your mother's flimflam hadn't backfired." She folded a cotton gown and laid it on top of a layer of tightly rolled garments.

"I've been thinking about that, Margaret. How could someone as savvy as you, detesting Swan the way you do, let her flimflam you?"

"Dazzled by visions of gold, I guess. And the prospect of getting some of my own back on Reiner Hess."

Dinah loosened her scarf and caressed her sore throat. "Hess seems to hover over our heads like a poltergeist, doesn't he?"

"Not over my head. I'm done and out of here."

"Don't you want to stay and find out who killed Alwin Pohl?"

"I don't care who killed him as long as I'm not the one who gets railroaded." She turned her back to Dinah and needlessly neatened the clothes in the suitcase.

Dinah said, "Swan seems to be the number one suspect."

"I'm sorry if that causes you pain."

"But you're not sorry about Swan's pain?"

"If you must know, I'm rather enjoying her predicament."

"Did you tell Lohendorf that you knew Pohl, and that she knew him?"

"Yes, I told him the truth. It's been in scarce supply of late."

Dinah stared at Margaret's back and doubt gave way to conviction. "You didn't tell *me* the truth, Margaret."

She rolled her shoulders, but didn't turn around. "I told you who Pohl was as soon as we got back from the morgue yesterday."

Dinah stood up and physically turned her around, gripping her arms. "You knew Pohl, but you also knew Hess. Make that present tense. You know Hess."

"Know him and hate him."

"Methinks you protest too much, Margaret. All that huffing about being deceived has all been an act. Mom didn't deceive you. It was the other way round."

"That's bull."

"Is it? I think you colluded with Hess and with Pohl from the get-go. Cleon wouldn't have told either one of them where he hid his money. You told them about the bank account in Panama and put them up to blackmailing Swan. You wanted revenge against her, not Hess. Am I getting warm?"

"Let go of me, Dinah, or I'll cough in your face."

Dinah let go with a little shove of disgust.

"She lied, I lied. It doesn't make us even, but it makes me feel better." Margaret pulled a tissue out of a box on the dresser behind her, blew her nose, and moved across to a chair next to the window. She sat down heavily and hiked her feet onto the footstool. "Have you ever been curious about your man's other women?"

Dinah flashed to Jennifer, she of the long blond hair, the good figure, and the permanent role of mother to Thor's son. "A little."

"Well, I've been curious about Swan from the day Cleon left me to move in with her. Oh, she was pretty. But what kept him mesmerized? As many times as she and I were thrown together at Cleon's mandatory gatherings of the clan, we never had a substantive conversation. Not even after she left Cleon and married your father. You'd think we would have had a field day dishing about the husband we'd shared and still held on to in a way. After I killed him, I wrote her a letter and tried to explain. She never wrote back or called. And then out of the blue, she calls me up with a proposition to travel to Berlin and blackmail Reiner Hess. I thought she'd gone barking mad."

"But you strung her along."

"Hell, yes, I strung her along. I was fascinated. She said she knew how much I hated Reiner and wouldn't I like to recoup the money he'd cheated me out of. I don't know why she thinks I hate Reiner. As a matter of fact, I used to go out with him from time to time when he lived in the States. After Cleon shafted me, he was balm to my bruised ego."

"You didn't disabuse her of the idea that you hated him."

"I reinforced it. Laid it on thick about how much I loathed the bastard just to hear more details of the scam. She said she had proof that Reiner had killed a couple of feds and he would pay dearly for it."

"You didn't believe her?"

"Reiner was a lawyer. If he was guilty of anything, it was moving Cleon's drug money into legitimate businesses, which doesn't seem half bad to me."

"Did you get in touch with your old flame to let him know what Swan had in store for him?"

"What makes you think I'd know how to find him?"

"Don't be coy, Margaret. Did you call him?"

"All right, Dinah. Yes, I called him. He was still at home in Berlin. It was before the German revenuers came down on him like vultures. We had a friendly chat. He said he'd received a letter from Swan asking for money, but he wasn't in a position to help her. I told him that she and I would be in town in late September, and that she claimed to have evidence of two murders he'd committed."

"What did he say to that?"

"He thought she was bonkers, but said he'd keep an eye on her. I didn't blow the gaff about your Panama account and I sure as hell didn't suggest that we put the screws to Swan. I didn't know she was being blackmailed until you told me. For what?"

"For half a mil," said Dinah, deliberately misunderstanding. "Did Hess tell you that he and his old chum Pohl were back working together?"

"He didn't say anything about Pohl. I doubt they've ever been chums. Reiner's nearly thirty years older and has a lot better manners."

Dinah remembered her comment about the subways being confusing and a fresh cloud of suspicion rolled in. "How did you get to Müggelsee, Margaret? Did you take the train? You'd have had to make several transfers. Or did Reiner act as chauffeur? Did he go with you to keep an eye on Swan?"

She didn't answer.

"I think he did," said Dinah. "I think he went into the woods and killed Pohl and you're shielding him, shifting the blame onto Swan."

Margaret swung her feet off the stool, leaned forward across her knees, and aimed her widow's peak at Dinah. "Reiner had no reason to kill the man, but if he did kill him, even if I knew that he did, I couldn't rat him out. After what I've been through, trust me, I wouldn't wish a charge of murder on my worst enemy." She hefted herself out of the chair and crossed the room to stand face-to-face with Dinah. "I owe you my freedom and I wouldn't *collude*, as you put it, to frame your mother for murder. I'll admit to you that Reiner was with me that night. But if you tell the police, I'll deny it."

"I assume the two of you have discussed Pohl's murder. Who does he think killed him?"

"He doesn't know. He was shocked."

"And I'm the Queen of Romania. Listen up, Margaret. The German police may not care if you leave Berlin, but I will regard your departure as a personal betrayal. If you know how to get ahold of Hess, you tell him to call me immediately. I want to meet this *rara avis*. Even if he didn't kill Pohl, he probably knows who did."

"If he agrees to meet you, will you promise you won't bring in the police?"

"Yes, I promise. You have my word on it."

There were no Truthful Whitefeet in Berlin.

# Chapter Twenty-one

To get to the Adlon Hotel from the Strasse des 17 Juni, you have to walk through the Brandenburg Gate. It is the only gate that survives from the original wall that encircled the old Prussian city. During the Cold War, the gate stood crumbling to ruin behind the hated Wall that divided East from West. No one could get through from the West and the GDR erected a parallel wall on the eastern side of the gate to make doubly sure that no one could get through from the East. Those caught in the no-man's land between the walls were shot. The Brandenburg Gate became a symbol of bitter division, and when the Wall fell in 1989, it became the symbol of reunification. As Dinah passed under the central archway, Swan's remark about the wall between them echoed in her mind. She tuned it out. She couldn't let herself be carried away by symbolism or wishful thinking.

The cobblestoned Pariser Platz on the east side of the Gate is a pedestrian square and always crowded. In front of the American Embassy, a mini-demonstration had drawn a ragtag group of young people. One waved a sign "STOP WATCHING US," a reference to Germany's outrage over the U.S. tapping of Chancellor Angela Merkel's cellphone. Another held up a picture of Edward Snowden, the American who leaked this bombshell, with a big "THANK YOU," and others wielded a banner "NO MORE SURVEILLANCE STATE." Nearby, a clown on a unicycle tossed candy to a flock of squealing children.

Dinah dodged around the commotion and proceeded toward the eastern end of the square, which was dominated by the Adlon. She walked through the door and the opulence made her immediately self-conscious. She doffed her trench coat, smoothed her sweater over her hips, and spiffed her hair. The convivial drone of conversation filled the lobby and, in the background, the mellow sounds of a piano. She sidled past a large urn of aromatic lilies and a pagoda fountain encircled by protruding elephant heads. Swan sat alone at the far end of the lounge, away from the music and the chatter.

Dinah was relieved to see a cup and saucer on the table in front of her instead of a bourbon glass.

"How's the coffee?"

"It's five-star, like everything else in this place."

Dinah hung her coat over the back of a chair and sat down. "If you were short of funds, why did you choose the most expensive hotel in the city?"

"Polly Wolly recommended it, and I didn't want him to think I was short of funds."

"Your choice of the Adlon wouldn't have anything to do with the fact that Stefan Amsel runs the place, would it?"

"No. I didn't know he was one of Florian's bunch until I checked in. Stefan is comping me the room as a guest of the club. Or that was the plan. I haven't spoken with him since before poor Polly got himself killed. It's funny how everybody slithers off into the tall grass at the first sign of trouble." She patted Dinah's hand. "Everybody except you."

Dinah didn't like to admit how longingly she had eyed the tall grass. "You didn't know him from Georgia?"

"No. I never heard of him 'til I checked in on the morning of the powwow. He came to the front desk to personally welcome me. He showed me up to the room like I was royalty and introduced himself as a Navajo, which tickled me to death because he's white as grits."

"If he knew who you were at the time you checked in, he

must have been expecting you. I thought Pohl was the only one you'd told about the Adlon."

"He was so pleasant and cordial, I didn't ask. My package was waiting for me in the room, along with a bowl of fruit and a complimentary bottle of champagne and the loveliest soap and shampoo in this world. Five stars aren't half enough for this place."

"Apart from the not-so-lovely fact that somebody filched your 'package,'" said Dinah. "Did it look as if anyone had tampered with it? Unwrapped it maybe?"

"It seemed to be intact, with the legal form typed and stamped and taped to the box. I took out the gun, a little twenty-two revolver, and put it in my handbag."

"Unloaded?"

"I already told you that it was. I left and took a taxi to visit Reiner's daughter Elke. I still thought he might could talk Polly out of his meanness, if he would. But he wasn't there and I came back to the Adlon. Polly called and told me when and where to meet him, then I went back to the Wunderbar and changed my clothes. I caught a train way yonder-and-gone to Müggelsee. Polly had given me instructions and a schedule. When I got off the ferry, Margaret was laying in wait for me at the dock, hoppin' mad. She asked me who it was I'd come to meet 'cause she knew it wasn't Reiner."

"Are you sure she was alone?"

"I think so. Who would be with her way out there? We're the only people she knows in Berlin."

"What did she say exactly?"

"Oh, that I was deranged, selfish, promiscuous, and on like that. With all her cussing, there wasn't much I could say except 'try to make the best of it.' She left mad as a hornet and I followed the trail up to the tower. I snuck through the woods and kept out of sight of the clearing where I saw them setting up the powwow."

"With the unloaded gun."

"That's right."

"Why did you have it if you didn't mean to use it?"

Her eyes skittered away. "I don't know. For protection in case he got rough, or if he didn't give me the tape." Her eyes came back from their wandering and she took a defiant tone. "His voice is on that tape, too, unless he erased it."

A server in a bright red dress refilled Swan's coffee and placed a napkin in front of Dinah. "*Was sie haben, Frau?*"

"I'll just have coffee," said Dinah. "*Schwarzer.*"

"*Ja*, black." She smiled and moved on.

"When you found Pohl dead, why didn't you walk back down the hill to the powwow and get help?"

"I don't know, Dinah. I saw a sign to Rahmsy-majigger…"

"Rahnsdorf."

"Yes, yes, and I just kept going, away from the blood and the trouble. I waved down a taxi and came back to the Adlon. I was scared and shook up. I took the gun out of my bag, put it in the chest-of-drawers and went down to the bar to have myself a bourbon. After a while, I went back to the Wunderbar. I wanted to tell Margaret, try and explain the strain I'd been under and why I'd fooled her. It's all so complicated. You know, really, I think I wanted her to come with me because she's so gutsy and independent. I didn't know how to travel on my own without a man. But Margaret was cold as the moon and after Sergeant Wegener came and told us there'd been a murder, Margaret wouldn't speak to me at all."

The server brought Dinah's coffee and she sipped for a minute and contemplated. If Amsel knew that Swan was a guest at the Adlon, it stood to reason that the whole club knew. Had one of them made off her gun? The only reason to steal it would be to further implicate her. If the police didn't find the murder weapon and someone stepped forward and reported that Swan had a gun, caliber unknown, shipped to her hotel, that would put the frosting on the case against her. Had Pohl been shot with a .22? Any gun was capable of killing someone, but Pohl was a big man and a .22 didn't have a lot of stopping power. Dinah needed to find out what the ballistics report said, but unless

Inspector Lohendorf was willing to bend the rules still more, the only person who could get her the information was Thor.

Swan said, "You look kind of woebegone, baby, like you've come to deliver the writ of execution."

"They found your DNA on Pohl's body, Mom. They're probably going to arrest you."

She winced. "'Barnaby Bowwow grew old and gray, condemned by the parson and hanged for a stray.'"

"It's too early to think about hanging. I made an appointment for you to see an attorney this afternoon at five. His name is Winheller. Promise me you'll stick to the truth and tell him everything you know about Hess and your movements on the day of the murder."

"Should I tell Mr. Winheller that Pohl was blackmailing me?"

"Yes, absolutely. He's your attorney. You don't want him to be blindsided. And tell him about the gun, too. The police will learn about it soon enough. I'll be back at four to take you to Winheller's office." Swan's eyes skirred away to the fountain and Dinah tried to imagine what the German lawyer would make of his new client and her litany of complications. As she got up to leave, she thought about Swan's natural inclination to smile and equivocate. "Tell Mr. Winheller everything, Mom. If ever there was a time when you don't want other people to think only what suits them, this is it."

Stefan Amsel's office was located in the Adlon Residenz, the newer wing behind the Adlon Palais on Behrenstrasse. He shook her hand with lukewarm propriety and gestured her into a chair. His hectic manner made it plain that he was a busy man with weightier things to do than waste time answering her questions. He sat down behind his desk and adjusted his wireless bifocals with both hands. Pudgy, with a doughy complexion and thinning ginger hair, he was nothing like the rambunctious Navajo with the porcupine roach who'd drunk too much schnapps and pounded his chest. Today he spoke not in short, staccato bursts, but in run-on sentences.

"When I saw her name, Mrs. William Calms of Georgia, on our reservations list, I knew immediately who she was because Florian had boasted that we would soon meet a Seminole woman from Georgia, although I do not say 'boast' to criticize, as Florian has invited many Native Americans to come to Berlin as guests of *der Indianer* club. We have had visits from a member of the Flathead Tribe of Montana, a member of the Shawnee from Oklahoma, a Cree from Canada, and an Arizona Navajo who gave me the name Doba, which means No War. I am opposed to all wars and I hope that you Americans will grow weary of starting them and flooding the E.U. with refugees."

"My mother…"

"Mrs. Calms, yes. Prior to her, we had never met a member of a Southeastern tribe. Although as matters stand, I believe I am the only one actually to have met her. I've heard a rumor that she was present at Müggelsee on the night of the powwow, but did not make herself known to us."

"She did not kill Alwin Pohl," interjected Dinah.

"No." He adjusted his glasses again. "Terrible what happened to Alwin and now the police must give us all *den dritten Grad*, the third degree as you Americans call it." A light on his telephone blinked red and he paused as if deliberating whether to pick up.

"Did all of *der Indianer* club know that my mother would be staying here at the Adlon?"

"I don't know. She made the reservation, herself. Ordinarily, if the Adlon has a vacancy, I offer it to the club's First Nations guests, but I had the impression from Florian that Mrs. Calms would be residing with her daughter. When I noticed her name, about a week ago I think it was, yes, when a package arrived for her, I held a room in the Palais wing."

"Did anyone open that package?"

He eyed her with contempt. "This is the Adlon."

"Meaning no?"

"Definitely no."

"Did Herr Pohl or any of the other members of the club visit her or come to the hotel? Viktor or Lena Bischoff, perhaps?"

"If they did, they would have announced themselves to the front desk, not to me."

She trotted out a mollifying smile. "I don't mean to be rude, Herr Amsel. As you said, the police are giving everyone the third degree and I'm trying to help my mother through the maze, help her understand the German system and avoid cultural blunders."

"Yes, it is hard in a foreign capital. I always feel unsure of myself in Istanbul in spite of the fact that Berlin has the largest population of Turks outside of Turkey. Attitudes about tea—"

"How well did you know Herr Pohl?" she asked.

"Not well. He was new to the club, although I believe that Reiner had known him in years past. There was a rumor, I don't say that Florian was the source although it may have come from him, that Alwin had been charged with, how do you say, *Totschlag*, and left for America because he did not wish to stand trial."

"What does that mean?"

"I believe you say manslaughter in English. But I may have that wrong. Slaughter is too strong a word when there is no intention, only carelessness." The red light on his phone blinked again and he raised a hand to answer.

Dinah rushed to get in another question. "What can you tell me about Reiner Hess?"

His hand froze in mid-air. "He is wanted by the police for tax fraud."

"Have you seen him recently?"

"No."

"Do you know how I might contact him?"

"It is rumored that he went to Switzerland. Or was it Liechtenstein?" He chortled. "To be with his money."

"I thought he'd gone to Cyprus," she said.

"That may be. We are not, how do you say, *in touch.*"

"Do any of your fellow club members stay in touch with him?"

The office door opened and a woman with slanted black eyebrows and a frantic demeanor poked her head in and spouted a stream of German.

Amsel jumped up, obviously relieved by the interruption. "My secretary needs me. I must terminate this meeting. If there is anything further, please call and schedule an appointment."

Dinah wanted to press him for an answer to her last question, but he was jabbering away in German to his secretary and waving her out the door.

She mumbled her thanks and left with at least one new nugget of information to mull. Alwin Pohl had been charged with manslaughter before he left Germany. That would have been more than a decade ago. Presumably, the German statute of limitations had expired or Pohl didn't expect to remain in Germany long enough for the authorities to notice he was back and reopen the case.

As she walked out into Behrenstrasse, the sun was making a feeble effort to burn off the fog. She wondered what repository of the German bureaucracy maintained records of *Totschlag*. That was a question for Mr. Winheller. In the meantime, she could do some research on her own. She headed toward Unter den Linden and the nearest branch of the Berlin State Library.

# Chapter Twenty-two

After two hours of searching through the digitalized archives of the *International Herald Tribune,* Dinah knew more than she ever wanted to know about the German crackdown on business moguls and banking bigwigs who sheltered their money in the tiny tax haven of Liechtenstein; and about the new international standards that forced Swiss banks to ask their clients if they had declared their assets on deposit; and about the harsh penalties imposed by both the U.S. and German governments on individuals who ignored reporting requirements. The afternoon's reading magnified her fears about the account in Panama, but she remained none the wiser regarding the personal history or local connections of Reiner Hess.

Her phone detonated inside her purse. Feeling the heat of a dozen withering stares, she silenced the plinking and fled, answering only after she had reached the exit.

"This had better be important, K.D."

"There's been an explosion."

"Jerusalem! Where? Are you okay? Jack?"

"We're fine, but somebody tried to blow up Margaret's hotel. I'm looking out our bedroom window at a fire truck and a row of cop cars."

"Can you see if anyone's injured?"

"There's a crowd in the street. I'm getting ready to go down and see what I can see."

"No! No, K.D. Lock the door and stay with Jack. I'm on my way."

She charged across Unter den Linden, inciting a cacophony of horns and angry shouts. Traffic had started to build and there were no taxis in sight. It was a straight shot back to the Gendarmenmarkt and she was a fast runner, but her Italian boots weren't designed for racing. Her heart beat against her chest as if it were trying to break out and run on ahead.

What conceivable reason would anyone have to blow up a little pension called Wunderbar? Maybe it was an accident—an unexploded World War II bomb unearthed by new construction. The country was peppered with buried ordnance. But there were no current excavations on Niederwallstrasse and the Wunderbar was at least twenty years old. Was it possible that the person who forced the Golf off the road and shot at them that first night was not Pohl? Did somebody else have a reason, not just to scare, but to kill?

Her lungs burned and she could feel the beginnings of a blister on her left heel. When she reached Französische Strasse, she stopped for breath and looked around for a taxi. No such luck. She pulled off the boots and cut across the square behind the Konzerthaus.

With Pohl dead, the only person who knew that Swan and Margaret were in Berlin was Hess. Was he afraid they'd lead the police to him? Swan had showed up at his daughter's house asking for him, and Margaret might have phoned him this morning after Dinah confronted her and demanded to meet with him.

She could smell the fire now. She ran through Hausvogteipl Platz and when she rounded the corner, she saw the fire truck. Black smoke wisped out of the second story—Margaret's window—and a helmeted fireman wearing a face mask and oxygen tank toted a fire hose into the building. Her chest tightened at the sight of Inspector Jens Lohendorf standing at the back of the truck. He was talking to the receptionist, who was crying. The other evacuees stood around drinking bottled water and looking dazed. Margaret wasn't there.

Dinah gravitated to Lohendorf. When he saw her, he stepped away from the truck and handed her a bottle of water. "She is receiving oxygen, but she is otherwise unhurt. She was in the *Toiletten* when the grenade exploded."

"Grenade?"

"That is a guess. The preliminary findings of the fire squad suggest a fragmentation device, most likely thrown from the street into Mrs. Dobbs' window, which appears to have been broken from the outside. The drapes and bed linens were set ablaze and when she opened the door to escape, the fire spread into the hallway."

"It had to be Reiner Hess," said Dinah.

"We are taking all reasonable measures to trace him. In cases where explosives are used, the federal police must investigate to determine if there is a link to any terrorist group. My officers will interview all of the potential witnesses."

"May I speak with Margaret?"

He conducted her to the rear of the fire truck and gave her a boost inside. Margaret lay on a stretcher with a mask on her face while an EMT monitored her vital signs.

"Margaret?"

Her eyes slotted open. She pulled the nose mask down and tried to sit up.

The EMT pushed her back down.

"If she can speak, let her," said Lohendorf.

Dinah took hold of her hands and raised her to a sitting position. She coughed and gathered her hair, which had straggled loose from the bun. "I feel like hammered dung."

"You look good to me," said Dinah. "One piece is good."

"What did you say? My ears are ringing."

"I was afraid I'd find you in small, unsightly chunks and we'd have to have a closed casket funeral."

One corner of her mouth tweaked up. "I don't suppose I can blame this one on Swan?"

"Lobbing grenades isn't part of her skill set. What about your friend Reiner? He's the only one who knows you're staying at the Wunderbar."

"You can't think he did this?"

"Let's ask him, shall we? Did you call him this morning as I asked?"

She drew a rasping breath and the EMT placed the oxygen mask back on her nose. After several chest-heaving respirations, she tugged it down again and looked out the rear door at Lohendorf, who was tuned in like a bug. "Like I told the inspector, I don't know where Reiner is."

Lohendorf said, "Mrs. Dobbs should go to the hospital for evaluation. Will you go with her, Frau Pelerin?"

"No." She looked at her watch. It was nearly four. "Sorry, Margaret. I have to be somewhere else. Will you be all right by yourself?"

"Par for the course. I hope they give me a gown and keep me overnight. I've got no place to sleep."

"Here." Dinah jotted down the code to her downstairs door and fished out her key. "If they cut you loose, come to my place. You know which house it is, the lavender with the red trim. And take this." She handed her a fistful of Euros. "For the taxi and a bottle of…of whatever medication you may need."

"Seems I'm beholden to you once again." She stuffed the bills into her bra and lay back down. "Wherever it is you have to go, you'd better put on some shoes. You'll catch cold running around barefoot."

Dinah watched the fire truck drive away with her and a geyser of aggravation shot to the surface. She ought to be grateful to Lohendorf for warning her to get an attorney for Swan, and she was. But if he hadn't listened in, she could maybe have talked Margaret into telling her where Hess was. If she knew. She said, "I thought you Germans were all in a tizzy about people who spy on private communications."

"When private communications bear on a murder, it is the duty of the police to listen."

He was doing his job, but she didn't have to like it. She turned and jaywalked across the street to her apartment.

She needed a shower and a Band-Aid for her blistered heel before returning to the Adlon to deliver her mother to the attorney's office. K.D. met her at the door with a barrage of questions. She answered them as economically as possible. "Margaret's room was damaged and when she's released from the hospital, she'll be bunking here with us."

"What bunk? There's no bunk. Why can't she just get another hotel room?"

"Because she's scared. She could have been killed. Because her clothes and money and phone are either burned or unusable. The police have cordoned off the Wunderbar. And because I want to keep an eye on her."

"Why? Did she waste somebody else?"

"I wish I had the bandwidth to cater to your feelings, K.D., but I don't. You'll have to grin and bear it. And also give her the bed. I'll share with her and you can go back to the sleeping bag. Jack can have the sofa."

"Fine, I'll give the old cow the bed. I probably won't get home until tomorrow morning anyway."

"You will or I'll change the lock and you can move in with Geert permanently."

For an instant, she looked as if she were going to throw a tantrum. Instead, her face spread into a grin. "Where will you sleep when Thor comes home?"

Dinah didn't want to think about Thor's homecoming. She would burn that bridge when she got to it. She cleaned herself up, changed into fresh clothes and in a guilty afterthought, she remembered Jack. She found him on his knees butting his head against the wall beside Thor's desk.

"Jack, stop!" Sorrowing Jesus, was he autistic? "You'll give yourself a concussion."

He angled his face and looked up at her. "I'm not hitting my head. I'm strengthening my neck muscles. Neck muscles are the most important thing for a race driver."

"Ah."

He bounced up and rubbed his hands on the seat of his jeans. "Did K.D. order the pizza yet?"

"I don't know. Are you hungry?"

"Yes. She scrambled eggs, but I don't like eggs and I don't like the kind of cereal you bought. I like chocolate. Mom buys me Chocapic at home."

On the spur of the moment, Dinah decided to take Jack with her. He could entertain himself looking at magazines or building his neck muscles while she conferred with the lawyer, and Baer Eichen impressed her as the sort of man who dined well. The kid needed at least one nutritious meal while he was in her care and he would be the perfect excuse to leave early. The stress of the last few days had taken a toll and she found herself hoping that she could stay awake long enough to discover what Eichen knew about Hess and Pohl.

# Chapter Twenty-three

Tall, trim, and stately, Klaus Winheller looked the very definition of rectitude. His confident voice and firm handshake conveyed a sense that Dinah's worries were needless. The "Win" in Winheller seemed like the stamp of destiny.

Swan complimented him on his excellent English and his superbly tailored suit. He squired her into his office and instructed Dinah and Jack to sit in the waiting room while he interviewed his client in private.

Jack played Crazy Taxi and Hot Wheels Showdown on his phone while Dinah's thoughts raced in circles, getting her nowhere. She worried about Swan's confabulations. She worried about Hess' intentions. She worried about Thor's failure to communicate and K.D.'s birth control. She worried why the attorney-client meeting was taking so damned long. An hour-and-a-half later, Swan and Winheller emerged smiling.

"*Dankeschön*, Klaus. I feel ever so much better now."

"*Bitte*, Swan. You must trust me now and let me do the worrying. When the police make their arrest, call me on my *handy* and I will come at once."

"I have a question," Dinah said. "Alwin Pohl was involved in a manslaughter case a few years ago before he moved to the U.S. I think you call it *Totschlag*. Could you find out if he left behind any old enemies from that event?"

"That *is* interesting. Yes, I will search the records and keep you informed."

She didn't want to add the story of the blown-up *Gasthaus* to his client intake notes, but she asked, "Do you have any idea how we can track down Reiner Hess?"

"We must rely on the police for that."

Or maybe Margaret, thought Dinah, if I can persuade her that he's the one who threw that grenade. She gave Winheller her phone number, made sure that she had the number of his "*handy*," thanked him, and hustled Swan and Jack out the door. She had a date with Baer Eichen and she didn't want to show up late.

Swan decided to walk back to the Adlon. Dinah grabbed a cab. Eichen lived only ten blocks from Winheller's office, but she had done enough walking for one day and her blister hurt.

"Are you hungry, Jack?"

"A little."

"Good. I have a feeling we're in for a very nice meal tonight."

"Who is this guy?"

"A banker by day and a Sioux warrior named Takoda by night."

"Does that mean we have to eat buffalo?"

"I doubt that buffalo will be on the menu."

They crossed the Marshall Bridge and got out of the cab in the middle of the block on Schiffbauerdamm. Dinah read Eichen's note. "Look for the cleft in the hedge and follow the grass lane. The house is by the river."

Jack frisked ahead and found the cleft. "It's here."

Dinah turned down the lane behind him and immediately felt hemmed in. The bordering hedges were head-high and pointed some forty yards away to the only house—a tall, narrow, gray stone affair reminiscent of an Italian townhouse. The river ran right outside his door.

Jack was already on the porch throwing pebbles toward the water by the time she hobbled up the steps. The ornately carved wooden door and the sweeping view of the city in the distance made it clear that Berlin's bankers lived well. As she rang the bell, her hopes for a fine dinner spiked. She halfway expected a butler to answer the door, but Baer appeared with a welcoming smile.

"Dinah. I'm delighted to see you." He wore an expensive suit, but the anomalous bolo tie with the turquoise clasp at his throat stood out like a blue-green goiter.

"Thank you for inviting me, Herr Eichen. I hope you don't mind. I've brought a friend, Jack Ramberg."

"Hello, Jack." He shook Jack's hand. "I'm Baer Eichen. Please come in and will you both please call me Baer?"

"Nice to meet you," said Jack. "If you're an Indian, don't you have a first name, like Standing Bear or Running Bear?"

Eichen threw back his head and laughed. "Baer is a German name and it does mean bear. My Sioux name is Takoda, which means friend. If you like, I will show you a book of old photographs of the Sioux people."

He didn't seem the least put off by Jack's unexpected appearance, but Dinah felt obliged to offer an explanation. "Jack's mom had an emergency and I'm looking after him for a while."

"It will be my pleasure to look after you both tonight." He hung their coats on a coat rack so loaded with coats it looked as if he had a whole house full of company.

"Do you have other guests?"

"Only you and Jack." He led them up a carved wooden staircase into a huge, sumptuous room, the focal point of which was a picture window with a view of the Spree and the Berlin skyline. He crossed a half-acre of richly-hued Persian carpet to an Art Deco style wet bar. Behind the bar, three mirrored panels reflected the fireplace and built-in bookcases across the room. "What will you drink, Jack? *Apfelsaft? Orangensaft? Johannisbeeresaft?* I don't have any other juices."

"What color is Johannisbeeresaft?" Jack asked.

"Purple, I should say. It is from the black currant."

"I'll have that."

"Straight, or with soda?"

"With soda."

Dinah had to smile at the deference he paid to Jack. While he spritzed soda into the juice from an antique siphon, her eyes roved around the room, taking in the understated splendor.

Across from the bar, an arrangement of comfortable-looking chairs had been grouped in front of a stone fireplace, mercifully unlit. A gilt mirror hung above the mantelpiece and on either side, bookshelves climbed floor-to-ceiling. A few exquisite wood carvings punctuated the rows of books, but there were no Indian artifacts. No photographs of family or friends, either.

He handed Jack his mocktail in an expensive cut glass tumbler. "And what is your aperitif of choice, Dinah?"

"I'll have a Kir if it's no trouble."

"Not at all."

She said, "You have a lovely house. Is it old?"

"Everything in this neighborhood dates only from nineteen eighty-nine when the Wall came down. It's new-fashioned, like most of the city. I am of the grandchildren generation. My contemporaries and I don't pine for the Berlin our grandfathers made." He handed her a Kir and mixed himself a Campari and soda. "Let's sit. I prepared hors d'oeuvres. I hope you like the selection of cheeses. And if you will excuse the immodesty, my Leberwurst is the equal of any French paté."

Dinah took a chair facing the view of the Spree. His hand grazed hers as he set the tray of appetizers on the cocktail table and took the chair facing her. His gaze was very warm. She sensed a sexual innuendo and was glad she'd brought Jack, who seemed captivated by something on the other side of the room. She sipped her Kir and started slow. "What bank do you work for, Herr...Baer?"

"I have been with Deutsche Bank for the last twenty years."

She said, "Did I read somewhere that Deutsche Bank financed the Northern Pacific Railway in the U.S., from Minnesota to the Pacific Coast after the American Civil War?"

"That is true. You are tactful to cite one of the more commendable projects from our history. Americans tend to recall our less admirable projects. I'm sure you've also read that Deutsche Bank funded the Auschwitz concentration camp. But enough about history and banking. Nations, institutions, individuals—we all have a past to live down. Please, try the Leberwurst."

She spread a layer of the soft schmear on a cracker and tasted. "It's luscious." She devoured it and instantly wanted another, but restrained herself.

"*Jøss!*" exclaimed Jack.

She had heard that same "yuss" from Thor when something surprised and pleased him. Jack set his juice on the floor and squatted in front of a small étagère. He looked back at Baer, wide-eyed. "It's a Ferrari two-fifty GTO."

"That's right. The nineteen sixty-two."

"May I touch it?"

"Yes. Do you like cars?"

"I'm going to be a race car driver."

"That is a model of the Ferrari made for the English Formula One driver, Stirling Moss. The real car sold recently for thirty-five million U.S. dollars."

Jack lifted the bright red model out of the case and held it as tenderly as if it were a newborn puppy.

Baer said, "I think cars are more to your liking than photos of old Indians. Don't be shy, Jack. They are all touchable."

"*Jøss!* It's the Pagani Zonda R that won at Nürburgring." He picked up another sleek, steel-blue model. "Did you used to be a race driver?"

"Just a fan, although I once drove the Nürburgring as a tourist."

"Wow."

Baer smiled. "Once at Nürburgring was enough to get the love of speed out of my system. Today I don't drive at all. One rarely needs a personal car in Berlin and when I travel outside the country, I travel by train."

Dinah slathered more of the Leberwurst on a fresh cracker. "You certainly have diverse interests, Baer. Native American culture, Formula One racing, paté making."

"What else does a lonely bachelor have to do with his time?"

His self-identification as a bachelor rather than a widower put her still more on guard. She said, "I imagine some of your time has been spent answering questions from the police."

"Yes. The murder was a great shock to everyone. Florian has suspended future meetings of the Indian club indefinitely."

"Were you and Pohl friends?"

"No." It was an emphatic no. "Alwin kept aloof. That is the stereotype of Germans, in general. But Alwin was especially remote. I often wondered why he joined the club. He had little interest in the romance of native cultures. He warmed up only when Lena Bischoff was around. I suppose you've heard they had a liaison."

"That's the kind of thing that would drive a lot of husbands to murder."

"Not Viktor. He is a passionate man, but he turns his passions inward. He has had a difficult life."

She said, "He told me about his grandfather and his father being Nazis. He seems to have a sackcloth-and-ashes mentality. He says he was born in the wrong century."

"Viktor was certainly born into the wrong family. His elder brother was an unofficial informant for the Stasi. Do you know about the Stasi?"

"They were the secret police in East Germany, the GDR."

"Yes. They co-opted a vast network of citizens to spy on their neighbors and even their families in order to root out dissidents and destroy them, either physically or psychologically. After reunification and the enactment of reforms, Viktor requested his personal file and learned that his brother had waged a psychological war on him for years. He repeatedly broke into Viktor's room and disarranged his record collection or turned pictures to the wall, always leaving some sign to let Viktor know he was being watched. Viktor is a man scarred by betrayals. But as I told Inspector Lohendorf, he could never harm another human being. He has neither the heart nor the mettle."

While Baer expressed the opinion more gently than Lena, the consensus seemed to be that Viktor wasn't man enough to kill Alwin Pohl. Having last seen Viktor half out of his mind with a butcher knife in his fist, she took this assessment with a grain of salt. "Do you know why Pohl left Germany, or why he returned?"

"Only what Florian has told me, something to do with a business opportunity. Would you care for another Kir?"

"No thanks."

"How about you, Jack? More juice?"

"No, thank you."

Baer went to the bar for more Campari and she segued from Germany to Georgia. "I understand that Pohl and Reiner Hess had known each other in the U.S. before returning to Berlin."

"Reiner." The name had a lead-balloon effect. It dropped without a verb and in the lengthening seconds of dead air, she turned to check on Jack. He was examining the undercarriage of a low-slung sports car as if it the secret of the universe were printed there. "Come and eat something, Jack. You said you were hungry."

"In a minute."

She looked back at Baer, who seemed to be studying her as intently as Jack was studying the model car. She said, "The name Reiner Hess seems to have a chilling effect. Do you mind telling me why?"

"It's difficult to speak about a friend after he has been accused of a crime."

She said, "He reminds me of a poem by T.S. Eliot about a mystery cat named Macavity. *You may seek him in the basement, you may look up in the air, but when the crime's discovered, Macavity's not there.*"

He laughed. "Deutsche Bank has had its own problems with tax evasion investigations. Twenty-five employees were charged last year with making false tax statements, money laundering, obstruction of justice. They are also my friends. Even our CEO was charged. The storm will blow over. Bankers are in greater danger from disappointing quarterly profit reports than from federal prosecutors. One can always amend one's tax declaration. I must therefore conclude that Reiner faces more serious charges."

"Is he capable of murder in your estimation?"

"Of Alwin's murder, you mean?"

She didn't think the question needed clarification.

He sat down again. "I've seen nothing that would cause me to believe that he is."

Baer's Sioux alias "Friend to All" was certainly apt. He seemed to count everyone he knew as a friend except Pohl. She said, "Do you know where he is?"

"Out of the country, I think."

"If he were still in Berlin, where would he be?"

He arched an eyebrow. "If he were in Berlin, it would be a great embarrassment to the police."

"I have reason to believe that he was at Müggelsee on the night of the murder. Do you know of any reason he might have had to kill Alwin Pohl?"

"Now I see it! I wasn't sure, but now I understand. You have undertaken to solve the crime, yourself."

He didn't sound insulted or defensive. He sounded…amused. He might be an ally or a he might be a snake in the grass, but at this juncture, she saw no downside to acknowledging what he would soon find out anyway. "My mother was at the scene of the crime. She touched the body. The police found traces of her DNA. If they can't come up with a more likely suspect, they'll arrest her. I'm doing everything I can to prevent that from happening. I met Pohl. He was a rotter. I believe there may be others who wanted him dead. Viktor has the most obvious motive, but Hess might have had one, too."

"And so could I. Is that why you agreed to have dinner with me? To uncover my dark motives?"

"Partly."

"And what is the other part?"

"I thought you'd take me to the best restaurant in Berlin."

He laughed so hard his wooden glasses slid down his nose. "And so I shall."

Jack came over and took a piece of cheese and a cracker. "Will we be eating soon?"

"Let's leave now," said Baer, tossing off his Campari. "Dinah can continue her interrogation at the restaurant. Wait for me downstairs. I will call a taxi."

Jack ran ahead and Dinah followed, checking her voicemail on the way. No news from Margaret was good news, no news from K.D. was at least neutral, and no news from Thor hurt less than a penknife to the heart. Or so she imagined. She put her phone back in her purse and lifted her coat off the rack. "What are you doing, Jack?"

He had squeezed behind the rack of coats and winter paraphernalia and the whole assembly was jiggling. "There's a big iron ring in the wall back here."

She pushed apart the heavy shroud of coats. "It looks like a piece of decorative hardware. Maybe it used to hold a picture."

"It looks like a door." He was pulling on the ring when Baer came down the steps. "Is there a secret passage, Baer?"

"See for yourself." He rolled the coat rack out of the way and wrenched the ring hard to the right.

A nearly invisible door slid open to reveal what looked like a well. A wooden ladder had been affixed to the concrete wall.

"What's down there?" asked Jack, peering down.

"Nothing but darkness," said Baer. "It's a bunker. This area is honeycombed with them. They were built by Hitler's army. Soldiers and thousands of civilians used them for bomb shelters during the Allied airstrikes. Hitler's private bunker and many others have been destroyed by our modern city managers. In Berlin, we have enough reminders of the past without looking underground. This bunker would have been destroyed, but the man who built the house had the idea that one day he would offer tours like the catacombs in Paris and Rome."

"Were you bombed?" asked Jack.

"The war was before my time. My parents used to tell stories, but they are not the kinds of stories one tells before dinner."

# Chapter Twenty-four

The shimmering, blade-like tower of the Zoofenster skyscraper cleaved the night sky above Charlottenburg district and the city zoo. Seen from the side, the building put Dinah in mind of a guillotine, not so much because she was en route to Berlin's most celebrated French restaurant, but because she felt she had lost her edge in this parley with Baer Eichen. Whether it was his charm or her haste to get answers, she was giving him more information than he was giving her.

The conceit of the guillotine played on in her imagination even if the swooshing elevator up to the Waldorf Astoria was an improbable tumbrel. She'd read somewhere that by the time Hitler came to power, German engineers had so improved upon the technology and efficiency of the guillotine that the Führer was able to keep a score of them chopping busily throughout WWII. It was fatal to underestimate German ingenuity, in weaponry or in wiles.

They stepped out of the elevator into the stylish environs of Les Solistes. Keep your head, she warned herself. Steal a page from Swan's book. Smile, but let him do most of the talking.

Pleading extreme hunger, she passed on a cocktail and they ordered food right away. The waiter helped Jack order, promising no broccoli, no beans, and no buffalo. Dinah ordered the langoustine to start and the pigeon entrée. Baer ordered foie gras and venison. He suggested a wine, but Dinah declined, and he ordered a bottle for himself.

Jack kicked off the conversation. "Who got murdered?"

"You have big ears," said Baer. "Will you be Watson to Dinah's Sherlock?"

"I don't know. Maybe she'll be Watson."

Baer laughed. "Either way, you make a formidable team."

Dinah couldn't tell if Jack had actually read the Sherlock Holmes stories or if he was being a wiseass. Another one not to be underestimated, she thought, and admonished him with a stern look. When Baer's laughter subsided, she said, "I'm afraid I lack Sherlock's deductive abilities. Please tell me about your fellow clubmen. I understand that Reiner Hess was given the boot."

"Reputation matters. No one wanted to see his name linked with Hess in the press. I like Reiner, but he has made a deliberate break. It is treacherous for a friend to say, and perhaps unfair, but I see Reiner as an opportunist."

"How so?"

"When Reiner joined the club, he lived part of the year in Berlin and part in America. He attended law school there and was licensed to practice in several states. He showed less interest in native cultures than in the skyrocketing value of native art. I have never been told and never asked, but I shouldn't be surprised if he assisted Florian in acquiring some of his more valuable pieces over the years."

"Acquiring them illegally?"

"If I were to learn that he cut corners or exploited certain loopholes in the law, it wouldn't surprise me. But that is conjecture. Nothing more."

"You must have some reason for the conjecture."

"The money, Dinah. What is the American expression? Reiner and Florian have made out like bandits."

The wine came, along with a plate of fancy palate teasers. While Jack sampled the goodies and Baer sniffed and swirled the wine, Dinah scripted out a massive antiquities smuggling operation in her head. She could picture Pohl and Hess casing Indian reservations and museums, acquiring the best items by hook or by crook, and funneling them to Germany for sale in

Farber's Happy Hunting Ground. Were they moonlighting from their usual jobs with Cleon, or had Cleon also dabbled in stolen art on the side?

"Is Florian another suspect?" asked Jack.

Dinah said, "If Florian is trading in stolen antiquities and Pohl threatened to expose him, he might have seen murder as his only recourse."

"There is always an alternative to murder," said Baer. "If one chooses to look for it."

"And what is your character analysis of Florian?" asked Dinah. "Is he someone who would look for an alternative?"

"Florian is an intelligent man. It would surprise me if someone as unintelligent as Pohl could force him into such straits that he would risk murder."

Jack picked the last morsel off the goody platter and turned his frank gaze on Baer. "What did Pohl do to make you not like him?"

A queer expression crawled across Baer's face. "Did I say that, Jack?"

"Sort of. When Dinah asked if you were friends, you said 'no,' but you said it like he was what my Dad calls a super weasel."

Baer sipped his wine and looked thoughtful for a few seconds. "I disliked the man for many reasons, but I would not call him a weasel. The weasel is a greedy and ferocious hunter, but he is cunning. Alwin Pohl was an unthinking brute."

The first course arrived with considerable fanfare and Baer turned his attention to the food. He contrasted the chef's Berlin restaurant with his flagship restaurant in Paris—which he had visited at the end of June, and reminisced about the cuisine at several other eateries in Paris and Berlin. If he seemed a little too eager to leave the topic of Alwin Pohl, Dinah was content to let it drop. Her suspicions about Farber had been furthered substantially and she knew what the next step in her investigation would be. But at the moment, she was famished and the langoustine was sublime. The aromas and flavors and Baer's foodie reviews provided a pleasant respite from the stress of the day. And when her pigeon came, she dispatched it with gusto and asked Baer if she might have a glass of his wine.

At the end of the evening, she thanked him for one of the best meals she had ever eaten.

"I'm pleased it lived up to your expectations." His eyes twinkled. "May I call you again, perhaps when there's no child-care emergency?"

Again, she detected a sexual innuendo. Uncertain how to respond, she essayed an ambiguous smile and Swan-like, left its meaning to his imagination. He put her in a taxi in front of the hotel and paid the driver in advance. Before he closed the door, he took out of his coat pocket an oddly shaped parcel wrapped in newspaper and handed it to Jack. "From one connoisseur to another."

"What's this?"

"Something to feed your dreams. Go ahead and open it."

Jack tore off the paper and pulled out the bright red Ferrari 250 GTO. "Wow. I can really have it, Baer?"

Dinah demurred. "It's too valuable a gift. It's very generous of you, but I don't think he should accept it."

"I insist. I am too old to play with cars. But mind you don't play too rough with it, Jack. The two-five-0 is a special car."

# Chapter Twenty-five

When Dinah and Jack returned to the apartment after dinner, they walked in on a bristling volley between K.D. and Margaret that featured the words "hag" and "piss ant" with several colorful modifiers thrown in for emphasis. Dinah shunted Jack into the office and took Margaret into the bedroom.

"How long have you two been at it?"

"Not long. She hadn't gotten around to calling me a murdering bitch yet."

Dinah scrounged up one of Thor's old shirts and a pair of sweat pants for her to sleep in. She gave her a towel and washcloth and one of those airline toiletry bags with the folding toothbrush and scratchy eye mask that she'd saved from a previous trip. "Keep out of the way for a few minutes, Margaret, and simmer down."

"She's the one who's acting out. I tried to be civil."

"I know you did. She's just not ready."

"I'll tread lightly. Who's the kid?"

"He's Thor's son. His name is Jack."

Margaret stripped off the clothes she'd been wearing when her room caught fire and pulled the clean shirt over her head. She had had a drink or two, but she wasn't tanked.

"I have to go out for a few hours, Margaret. I'm going to take K.D. with me. Will you look after Jack? See that he puts on his PJs pretty soon and don't let him swallow drain cleaner or anything."

"Sure. I'll mind him."

"Thanks." Dinah went back to the living room. Jack had come out of the office and was lining his cars up in race formation along one wall with the new Ferrari out in front. K.D. lounged on the sofa, texting.

"Sign off, K.D. I'd like a word." She led her into the kitchen. "I know you have plans tonight, but I need your help."

"What?"

"I need you to help me break into an art gallery."

"Whoa. That's rich."

"It's a one-time thing, K.D. Burglary is a crime. It's wrong and I wouldn't do it if there were any other way. If there weren't, you know, extenuating circumstances."

"Okay. But afterward, I'm going out with Geert and you have to promise me—no sermons and no flak when I get back. Geert can drive us to this gallery and stand lookout."

"Did you hear me say it's a criminal offense? We can't involve another person."

"Don't worry. Geert's cool."

"I don't care how cool he is, K.D. This isn't a symposium. No third party."

"So I won't tell him what we're doing. I'll say we're out to score a few cartons of untaxed cigs. I've seen several Vietnamese dudes selling them on the street. As much money as Geert spends on smokes, he'll totally go for it. All he has to do is text me from across the street if the cops show up."

"Won't he expect a carton in return for his help?"

"I'll just say the seller never showed."

Dinah didn't know what Geert had said to earn K.D.'s trust as an accomplice, but whatever it was, it didn't boost Dinah's confidence. Even so, it might be a good idea to have some muscle as backup, not that Geert had much to show in that department. She changed her clothes and the three of them set off in Geert's Opel.

"You won't let her get drunk at the club, will you, Geert?"

"Seventeen, she can only drink beer and wine. It is the law."

"Or let her be drugged and dragged off by a rapist?"

"No drugs," he said. "No rapists."

Other than yourself, thought Dinah, but K.D. wasn't your typical teenage ingenue. She could fend for herself.

Geert parked the Opel on a side street six blocks from the gallery and they walked back toward Kürfürstenstrasse through a spitting rain. At midnight, street traffic was sparse, but there were still plenty of pedestrians on their way to and from the local theaters and clubs. Geert positioned himself in a doorway across the street from the gallery. Dinah and K.D. cut down the alley behind the Happy Hunting Ground. The back door was easy to find. The yellow tepee was still up. Dinah opened the flap and aimed her light inside. It was empty.

K.D. inspected the gallery's backdoor lock. "It's a tumbler. Piece of cake."

In the actual commission, Dinah felt feverish and jittery and she couldn't block out thoughts of Thor. This caper would confirm his worst assumptions about her. Not that he was such an almighty straight arrow. "What about the alarm system?"

"That's the tricky part. My bump key will jump the driver pins and I can open the door, but that'll probably break the electric circuit and brrrang!"

"Won't it shut off if you close the door in a hurry?" Even as she said it, Dinah couldn't believe that a gallery housing pricey objets d'art would make burglary as easy as closing the door behind you. "I guess not."

"Not." K.D. ran her flashlight up and down the jamb and seam. "There's probably a control box inside, hooked up to more alarms. If that's the setup, there'll be a keypad and security code. We'll have maybe thirty seconds, sixty tops, to find the alarm panel and smash it."

"How did you get past the keypad security in my building without smashing it?"

"Hello-oh? I lived there for two weeks." She scouted around the side of the building and looked in a low window. "I can see a blue LED light a few feet down the hall. It could be the alarm panel. Or not. The owner may have installed a dummy."

Dinah was loath to inquire how the girl had come into possession of a burglar's bump key, or where and why she had picked up her flair for breaking and entering. If she didn't clean up her act, she'd end up in the cooler. Dinah faulted herself. *I should be counseling reform and setting a good example. Instead, here I am urging her on. If we're caught...*but she couldn't think about that right now. "What's your best judgment?"

"I'm thinking." The expert ran a finger along the downspout. "No anti-climb paint. Shows they're not too hyper about security." She clutched her hoodie and looked up. "It wouldn't be hard to shinny up the downspout to the roof. Is there a skylight?"

"No. Sunlight would discolor the art."

"We go through the door then. But unless you know the code, I'll have to break the control box and they'll know somebody was here. If I can't find the box before the alarm goes off, we could have five-0 down on our necks and have to book, like really fast."

"If that happens," said Dinah, "run toward Kurfürstenstrasse. Try to blend in with the crowd."

"Duh." K.D. gave her a reproving look. "What do you expect to find in here, anyway?"

"A secret someone would kill to keep."

"Okay. Here goes. Hold the light for me." She leaned one shoulder against the door, bowed her head, and gently slid the key into the lock. So quick as to be virtually simultaneous, she gave the key a deft forward thrust and pushed the door open.

A flurry of beeps commenced and Dinah's heart speeded up as if to keep time. K.D. took back her flashlight and the baseball bat Dinah had been holding and walked inside. Dinah followed, closing the door behind her. The beeping continued.

"Whoa, somebody's been toking up," said K.D., not bothering to lower her voice.

"Weed with a soupçon of desert sage," said Dinah.

K.D. ignored the keypad just inside to the right of the door and moved on to the blue light on the wall across from Farber's desk. "This isn't the control box," she said. "It's a thermostat." She advanced farther into the gallery, her light scaling the wall from floor to ceiling. "Geert says marijuana's legal in Berlin. Is that right?"

"Keep your mind on the job, K.D." Her cool was more unsettling to Dinah than panic. Time was running out. How many seconds of beeping remained before hell broke loose? She ran her light around the gallery walls. She was the supposed grown-up and the instigator of this exploit, plus which, she had been in the gallery twice during daylight hours. She ought to be able to offer some kind of guidance.

Her light lit on the *katsinam* mask. It was half of a hollowed-out squash with a crudely painted face as ugly as dried mud, but to the Hopi, a *katsinam* was the personification of a helpful spirit. Was it really as fragile as Farber said? He had reacted with such sudden vehemence when she tried to touch it.

She stepped around K.D. and touched the edge of the mask. It felt sturdy enough. Gently, she lifted it off its nail. Behind it, a plastic apparatus the size of a playing card had been wired into the wall. "Is this it?"

"Yep. Move back." K.D. swung the bat like a power slugger. The beeping stopped. Pieces of plastic clattered onto the floor and the gallery went quiet.

Dinah's heart seemed to pause as she waited for the wail of a siren and the flash of bright lights. But seconds passed and nothing happened.

"Good guess," said K.D. "How'd you know to look there?"

Dinah wasn't ready to admit that her good guess was based on superstition and blind luck. She felt stupid enough as it was. "Thanks, K.D. I know it sounds hypocritical, but I'm sorry I had to involve you in this. Please don't use your magic key again. Promise?"

"Only if I'm asked by a responsible adult."

"I deserved that, but we'll have that conversation another time. Get out of here and take extra care at the club tonight. Stick close to Geert and don't—"

"Do anything you wouldn't do?" She snickered and pranced out the door giving Dinah no chance to reply, not that she had a reply.

Alone in the Happy Hunting Ground, Dinah rehung the *katsinam* over the broken control device and walked slowly around the place, shining her light on the masks and other artifacts. If they had been purchased from American dealers, there would be documentation showing the provenance of each piece and the validity of the seller's title. If there were gaps or discontinuities in the record of ownership, that should also be documented. She had constructed a narrative in her head in which Pohl and Hess stole, or procured stolen art, and Farber and Bischoff fudged the paperwork and either resold it directly or put it up for auction. When Pohl fell for Lena and announced that he wanted to cash out, one of the others—or all of them acting in concert—decided it would be safer and more economical all around to kill him. If she could scare up evidence of motive, maybe Lohendorf would look beyond the fact of Swan's DNA.

She sat down at Farber's desk. She wished she could have gotten inside the gallery without leaving behind evidence of the break-in, but one brilliant thing that she had done was to memorize the password he used when he opened his laptop to show her the slideshow. His business records were probably stored on that computer and for transactions involving Native American art, some of the documents would be in English. She looked high and low, drawer by drawer. The laptop wasn't there. She sorted through the papers on top of the desk, but they appeared to be mostly advertisements and art catalogs. She riffled through the file folders, but there was nothing in English, nothing with the words auction or *auktion*, no correspondence from or to Reiner Hess, nothing to show for this risky sortie but a surfeit of adrenaline.

The marijuana odor was stronger here and she got up to nose it out. A light parka hung on a peg behind the desk. She gave it a sniff. It was redolent enough to get high just from touching it. She didn't know if Farber smoked, but Viktor did. On the off chance she'd find something to make this night's risk worthwhile, she went through the pockets. The left yielded nothing but few bits of loose grass. The right held a nubbly something that felt like a heavy key fob.

"*Schiesse! Die Tür wird entriegelt.*"

She froze, her hand still inside the pocket. Somebody was coming through the back door. Somebody who sounded seriously angry. Breaking the alarm box must have alerted the police after all. Maybe it was designed not to make a noise on this end so as to catch an intruder red-handed, still inside the premises. She looked around in desperation. The only thing big enough to hide behind was that stone lion-bear chimera in the corner. She killed her light, crammed it in her coat pocket, and slunk into the shadows, feeling her way along the wall and around the statue with her left hand. Her right was still clenched around the key fob. The space between the back of the statue and the wall was miniscule and she was barely able to squinch through.

There were two voices, both male. One belonged to Farber. The other, she didn't recognize. They spoke in rapid German. This had happened to her once before in Greece, trapped in a tight spot while her captors gabbed in a language she couldn't understand. Why did she never get in trouble in places where people spoke Muscogean or Quapaw? She could at least have picked up a smattering.

The overhead lights came on. She dared not move, though she couldn't if she wanted. There wasn't enough room to crouch. She couldn't bend her knees or turn sideways. Her shoulders and heels were flat against the wall, her nose against the rough-hewn stone. It smelled like dirt. Like a fresh-turned grave.

Farber ranted, his voice traveling around the gallery. The other guy sounded phlegmatic, but somehow more frightening. She couldn't see, but he didn't seem to be firing off questions the way a cop would have done. Whatever they were saying, they would have seen the pieces of the broken control box on the floor. Maybe they'd calm down when they saw that none of the art had been stolen. The only thing she had taken was Viktor's key fob.

She heard desk drawers being opened and closed with force and what sounded like some serious swearing. Had she put papers back in the wrong order?

She glanced down at the object in her right hand and her eyes dilated. Not a fob. Mother of God. It was a grenade.

Her brain shut down. She couldn't scream. She couldn't breathe. She no longer heard or cared what the Germans were saying. She saw her obituary as clearly as if it had been printed in boldface on the inside of her eyelids.

*After a lengthy battle with stupidity, Dinah Pelerin was splattered across the walls of The Happy Hunting Ground art gallery by what might have been a WWII grenade, which she had nicked out of the owner's pocket during the course of a break-in.*

Farber's voice dropped to a less furious pitch. She willed herself to concentrate. She was alive. The critical question was how to stay that way. As her brain rebooted, she recalled that grenades had pins and the pin had to be pulled before the world went kaboom. This particular grenade had a metal tail that ran the length of it and a ring. Her fingers curled around the grenade under that tail. So long as she didn't mess with it, or with the ring, she would probably remain in one piece. She was also beginning to think that Farber and friend weren't going to look behind this statue. Their tour seemed to be winding down. If they left, she could squeeze out of this cranny and escape. If they stayed, she'd have to decide whether to show herself and brave the consequences, or wait them out. She didn't think she could stand in this cramped and rigid posture much longer.

She squirmed and wiggled her left hand up to her nose to stop a sneeze. The dirt smell wasn't helping. She tilted her head back for air. Just above eye level was a label. MALAWI NATIONAL MUSEUM, Minya, Egypt. That museum had been in the news just a few days ago. Over a thousand artifacts had been looted. Did Farber deal in stolen art from other parts of the world? It made sense. An unscrupulous art dealer might specialize, but he wouldn't turn up his nose if loot from a different source became available.

The phlegmatic voice said in perfect English, "I'll take care of it," and somebody doused the lights.

They were leaving. Dinah let out the breath it seemed she'd been holding forever. She counted slowly to five hundred after she heard the back door close before she sucked in her stomach and squiggled out into the open. With her left hand, she took out her flashlight and with her right, as carefully as if she were replacing a baby bird in its nest, she replaced the grenade in the parka pocket. First thing tomorrow morning, she would call Lohendorf and tell him about her discovery. If he arrested her for burglary, so be it. She could point to stone cold evidence that Florian Farber was an art thief, and to circumstantial evidence that the owner of the jacket hanging behind Farber's desk had tried to kill Margaret. Taken together, the facts should give the police ample cause to question both Farber and Viktor again regarding Pohl's murder.

If only she could have gotten to her phone and recorded the voices to play back to Margaret. She had a strong feeling that the phlegmatic voice belonged to Reiner Hess.

# Chapter Twenty-six

Dinah dragged in the door dead-tired. She turned on a lamp, peeled off her damp coat, and hung it on the peg on the back of the door. It was almost three a.m. Soon the caged cuckoo would be moaning. It was ridiculous to feel pity for a mechanical bird, but after what she'd been through in the last few hours, she decided to let the pest fly free as soon as the sun came up, regardless of the racket. He might not be as raucous as he had been. The clock hadn't been wound in a week. Thor was the only one who knew how.

Jack was asleep on the sofa, apparently none the worse for her neglect. She picked up the blanket he had kicked onto the floor and covered him. How weird would it be to have a child? To be on duty full-time? To always be conscious that someone was counting on you to do the right thing, looking up to you as a role model and making life choices based on your advice and example? Responsibility like that would petrify her.

Thor hadn't been petrified. Why not? He couldn't look after Jack all the time during those six-month visits. His job demanded that he be available on a moment's notice. Did he have a live-in nanny?

Jennifer probably had a career, too, but from what Dinah could tell, she'd done a terrific job with Jack. When she left him in Berlin, she obviously trusted that Thor had paired up with a conscientious girlfriend. If she'd thought for a minute that this girlfriend would leave her son in the care of a dipsomaniac while she went out to burgle a local business, she would be petrified.

The bedroom door was closed, but she could hear Margaret sawing logs on the other side. She wondered if she'd left any gin in the bottle. After that close call with the grenade, she could use a tranquilizer. She plodded into the kitchen. A half-full bottle of Monkey 47, Schwarzwald Dry Gin, sat on the table and next to it, a packet of little green pills. Bionorica Sinupret extract. Must be some sort of sinus remedy. In her terror, she had almost forgotten her sore throat. It was probably some kind of allergy. To stress, most likely. But an ounce of prevention couldn't hurt. She grabbed a glass, poured herself a jigger of the Monkey, swallowed two pills, and chased them down with a sip that scalded. It tasted like a mixture of Pine-Sol, kaffir lime, cardamom, and something perfumey. Honeysuckle? Whatever it was, it was fantastic. Being alive and in one piece was fantastic. She savored another sip, closed her eyes, and heaved an enormous sigh.

"Hard day?"

Her eyes flew open. Thor stood in the doorway, one shoulder leaned against the jamb. He was barefoot and shirtless and his drawstring pants hung low around his hips. Her first impulse was to jump up and throw her arms around him, but he stayed put, arms folded across his chest. The air between them had changed. They weren't the same people they'd been four days ago, not to each other. She stoppered the bottle and feigned a blasé expression. "When did you get home?"

"Around eleven. Margaret said I'd just missed you. She's quite a character, by the way. She tells some interesting stories."

"I wouldn't put too much stock in them." She gave a careless little wave. "Come in and have a drink of the very aptly named Monkey."

He picked up a chair, twirled it around, and sat down with his chin resting on the back. "If I were to ask you for a rundown of the last few days, what would you tell me?"

"Rain, lies, houseguests, murder. That about sums it up."

"That's pretty thin. You've left out some important details, haven't you?"

"You're the expert in leaving out details."

"Okay, Dinah. You've been handed a surprise, for which I'm sorry. Don't generalize about my trustworthiness in every other way."

"All right, I won't. You've proven yourself to be an absolute puritan when dealing with professional matters. But that kind of selective trustworthiness is not what I need. You'll just take anything I say and repeat it to your friend Lohendorf."

"You know I wouldn't do that."

"I thought I knew what you wouldn't do."

"Is it that you don't trust me to know the facts, or you don't trust me to know the truth?"

"What's the difference?"

"Facts can change, not truth."

"Oh, give me a break. I held a grenade in my hand tonight, Thor, and thought about death. Don't come in here with your pants at half-mast looking like a *Playgirl* centerfold and try to, to mousetrap me with philosophy."

"A grenade! Are you serious?"

"As a lit fuse."

"Jesus, Dinah. Where? What happened? I swear to you, it won't go any farther if you don't want it to."

She took another sip of gin and told him about her night at the gallery, making no apologies for the break-in. "It's clear that Farber is crooked and the man who was with him was probably Hess. I wouldn't be surprised if Hess is hiding Farber's money for him in a secret account in Cyprus, and Farber is hiding Hess from the police while he's in Berlin. Anyway, you don't have to worry about me holding out on the police. I plan to call your pal Lohendorf as soon as his office opens and sing like a canary."

"He could arrest you, you know."

"I don't think Farber will report the burglary. I don't know how he had rigged his security system, but it wasn't designed to bring in the police. The last thing he wants is for people to start poking around and asking about the provenance of his inventory. Anyhow, I didn't take anything. Maybe he thinks it was vandals or kids looking to score drugs. Somebody, probably Viktor, spends a lot of time with his Aunt Mary Jane. The coat with the grenade stunk to high heaven."

"Tell me what the grenade looked like."

"A pound or pound-and-a-half, olive drab with indentations or grooves. It had a curved lever like a tail, and a ring."

"Sounds old, and American made. The Germans used stick grenades, no ring."

She shivered and took another sip of gin. "In the dark, I didn't know what I'd grabbed. I felt that ring and like an idiot, thought it was for keys. I could have been blown to bits, along with one of Egypt's pharaonic treasures."

He reached out a hand and stroked her hair. "I just thank God that the Egyptian patrimony was saved."

She looked into his eyes and laughed. "Yeah. If I'd pulled the pin, I'd have landed in Egyptian hell, tormented by demons and damned to swim in my own blood for eternity." The laughter was cathartic, but his touch sparked side effects that disrupted her defenses. She got up from the table and stood next to the counter. "What I can't figure out is why Farber, or Viktor, or Hess would try to kill Margaret. It's possible that she knows where Hess is hiding out, but it would be a lot easier for him to move than to kill her and call down the wrath of the entire Berlin police force on his head."

"What makes you think that Hess was the other man in the gallery tonight?"

"I don't know. His voice sounded so commanding, like he was the honcho and Farber had better do what he said or else. Hess was with Margaret at the lake on the night of the murder and I think he's into a lot shadier schemes than hiding his money in Cyprus."

"Cyprus is the go-to spot for tax evaders these days. The richest man in Norway lives on Cyprus as a tax exile. Norwegians call him the 'big wolf.'" He unstopped the Monkey 47, poured another jigger into her glass, and tasted. "Potent stuff."

"Dynamite. I think I'll keep a bottle on hand as a restorative in the event I have any more near-death experiences."

"Look, Dinah, I won't interfere if you don't want me to, but say the word and I'll go with you tomorrow to talk with Jens. I can vouch for your detective's intuition." He grinned. "And I can post bail in case he jails you."

"Thanks, Thor. I mean it. Thank you for your advice and your moral support, and for that pile of household cash you left in case the furnace blew and I needed a repairman. I spent it all on the lawyer's retainer. And thanks for passing on Lohendorf's warning. That wasn't strictly by the book for either of you. But you should know that Mom is going to correct her statement to the police and admit that she went to meet Pohl, but found him dead. After the grenade attack on Margaret and what I saw at Farber's gallery, I think Lohendorf will realize that the DNA he found was the result of accidental contact with the body. I think he'll refocus his investigation on Farber and we can all stop worrying."

"You don't have to thank me for anything, Dinah. If one of us is in trouble, the other is. That's what it means to be a 'household,' isn't it?"

She felt a rush of warmth and pent-up guilt and self-reproach. Maybe it was the resurgence of conscience or the fleeting courage of the Monkey 47. Almost as an out-of-body experience, she heard herself say, "I have two million dollars in an offshore account in Panama. I inherited the proceeds from an illegal drug operation four years ago."

He stared, a look of amazement drawing his forehead into tight ridges. "*Uff da.*"

"Whatever that means, I'm sure I deserve it. But I don't want you to be in trouble just because I am. I was stupid, but I'm not going to stick around and let you be tarred with the same brush. I don't think Lohendorf will find out, at least not immediately, but I'll clear out before your connection to me can tarnish your career. I'll take K.D. and Margaret and move into the hotel with my mother tomorrow."

He continued to stare.

"Aren't you going to say something? Anything?"

The cuckoo moaned.

With each mournful caw, her self-esteem shriveled. His face was a study. "Well, say something for crying out loud."

"You should have told me you didn't like the clock."

She didn't know whether to laugh or cry. The way her throat felt, it was hard to tell.

He got up and took her hand. "It's three o'clock in the morning. Come to bed with me. We'll talk about it when we're fresh and thinking straight."

She shook her head. "I'd love nothing better than to jump into bed with you, Thor. How's that for honesty, coming from one of the world's leading specialists in detours and denials? But we can't just pick up where we left off. I'm not who you thought I was and vice versa. Jack is no small vice versa. I'm not parenting material, not even part-time, and if you can turn a blind eye to my criminal carryings-on—a stash of dirty drug money, for heaven sakes—then you're not the man I thought you were. We don't know each other. And besides, there *is* no bed. Margaret's in the bedroom and K.D. has dibs on your sleeping bag when she gets home."

"We know each other, Dinah. The facts are still coming in, but we know the important things. The core truth." He gave her hand a tug. "Come on, I've set up an air mattress in the office."

# Chapter Twenty-seven

Loud noises roused Dinah from sleep. She rolled over and reached for Thor, but he was gone. She heard him speaking German in the other room. He sounded pretty damned boisterous for—she looked at her watch—eight o'clock in the morning. What was he doing, roughhousing with Jack? No, Jack didn't speak German.

Something heavy clunked on the floor and Geert cut loose with a rush of excited German. What was Geert doing here? Had something happened to K.D.? Had he brought her home falling-down drunk?

She sat up, rocked on her butt a few times, and sprang to her feet. Something would have to be done about the sleeping arrangements. Being forced to spend the night on an air mattress in her own apartment was above and beyond the call of Southern hospitality. She yanked on her clothes and raked her fingers through her hair. What were the odds that the bathroom would be free? She shambled into the living room. Lena Bischoff hung limp as a noodle between Thor and Geert and they were dragging her toward the bedroom.

"See who we brought you?" gloated K.D. "As soon as she wakes up, Lena's going to give us the skinny on her dorky husband Viktor. She and I totally bonded at the club last night."

"Thor, wait." Dinah was still struggling to wake up and she wasn't receptive to the idea of yet another new roommate. "You can't put her in the bedroom. Margaret's in there. Why can't Lena sleep it off in your apartment, Geert?"

"I don't want her," said Geert. "She is wild. The witch clawed me." He showed her red marks on the side of his face.

"You brought her here against her will?"

"She totally wanted to come," said K.D., opening the bedroom door.

"Shh!" Dinah pointed to Margaret, who was still out, flat on her back, eyes covered with the airline eye mask, and snoring like a Mac truck.

K.D.'s whisper wasn't much softer than her normal speaking voice. "Lena got a little high and mistook Geert for Viktor, that's all. She'll only be here for a few hours and you're definitely gonna want to hear what she has to say. Margaret can share."

Aphrodite nestled on the pillow next to Margaret's head. She switched her tail and hissed as the invaders closed in. The Mac truck made an abrupt gargling noise as if downshifting and the cat bolted out the door. Margaret didn't stir. Thor eased Lena down next to her and K.D. straightened Lena's legs and took off her shoes.

"Jerusalem." Dinah didn't wait to be briefed. She needed the bathroom and she needed coffee. Her first need was blocked by a locked door. As the only one missing from the scene was Jack, she could only hope that he didn't waste a lot of time on hygiene. She went to the kitchen and put on the coffee.

From the kitchen window, she could see the front of the *Gasthaus*, its entry boarded up and a few red and white striped traffic cones on the sidewalk in front. She wondered if Margaret's neatly packed suitcase had survived the blast. If it had, surely Lohendorf could have no objection to returning it. If she had a change of clothes, Margaret could move out to another hotel.

After a few minutes, Thor sauntered into the kitchen and put his arms around her. "Feels good to be home," he murmured in her ear and kissed the back of her neck.

She wasn't sure what last night's lovemaking had meant, but the concept of home left a lot to be negotiated. Her throat still didn't feel right. "It'll feel less good if you caught whatever germ I've got."

"My daily spoonful of cod liver oil makes me bulletproof."

"Don't say that. Touch wood." She rapped a knuckle against the wooden windowsill and gazed at the gray, rain-slick street below. "Is Jack out of the bathroom?"

"Yes. I think K.D.'s gone in now. Jack just asked me if I knew who had murdered Alwin Pohl. Have you been talking to him about the situation?"

"Not exactly." She poured herself a cup of coffee. It hadn't taken long for her negligence in the matter of child rearing to come to the fore. "Jack's an inquisitive kid. He may have over-heard an adult conversation. It's not my fault if he arrived in the middle of this chaos."

"I wasn't accusing you, Dinah. I don't want him to grow up in an ivory tower. His knowing about the murder surprised me is all I meant."

"Well. Surprise seems to be the order of the day around here, doesn't it?" She took one sip of coffee and fumed off to the bathroom. "K.D., there are other people in this apartment. Do the necessary and save the beauty treatments for another time."

The door opened and K.D. came out, eyes blazing. "After all I've done for you, you could show a little gratitude."

Dinah didn't regard Lena as a gift deserving of gratitude. She do-si-doed around K.D. and locked herself in the bathroom. She wished she could hide out in here all day. Maybe she had late onset bipolar disorder. Her mood had plummeted since the three a.m. high and she had a premonition that some god-awful "other shoe" was about to drop.

A hot shower helped clear her sinuses and restore a sense of resolve. She psyched herself up for the conversation with Lohen-dorf. When she walked out of the bathroom, she felt ready to parry any questions he might ask.

Margaret waited outside the door, cocooned in a white blanket from neck to knees. Her skin was ashen, her mouth downturned, and her hair hung around her face and shoulders like loose straw. "You need a second john."

"So it seems."

"Who's the blonde I woke up with?"

"Her name's Lena Bischoff. She may have information about Pohl's murder."

Margaret snorted. "Dressed like a hooker. I wouldn't believe anything she says."

She disappeared into the bathroom and Dinah went back to the kitchen for more coffee. Jack was on all fours, head pushed against the wall, strengthening his neck muscles. Thor was talking on his cell.

"Yes, he's fine. Settling in, no problems. Right. I'll make sure he does." He smiled at Dinah. "Dinah got him a new car, which he's pretty excited about. A Ferrari GTO. Right. Don't I know it. Uh-huh. How's your dad?"

Dinah took her coffee and headed for the office. She passed K.D., dossed down on the sofa with earbuds in her ears. Not once since she arrived had K.D.'s mother called to see if she was safe. For all she knew, the kid could have been sold into slavery. Small wonder K.D. waged war against everyone over the age of thirty. Dinah wanted to ask her what Lena had said last night. There was no reason to believe that Lena would tell the same story when she woke up sober. But there was no rush and both she and K.D. would be more agreeable after a couple of hours sleep. Anyway, there were other leads to follow.

She started into the office when out of the corner of her eye she noticed the clock. She glanced at her watch and, setting her jaw, she ripped the duct tape off the cuckoo's door. She waited a minute and at the stroke of nine, the bird popped out and began its obnoxious two-toned whistle. "Don't hold back, bird. Here on the Niederwallstrasse, we're all about sharing."

Still on the phone to Jen, Thor came to the kitchen door and grinned. She made a face and closed herself in the office. She meant to give Lohendorf plenty of ammunition about Farber's art thefts and initiated a computer search for news of the Malawi

Museum robbery. Located on the Nile a hundred and fifty miles south of Cairo, the museum had almost no security. The looters broke in during a protest by supporters of the deposed President Morsi, murdered the ticket agent, and ransacked the place. The scale of the devastation shown in the pictures sickened her. What the looters hadn't hauled away, they had trashed. Antique glass display cases had been splintered and brightly painted coffins battered to kindling. Stolen items included amulets, necklaces, funerary masks, votive statues, animal mummies, and even jars containing the two-thousand-year-old preserved organs of Egyptian dead. Some larger statues had also been removed, including one from the Tomb of Amenemhet.

Egypt wasn't the only country whose heritage was endangered by political unrest and civil strife. There were numerous articles citing the loss and destruction of other national museums and World Heritage sites. Looters had pillaged the National Museum of Iraq during the U.S. invasion, and scavengers used bulldozers to dig up archaeological relics from the ancient Hellenic city of Apamea during the Syrian uprising. The smuggling and selling of stolen antiquities had become a booming business with global reach. With so many Crusader castles and mosques and churches being pulverized by rebels and militias, Dinah wondered if ordinary thieves might be doing posterity a dubious favor. At least, they aimed to profit from their loot, not pulverize it.

Somebody knocked. She was about to say "go away," but Thor stuck his head in. "Ready for that call to Lohendorf?"

"Yes. I think that statue in Farber's gallery came from the Tomb of Amenemhet. I can do a search of the museum's collection before the robbery and find a picture."

"I'm not sure what he can do about looted Egyptian art. Germany still has no law that addresses the restitution of art the Nazis stole from its Jewish citizens. Everything proceeds on a case-by-case basis."

"That's terrible. But they must have laws against theft and smuggling. There has to be a law that applies to this sort of wanton plunder."

"Let's start with an up-front admission that you broke into the gallery last night. If you're right that Farber didn't report the burglary, that'll be persuasive. I'm sure Jens will pass on your concern about Amenemhet's tomb to the proper authorities. But he'll be more interested in that grenade. Grenades are banned under the German Weapons Act."

He dialed the number and Dinah felt a weight lift. Regardless of nationality or specialty or beat, cops related to other cops. They respected one another, trusted in hunches, and cut each other slack. And Thor was her cop, advocating for her.

It took a few minutes to get through to Lohendorf and the weight began to build again. What if she'd gotten it all wrong? What if the Malawi Museum had sold Farber that statue or given it to him on consignment? What if he *had* reported the burglary? What if he had installed electronic cameras that K.D. hadn't seen? It wouldn't be just Dinah that Lohendorf arrested. It would be K.D., too.

"Jens. It's Thor. I'm back in Berlin and Dinah and I have some news to report in connection with the Pohl case." He listened for a long time without speaking. "Yes, Dinah told me her mother had retained counsel. That's good. Right, right. At least you're not wasting time on a red herring."

He listened some more and his eyes augured bad news. "When? How?"

She held her breath.

"No. Not the sort of thing I'd chalk up to coincidence. How soon will your medical examiner be able to give you a cause of death?"

"Who?" she mouthed.

Thor held up a hand. "I understand. Can you come to our apartment this morning? Eleven's fine, and bring your sergeant. We have Lena Bischoff here."

He disconnected and she almost screamed. "Who's dead?"

"Viktor Bischoff. There was a house fire early this morning. He was pronounced dead on the scene. It could be a suicide. Jens has his doubts."

# Chapter Twenty-eight

"Lena showed up at the club around two," said K.D., basking in the attention. She sat at the kitchen table with Sergeant Wegener, who took notes, and Dinah, who couldn't stop thinking about Viktor. Would he be alive today if she'd called the police the night she was there? If she'd reported that his carelessness with fire posed a danger to the neighborhood and himself? One more thing to feel guilty about.

Unaware that Viktor was dead or that Lena might be a suspect, K.D. didn't stint on the details of her night at the club. "They play acid techno on the weekends, only it's way hardcore and they spell it *tekkno*. So I was dancing with this German dude and it was like being in the center of this whirlwind of sound. We were totally into it, but it gets really hot with the lights and all those bodies jumping around. After a while, I needed a break and we go to a table at the far end of the dance floor near the door. Geert brought us a beer and we're chilling when in walks Lena."

Lohendorf and Thor were questioning Lena in the living room now. Dinah wished she could be in two places at once.

"Did Mrs. Bischoff join you at your table?" Wegener asked K.D.

"No. I waved and called her name. She looked at me, but I don't think she recognized me. She was pretty damaged."

"Damaged how?" asked Wegener.

"Buzzed. On the way to being crunked."

Dinah said, "Stick to standard English, K.D. Sergeant Wegener isn't here for a seminar on American slang."

K.D. tossed her hair. "She was high, okay? Glassy-eyed and unsteady on her feet. But she goes straight onto the dance floor. She looks like she's about to fall on her face, so I go up to her and say, 'Come sit with me, Lena.' And I sweet-talk her to my table."

"Was she lucid?" asked Dinah.

"The music was real loud and you sort of had to fill in the blanks, but yeah. She talked about her poor dead *schatzie*, Alwin, and how he liked to dance and drive fast and spend his money on clothes and travel. He knew how to have a good time. Not like Viktor and his boring old Indian pots."

Lena had been ruthless in breaking up their household, but was she capable of burning the house down around Viktor's head? Recalling the knife she'd plunged into Viktor's drum, Dinah thought she just might be.

Wegener folded over a page in her notebook. "Did she speak of the night Alwin was killed?"

K.D. toyed with her hair and flicked a questioning look at Dinah.

"It's all right. Tell the Sergeant the truth."

"She said he had a date to meet Swan in the woods before the powwow. I was asking her if he had any other meetings that night when this dude struts up to the table like he owns her and tells me to *abhauen*. He totally snarls the word and jerks his thumb. No big braintwister what he meant. I had lost sight of Geert, who was supposed to be looking out for me, so I scrammed."

"Can you describe this man?" asked Wegener.

"He looked like he could be her father, but if he was, she didn't get the ugly gene. He was a real double-bagger." She rolled her eyes at Dinah. "Meaning like *not* a handsome specimen. Ratty hair, thinning. Kind of a schlub."

"Hair color?" asked Wegener.

"There was a light show going on, strobes in all colors. It was hard to tell."

"Is this the man?" She showed her a picture of Viktor.

"No." K.D. swept Aphrodite up in her arms and cuddled her. It amazed Dinah that she could make the little beast purr. "The jerk she met wore glasses. Anyhow, I told Geert what he said to me. Geert wanted to punch him out, but I'm like no, we should wait and see what goes down between him and Lena. We watched and after like, a half-hour, the dude gets up and leaves. I went back to talk to Lena, but she'd had another drink and she was wasted. She definitely couldn't go home by herself and we brought her here. She was hallucinating in the car and thought Geert was Viktor. She does *not* want to go home. She said she's crashing at her sister's place."

"What kind of glasses did the man wear," asked Dinah.

"I don't know. Ordinary."

That eliminated Baer. Amsel had a face like an unbaked biscuit, which met the ugly test. He had thinning hair and wore ordinary bifocals. Farber was equally unattractive, had a skimpy mohawk and wore black wire rims. She said as much to Wegener. "With Alwin dead and Viktor set against her, Lena may have needed money. Maybe somebody hired her to set the fire and afterward, she felt guilty and got drunk. The man who met her at the White Noise could have shown up for the payoff."

Wegener's eyes sparkled with scorn. "It is not yet certain that Herr Bischoff was murdered. It is more likely that he killed Pohl and felt so guilty that he killed himself."

"If Viktor was going to commit suicide, I think he would have done it a long time ago," said Dinah. "The man who met Lena has to be found and questioned."

"Naturally, we will locate this person, but there are many men who wear eyeglasses."

"I've simply suggested two," said Dinah. "Could you show K.D. pictures of Farber and Amsel?"

"If Lena doesn't give Inspector Lohendorf the name of the man, I will have their driver's license photos sent to my phone."

"My bad," said K.D. "I should have taken a picture. Guess I was overwound from all that wickedness with you earlier in the night."

"What wickedness?" asked Wegener.

"A chocolate cream pie," said Dinah. She had made a clean breast of her break-in at the Happy Hunting Ground, but she had prevailed on Thor to keep K.D.'s name out of that adventure and she'd warned K.D. to keep her mouth shut. If things worked out and she stayed on in Berlin, there was no sense starting out with a rap sheet. "Is that what you mean, K.D."

"Yeah. I was crunked on sugar."

Dinah needed to get back to the Adlon to make sure Swan hadn't committed any additional crimes. She and Winheller had met with Lohendorf this morning and Swan was no longer the prime suspect in Pohl's murder, but Dinah wouldn't feel safe until her passport had been returned and she was winging her way back to the States. "Have you finished with your questions, Sergeant Wegener?"

"That is all for now."

"Then if it's permitted, I have to go out for a while."

"Don't leave town."

Dinah couldn't decide if she was making a joke. If so, she had forgotten to smile. Dinah gave K.D. a final warning. "Remember our agreement, K.D. I'll see you later."

She had left her purse in the office and had no choice but to forge through the living room past Lohendorf, Lena, and Thor. Lena sat forward on the sofa with her hands over her eyes. Lohendorf stood directly over her. Thor leaned against the office door. No one was speaking. Dinah met Thor's eyes briefly. He stepped aside and she slipped into the office. Jack was doing a headstand on the air mattress while watching TV, *Charlie's Angels* dubbed in German.

She laughed. "Upside-down and in German. You must be bored."

"Can I come out now?"

"Not yet. There's some heavy adult conversation going on out there."

"Another murder?"

"You'll have to ask your dad. The inspector won't allow me to sit in and listen."

"Me either." He rolled into a ball and somersaulted to his feet. "K.D. says Margaret murdered somebody. Is that right?"

Dinah took her phone off the charger and put it in her purse. "Yes, technically."

"She seems nice, but K.D. says she's evil."

"Sometimes nice people find themselves in not-so-nice situations they can't see their way out of. They may not always do the right thing. That doesn't make them evil."

"Isn't all murder evil?"

"Yes, but…" She'd given Thor grief for splitting philosophical hairs and here she was espousing moral relativism to a nine-year-old. "Yes of course it is."

"Dad's job is to keep people from getting murdered."

"I'll bet that makes you proud of him."

"Yes. If I don't race cars, I'll probably be a secret agent and do what he does. I like it when he tells me stories, but Mom says he talks about his job too much and he shouldn't talk about it at all with me."

"What does Thor say?"

"He says I should know what he does, but he doesn't tell me the gory stuff."

She felt marginally less guilty about discussing Pohl's murder in front of Jack, although Jennifer had a point about overdoing things. Thor seemed to have insinuated himself into Lohendorf's investigation and might be discussing murder all day. Being as how Dinah didn't plan to talk about any gory stuff with Swan, it wouldn't hurt if Jack tagged along with her to the Adlon. He'd probably enjoy a break from TV, and she'd like to know more about Jennifer. "Would you like to get out of the apartment for a while, Jack?"

"*Jøss!*"

"Are you a good walker?"

"I ran a five k race with Dad last spring."

"Then let's ask him if it's okay for you to come along with me."

"It's okay. Mom said I should do what you say, same as Dad."

"Let's at least tell him where we're going."

As they walked out of the office, Lohendorf was helping Lena to her feet. She looked bewildered and scared and terribly young. It would be next to impossible to convince a jury that she killed her husband. If Dinah hadn't seen first-hand evidence of her destructive temper, she wouldn't believe it.

"Thor, is it okay with you if Jack and I go for a walk and visit my Mom?"

"Good idea. I have work to do, but I'll pick you up at the hotel in a couple of hours."

While Lohendorf conferred with Wegener, Dinah whispered, "Who did Lena say came to meet her at the White Noise?"

"Later."

It would have been as easy to say the man's name as "later" and she was champing at the bit to learn what kind of bullet killed Pohl. The mystery of Swan's missing gun still chafed. Until she knew for certain that the murder weapon wasn't a .22, she couldn't breathe easy. But Lohendorf motioned Thor to join the conversation across the room and there was nothing she could do but worry and wait. She jogged down the stairs behind Jack, pointed him toward Hausvogteiplatz, and did her best to keep up.

At least it wasn't raining. She glanced up at the Einstein quote. "When concerning oneself with matters of truth, there's no difference between small and big problems." Einstein had also said that it was important to see old problems from a new angle, but the only angle she could see for Viktor's murder was a falling-out among thieves. He worked in the gallery. He had to know about the illicit art and probably doctored his histories of the pieces to make them saleable to collectors. Or did he? There was something so, so guileless about him.

"Left on Taubenstrasse," she called out to Jack.

Jack was an entirely new problem and one that Einstein couldn't help her with. She thought about what her life would be like if she stayed with Thor. He could never be sure when he might be sent to Kenya or some other hot spot. If he were called away during one of Jack's visits, she would become the de facto parent. She loved Thor, but she hadn't signed up for the full domestic package. And what if she grew to love Jack and then she and Thor split up? He obviously didn't mate for life. She had yet to ask if it was he who grew tired of Jennifer, or the other way around.

Brimming with energy, Jack roared up to an intersection. "Stop," she called. "Mind the cars."

While they waited for the little green man, she asked, "How long did your mom and dad live together before they separated?"

"What do you mean 'separated'?

"Lived apart from each other?"

"They've lived apart as long as I can remember."

The light changed and Dinah gnawed on that for several blocks. She was so engrossed in her thoughts that the verdigris horses atop the Brandenburg Gate came into view before she realized it.

Arms outstretched, Jack banked and air-planed through the gate and Dinah followed. There were no demonstrations today, just the clown on the unicycle. Jack spiraled a few times, forcing the cyclist to pedal backwards.

"*Achtung!*"

"Excuse us." She caught Jack by the collar and propelled him down the boulevard and into the lobby of the Adlon.

They were waiting for an elevator when he turned and pointed. "It's Baer."

He was standing at the reception desk talking with Stefan Amsel. The elevator doors opened. Dinah held back, her imagination bubbling with dark possibilities. But there was nothing furtive or criminal about two members of the same club meeting at the hotel where one of them worked. She pushed Jack into the elevator wondering what the Indians would make of the latest death.

# Chapter Twenty-nine

Swan appeared unusually cautious when she opened the door. Her eyes swept the hall. "I didn't expect you until later today. And who might you be, young man?"

Dinah answered for him. "He's Thor's son. Jack Ramberg, this is my mother. I'm sure she won't mind if you call her Swan."

"Not at all. Y'all come on in." She looked up and down the hall again and closed the door. "Have a seat. Help yourself to the fruit basket, Jack. They put everything but the kitchen sink in that thing. Cheese and chocolate bars and little wrapped weiners."

"Thank you." He went to explore what was on offer.

Dinah breathed in the fragrance of Chanel, but she scented an unpleasant surprise in the offing. "You're awfully edgy, Mom. Is something wrong?"

"Not as wrong as yesterday. Klaus and I spoke with Inspector Lohendorf this mornin' in his office. Klaus is just a wonderful lawyer. Very protective and very professional. I can't say that Lohendorf was any too gracious. He badgered me about why I had agreed to meet Pohl and what I knew about Reiner. But in the end, he acted like he'd been persuaded that I wasn't a killer." She put a finger to her lips. "Maybe Jack shouldn't be hearing this kind of talk."

He looked up from the fruit basket. "I know about Pohl's murder. There was another murder today."

"No! Who?" Swan blanched white under her blusher.

"Viktor Bischoff," said Dinah. "He was Florian Farber's assistant at the gallery. Did you meet him in person or on Facebook?"

"No. What happened to him?"

"We don't know for sure that it was murder." Dinah hadn't intended to talk about murder and she didn't want to think about the gory details of Viktor's death, whether or not it was murder. She picked an apple out of the basket and dropped into an armchair. "You said that Florian had friended a number of Indians on Facebook."

"That's right. He said he had friends from almost all of the five-hundred-and-sixty-six registered tribes."

"Did he or Pohl ever ask you about Seminole art or archaeological artifacts?"

"Not Pohl. Florian asked me about the Ah-Tah-Thi-Ki Museum on the Big Cypress Reservation, but I don't know anything about it and told him so. Why? Is that important?" Her eyes flitted back to the door.

"Maybe. Are you expecting someone else?"

"Yes, I guess he'll be back soon."

"Who?"

"Mr. Amsel. He evicted me this morning. He was here, inside my room sitting in this very chair when I got back from the meeting with Lohendorf."

"He just let himself in?"

"And he was nasty about it, too. He said he could no longer allow me to stay at the Adlon, not even if I paid. He said he had a duty to protect the hotel and all of its guests and I was 'bad medicine.' That last was kind of a slur, don't you think? I mean, it sounds like lingo from an old cowboy movie."

"Maybe he thinks somebody will try to blow up this hotel like they did Margaret's," said Jack.

Swan gasped. "Somebody blew up the guest house?"

"With a grenade," said Jack. "Margaret had to go to the hospital, but they didn't keep her."

Swan's hands flew to her face. "Mercy! Is Margaret all right?"

"She's fine, Mom. She inhaled a lot of smoke, which aggravated her cough, but otherwise she's okay. And most of the damage to the guest house was confined to your, to *her* room."

"Thank the Lord."

So much for keeping Jack shut up behind closed doors, thought Dinah. Margaret could have told him about the fire, but he must have eavesdropped on Thor and Lohendorf in order to have heard about the grenade. She wondered what other information he'd gleaned. "Did you hear what Lena said to Inspector Lohendorf, Jack?"

"I only heard her crying. She said she didn't know Viktor was dead and then Dad saw the office door was cracked and he closed it and made me turn on the TV."

She bit into the apple and thought about the grenade. Viktor must have kept them as souvenirs along with the old gas mask and the binoculars she'd seen next to his grandfather's photo. But what possible reason could he have to try to kill Margaret unless somebody—Hess?—sent him to do it? Or was Margaret who they were after?

"Where is Margaret?" asked Swan.

"She's staying at our apartment temporarily, until we can get her some clothes and a new passport."

"Poor woman. I tricked her into coming to Berlin and almost got her killed."

"You weren't the only deceiver, Mom. Margaret spoke with Reiner Hess before she left Georgia. She's met with him at least once here in Berlin."

"But why didn't she call me out sooner?"

"Come over here and sit close. Jack, turn on the TV, and up the volume."

He made a face, but did as he was told. Swan balanced on the arm of Dinah's chair and leaned in.

While Jack channel-surfed, Dinah tried to interpret Margaret's motives to her mother. "You're the other woman, the black swan that changed her life. In part, she wanted to see what made you tick and in part, she wanted to see you humiliated. She needs money and at first I thought she might have told Pohl and Hess about Cleon's secret account and put them up to blackmailing you, knowing that I'd give you the money. But she denies it and I want to believe her. She's broke and lonely and depressed. She may not know, herself, why she did it."

Swan sighed. "Margaret and I are bound together by history and bad luck and circumstance. We ought to make peace before we die. If she knew the heartache Cleon's so-called love has brought me over the years, her envy would turn to pity."

Dinah marshaled her courage. This was it, the time to ask the big question, to go over the wall or live behind it forever. "Mom, I've never had the nerve to ask you before, but did you have any idea that Cleon killed—"

The room phone rang. "It's that awful man." Swan jumped up and tottered into the middle of the room. "What should I say?"

"I'll speak with him," said Dinah. "Jack, you can turn the TV down now." She answered the phone in an assertive voice. "This is Dinah Pelerin."

"Hi, *kjære*. You sound very forceful."

"If wishes were horses. Where are you?"

"Downstairs. I have news."

"Why didn't you call my cell?"

"Because I'm here. Shall I come up?"

"Sure." She hung up and chucked the apple in the wastebasket. "That wasn't Amsel?"

"No. I don't know why you're so worried about him. We'll find you another hotel this afternoon. Something inexpensive and closer to our place. Thor is on his way up. Please act natural."

Thor arrived and Swan opened the door with melodramatic panache. "Good heavens, you didn't tell me he was so handsome."

Here we go, thought Dinah. Feeling awkward as a teen on prom night, she made the introduction.

Thor smiled and held out his hand, but Swan leaned up for a kiss. He planted one on her cheek. "I've wanted to meet you for a long time, Mrs. Calms."

"Call me Swan." She turned to Dinah. "I love him already. It's plain as day that you were meant for each other."

Thor grinned at Dinah. "It's that obvious?"

"You're the first Thor I've ever met. Such a fascinating name. Sort of swashbuckling. Come in, come in and sit down."

I should have told her to act unnatural, thought Dinah.

Thor kept his face remarkably straight. "I can't stay. I'm on my way to the Embassy, but I wanted to stop by and fill you in."

"The sooner the better," said Dinah. "What did Lena say? And no need to stuff cotton in Jack's ears. He'll find out anyway."

"It was Lena who threw the grenade. When she left Viktor, she took two grenades from his collection. She found out you were staying at the Wunderbar, Swan. She didn't know you had moved and I guess the hotel's front desk didn't know either. It was you she wanted to hurt. She believes you killed Alwin Pohl and she wanted revenge."

"Oh, dear."

"How did the other grenade wind up at the Happy Hunting Ground?" asked Dinah.

"She wore Viktor's coat and pulled a cap over her hair so no one would recognize her. After she threw the first shell and saw what it did, she panicked. She went to the gallery and left the coat with Farber. He didn't know what was inside. Inspector Lohendorf has placed her under arrest for attempted murder, arson, and possession of banned weapons."

Swan appeared stricken. "Margaret almost killed and a young girl going to prison, all on account of me."

"You've caused your share of trouble, Mom, but assault with a deadly weapon is one hundred percent on Lena's head. She didn't know how many people it might kill and apparently she didn't care." Dinah turned to Thor. "Did she set the fire that killed Viktor?"

"She denies it. She seemed shocked and broken up at the news of his death and her alibi checks out. She spent the early part of the evening at her sister's house in Prenzlauer Berg, and

K.D. and Geert saw her at the White Noise at two. The fire was reported by Viktor's neighbors at about three."

"Who was the man she met at the club?" asked Dinah.

"Stefan Amsel."

"Why? What about?"

"She says he tried to talk her into going back to Viktor."

Dinah was skeptical. "You believe that?"

"Lohendorf has already corroborated her story with Amsel. Viktor phoned Amsel last night, drunk and threatening to kill himself. Amsel says he called Lena's sister and she told him where Lena had gone. He went to the club to try and get her to talk to Viktor. Viktor also called another of his friends, Baer Eichen. Eichen was with Amsel when Lohendorf reached him."

"Did the inspector also speak with Eichen?"

"Yes. He said much the same thing. Viktor was drunk and rambling about Lena and Pohl. The easy answer is that Viktor killed Pohl and, unhinged by guilt and Lena's desertion, he killed himself."

"Did they find the gun he used?" asked Dinah.

"They're still searching."

"Poor soul," said Swan. "Such a tragedy, but I can't tell you that I'm not relieved to be out from under that Inspector Lohendorf's microscope."

Thor smiled. "He didn't enjoy pressuring you, Swan. He was doing his job."

Dinah was still processing the "easy answer." Something didn't compute. "What about Farber? He's still a suspect, isn't he? Is Lohendorf going to investigate the *katsinam* mask and the statue from the Malawi Museum?"

"There's a special task force that traces stolen art. In fact, there are several task forces, most assigned to track down art stolen by the Nazis in the thirties and forties. Jens will report what you saw and I'm sure the statue will be recovered eventually. But after what he's heard today, he has no grounds to suspect Farber of murder."

She said, "It's not right. And what about Hess?"

"The tax authorities will keep searching."

She wasn't consoled. "It's not right."

Swan said, "It's all over now. We need to have a family dinner, celebrate and get to know each other. Margaret and I should talk to one another and let bygones be bygones. And poor little K.D. Life's too short to carry hard feelings. How about tomorrow night?"

"I'll look forward to it," said Thor. "You and Dinah can work out the time and place. Jack, you come with me. I want to show you the Scandinavian Embassy complex where I work. Maybe you'll decide you want to be an architect or a diplomat instead of a race car driver."

Jack took a chocolate bar out of the fruit basket and joined his dad at the door. "Thank you, Swan. It was nice to meet you."

"Lovely meeting you and your father, Jack. I'll see you both again tomorrow."

Thor's hand brushed Dinah's. "I'll see you later tonight."

"It'll be late. I'll take Mom to dinner first." She watched him walk away down the hall and abruptly remembered. "Thor!"

He turned.

"Did Jens tell you anything about the gun that killed Pohl?"

"It was a nine millimeter. It will make the case extra neat and tidy if he finds it in the ruins of Viktor's house. They're still searching."

She stared after him in bafflement. It made the theft of Swan's .22 nonsensical. She closed the door and Swan raised her arms and did a *Sound-of-Music* pirouette. "Baby, I can tell from the way he looks at you that he's head over heels. And the little boy is adorable."

"He is, isn't he?" Dinah's thoughts were still bucking against the easy answer. She said, "I can't believe that Viktor killed Pohl."

"If the professionals are satisfied, why can't you be?"

"I don't know. I just can't see it."

"'Riddle me, riddle me, riddle me ree. None so blind as those who won't see.'"

Dinah laughed. "Maybe it's Lohendorf and Thor who won't see."

"Even if you're right, you shouldn't call Thor's judgment into question, honey. Men get prickly about that sort of thing."

Dinah tamped down her own prickliness. She just had to keep reminding herself that Swan lived on a different planet whose language she neither spoke nor understood. So long as she thought of her as an extraterrestrial whose visit to Earth she had been assigned to monitor and control, everything would be all right. Now that Swan was in the clear for Pohl's murder, Dinah felt a great burden lift. It was time for the two of them to decompress and let down their hair. "Would you like to go shopping before dinner? It's not raining. We could wander along the Unter den Linden."

"I can't have dinner with you tonight, baby. Klaus is taking me out to celebrate. I should rest and do my hair this afternoon."

Dinah did a slow burn. "You never have any time for reflection, do you? Always off to your next dalliance. Is that because you can't stand to think about all the lies you've told?"

"I told you why I lied about Alwin Pohl."

"I'm not talking about that batch of lies."

"What then?"

"Cleon murdered my dad. Did he tell you?"

She recoiled as if she'd been slapped. "That's crazy."

"Oh, but it's true. Didn't you know?"

"No." She backed against a chair. Her knees buckled and she sat. "How can you say such a thing?"

"How can you be surprised?"

Swan shook her head from side to side.

"He did it to get you back," said Dinah, "although I'm not sure he ever really lost you. The two of you were as close as a pair of sealed lips, but Cleon owned up in the end. And in case you're curious, he didn't show a flicker of remorse."

"I don't believe you. Cleon wouldn't have done anything to hurt me. He loved me."

"That's precisely why he killed your husband. What I need to know is whether you knew he was going to do it."

"No!"

"Did he tell you afterward? Did he come to you with a new proposal of marriage?"

"He wanted us to remarry. That doesn't mean he killed Hart." She braced up and regained a dash of defiance. "I don't care what Cleon said to you, I don't believe it. He had cancer. He was taking painkillers. He wasn't in his right mind. Anyway, I said no when he suggested we get married again, so you can't say I led him on in any way."

Did that self-serving denial of responsibility constitute an admission of knowledge? Swan seemed scarcely to comprehend the evil of murder, much less empathize with the murdered. Dinah pushed harder. "All those years later, after Cleon came out of that house with blood on his coat, after he told you he'd murdered two federal agents, did you never look back and wonder what other ungodly things he might have done?"

"He had changed by the time he shot those agents. After he got into the drug business, he wasn't the same man." She bounced up with a smile, like an actress who'd finished a difficult scene and gone back to her normal persona. "Don't you remember how good Cleon was to you when you were little? All the books and trips? And that funny little Shetland pony. What was his name? I remember you called him Neddy, but your brother called him Stewball."

Dinah might as well have been talking to an alien life form. "'None so blind as those who won't see.'"

Either Swan didn't hear or pretended she didn't. She preened in front of the mirror, whishing her hair this way and that. "What should I do if Mr. Amsel comes back and tries to kick me out?"

"Tell him Inspector Thor Ramberg of the Norwegian Criminal Investigative Service has ordered you to remain in this room until further notice."

"But Thor didn't say that."

Dinah laughed an ironic laugh. "I wouldn't worry about it if I were you."

# Chapter Thirty

The row of white metal crosses on the fence across the street from the Brandenburg Gate stopped Dinah every time she passed by. Each one paid tribute to an East German citizen who died trying to escape over the Wall. The saddest to her was the one farthest to the right, Chris Gueffroy. He heard from an East German guard that the GDR had revoked its shoot-to-kill order and on February 5, 1989, he made a run for it and earned for himself the distinction of being the last person shot going over the Wall. He wasn't the last victim. A man named Freudenberg toppled out of his hot-air balloon trying to fly over the Wall in March. But today in particular, Chris' death resonated. She fancied she could hear his ghostly lament, *Don't believe everything people tell you.*

A gust of wind ripped through the trees and she was caught in a hail of chestnuts. She picked one up as a worry stone and walked. She had no reason to go in one direction or another. She just knew that she had to walk and hoped that the exercise would stir some fresh insight. She turned the corner onto Scheidemannstrasse. Ahead, she saw the Reichstag, Germany's historic parliament building. Its recently added glass cupola was an architectural tour de force and visitors to the city lined up to get inside for a look at the dazzling inverted cone of mirrors.

To escape the mob, she cut through the Tiergarten. The big yellowing oaks gloried in the sunshine and the lindens and maples blazed like struck matches. The nip of autumn in the air and the earthy smell of decaying leaves brought down by yesterday's rain and wind, energized her and she understood why the park was called Berlin's green lung. She rubbed the chestnut in her hand as if it might magically summon a genie who could answer all her questions.

If Lena didn't know that Swan had gone to the Adlon, if *she* hadn't taken her gun, who had? It must have been Stefan Amsel, but why? The murderer would know that it wasn't the same caliber as the murder weapon. Either Amsel had Swan's gun or he knew who did. With Viktor now the presumed killer, he could have no reason to lie, whether to protect himself or anyone else.

She crossed Strasse des 17 Juni and paused next to a mossy pond to watch a man and a little boy feeding a pair of swans. It never ceased to amuse her when she remembered that swans mate for life. But then, her Swan had been named for the river, not the bird, and she wasn't the only one who couldn't hack the 'til-death-do-us-part thing. Thor and Jen didn't last long enough for their son to remember them as a household. After a few minutes, the man and boy ran out of bread and continued hand-in-hand down the path. She rotated her shoulders sideways, brought the chestnut forward from behind her head, and whipped it thirty feet across the pond. Not bad for a girl, she thought, and walked on.

Viktor's death had saddened her in a way she couldn't quite articulate. Of all the wannabe "Indians" she'd met, he had seemed the most sincere. She recalled some of the criticisms she'd read online about Karl May. Criminal. Con man. Pathological liar. And *hochstapler*, which translated as "a swindler and a deceiver." He lied about having lived among the Apaches in America, but he had so melded fiction and reality that he believed his own myth. He regarded Winnetou as a real person and himself as Winnetou's loyal friend and comrade. She had the sense that Viktor was a lot like Karl May. They both found escape in the persona of nobler beings.

She wondered if Baer had returned home after his meeting with Amsel. She felt an urge, almost a compulsion to talk with him, not so much to gather information about Hess or Amsel as to hear his thoughts about Viktor, or perhaps to receive absolution. She couldn't shake the thought that she might somehow have prevented his suicide if she had reported his morose mental state. Was guilt the reason a contrarian voice in her head howled murder?

Thor and Swan were both busy. She had time on her hands and questions on her mind. There was nothing to stop her from paying a surprise call on Baer. As she circled back through the park, she recalled his intimation of sexual interest. Would he misinterpret her visit as a sign of reciprocal interest? Not today. He'd be too upset about Viktor's death. And if he made any untoward moves, she could lower the temperature very quickly.

On Schiffbauerdamm, she kept her eye out for the gap in the hedge and the narrow passageway to the river. When she looked down the closed-in corridor to his house, a twitch of anxiety ran through her and she reached automatically for her Berlin Wall worry stone. She must have left it in a different jacket. She wished she hadn't thrown the chestnut away. Now that she was here, she couldn't think of a single thing to say. Just offer your condolences and leave, she told herself. Ad lib, as usual. She straightened her shoulders and marched down the path.

She rang the bell and promptly heard footsteps descending the stairs. The door opened. His face was haggard, as if he hadn't slept, but his eyes brightened when he saw her. "What perfect timing. I am in need of pleasant company."

She said, "I heard about your friend Viktor."

"It's hard to believe he's gone. I may have been the last person to speak with him. Come, let's go upstairs and sit." He helped her out of her jacket and hung it on the rack. "Can you believe that on the day when rain might have extinguished that fire and saved Viktor's life, the sky was clear and full of stars?"

She didn't think rain would have helped much, but she didn't say it. She shuddered slightly and followed him up the stairs.

"Please, sit down. May I get you something to drink?"

"No, thanks. I'm sorry to intrude. I came on impulse." They took the same chairs they'd sat in before. In spite of the huge window and the mirrored panels behind the bar, the room seemed gloomier than it had on her first visit. Certainly, her host did.

He took out a cigarette. "Do you mind?"

"No."

He looked as if he needed it. His hands shook slightly as he lit up a Raucher sterben früher. "Stefan Amsel and I will arrange the funeral. The last thing Viktor would want is a traditional mass. We will have a drumming ceremony. There is no one to object. His parents are no longer living, he was estranged from his brother, and Lena wouldn't know what to do even if she cared to do it."

"She probably won't attend the funeral," said Dinah. "She was arrested this morning for firebombing the guest house where she thought my mother was staying."

"Was anyone injured?"

"Luckily, no. Lena used an old American grenade she found among Viktor's belongings. Why do you suppose a man of peace kept live grenades around the house?"

"I didn't know that he did. There is so much left over from the war. Perhaps they reminded him of the destructiveness and futility of war. He had curious ideas about atonement."

"You told me that you thought Farber might be acquiring some of his art pieces illegally. I'm sure of it. The Hopi people would never have sold a *katsinam* mask. Viktor must have known that some of the things coming into the gallery were stolen."

He pinched off the ember of his half-smoked cigarette, placed the butt on an oyster shell for reuse, and went to the bar. "Are you sure you won't have a drink?"

"Yes."

He poured himself a glass of something amber and chugged it. "The right woman might have saved Viktor. Even the wrong woman might have saved him, if she had gone to him in his hour of need." He replenished his glass and brought it back to his chair. "I never understood what he saw in Lena, or she in him.

In terms of character, she was tailor-made for Pohl. If Viktor did anything illegal, and I can't believe that he did, it was for her."

Dinah harked back to Viktor's poignant remark that Baer had been lucky that his wife died young. Dinah wanted to ask about her, but was afraid he would clam up. "Did Viktor tell you that Lena had smashed his pottery?"

"Yes. He talked to me the day after her tantrum. He was despondent, of course, but resigned. I don't know what sent him over the edge."

"You do believe it was suicide then?"

His eyes hooded behind the wooden glasses. "Ah, you are investigating still. Do you have reason to suspect foul play?"

"It's a stupendous coincidence."

He set his drink on the coffee table and relit the cigarette. This time, his hands didn't shake. "Why are you pursuing this, Dinah? There is no connection between Viktor and your mother. If the police have transferred their suspicions to Viktor, her troubles are behind her. Is that not so?"

"Yes, and I'm extremely relieved that she's out from under the cloud. I just don't like coincidences."

"But Viktor's death is a coincidence that makes logical sense. He was an unhappy man, his wife betrayed him with Pohl, depleted his savings, and destroyed the things he valued most. Her leaving was *der letzte Strohhalm,* the last straw. Even if she didn't set the fire, she is responsible for his death."

Was that speech a shade contrived? Remember Chris Gueffroy. *Don't believe everything people tell you.* She said, "The police think Viktor killed Pohl and then killed himself, either because he couldn't live with the guilt or because he didn't want to face the consequences."

He inhaled deeply and turned to look out at the river, the color of lead in the fading light. A tour boat glided past and he followed it with his eyes. "Nothing is without consequences. They follow our sins as surely as a wake follows a boat. Sometimes the consequences are worse than the original sin."

When last they'd talked, he had insisted that Viktor was incapable of murder. Today he sounded reconciled to the fact. "When Viktor called you in the middle of the night, did he confess that he'd killed Pohl?"

"No."

"You've spoken to Amsel. Did he confess to him?"

"No. Neither Stefan nor I would have blamed him if he had done it. After the shabby way Lena treated him, he showed a kind of tragic nobility by not killing her."

Baer's antipathy toward Lena made Dinah wonder if his late wife had betrayed him in similar fashion. She hazarded a push into more personal terrain. "Viktor mentioned that your wife died young. Did he know her?"

"No." He crushed his cigarette in the shell and, like a brooding Bogart, withdrew to the window to stare out at the Spree.

Dinah couldn't decide whether he was composing himself to speak or whether he meant to stand there with his back to her until she slunk away down the stairs and left. She said, "That was presumptuous of me. Sorry if I roused painful memories."

He turned and his face had relaxed. "It is I who must apologize. I forget how open Americans are, how natural and unoffending such a question would seem to you. We Germans tend not to reveal ourselves so directly to people we don't know. In truth, we are reticent even with those we call friends." He returned to his chair and picked up his glass of amber. "My wife Sabine died before I moved to Berlin. At the time, she was about your age, I'd guess, with dark eyes and a smile very like yours. She died while carrying our unborn child."

Dinah was about to utter some bromide about losing a loved one when he asked, "Will you attend Viktor's funeral with me?" There was nothing seductive in his manner. He seemed like a man grieving for a friend and in need of company.

"When will it be?"

"We don't know yet. There's to be an autopsy. We must wait for the police to release the body. We will have our answer then, as between suicide and murder."

"If it was murder, if you had to guess who did it, who would you guess, Baer?"

"The person who would want to kill Pohl and the person who would want to kill Viktor are fundamentally incompatible. And yet I understand that in crime fiction, it's a mistake to postulate more than one murderer."

That postulate was going to take some time to consider. She said, "Call me and let me know the day and time of the funeral ceremony, Baer. I'd like to be there."

The doorbell rang and he looked at his watch. "Stefan is early. We are going to dinner tonight to discuss the arrangements."

"I'd better go," she said. "I have to prepare for my class at the University on Tuesday."

"Thank you for coming." He walked down the stairs in front of her and she noticed a limp she hadn't noticed going up. Of course. She remembered Florian saying he had an artificial foot. In the entryway, he helped her into her jacket and opened the door.

A sixtyish man with a blocky build and collar turned up to his ears was waiting on the other side. He skimmed a surprised look over her head to Baer, who forgot to make the introductions. The visitor said something in imperious German. Whatever the gist, it was obvious from the hostile sheen in his eyes that he was less than thrilled at the sight of Dinah.

She covered her own surprise, said "*Auf Wiedersehen*," and started down the path. She turned her head for a second look, but the man had already disappeared inside.

# Chapter Thirty-one

It was the same voice she'd heard talking to Farber in the gallery. She was positive of that much, but was the man Reiner Hess? If she called Lohendorf this minute and told him to get to Baer Eichen's house ASAP, would he find a wanted tax evader or a gruff-voiced member of *der Indianer* club who had helped Farber reset his burglar alarm and who was now helping Baer plan Viktor's funeral? Would Lohendorf take a chance on her flimsy suspicion if, as Thor said, tax evaders and art thieves weren't his bailiwick?

Like a dope, she realized that the photograph Lohendorf had shown her on the Müggelsee ferry must have been Hess. She had been so sure that Pohl was Hess that she had scarcely given it a glance. It could be the same man she saw today. Or not.

As she walked back toward the Gendarmenmarkt, Baer's question repeated in her head. Why was she pursuing the matter? Unless Viktor's autopsy showed a wound he couldn't possibly have inflicted, or a dose of poison he couldn't possibly have administered, the case was closed. She should back off, put her energy into resolving her personal problems, count her blessings. She was alive. All the people she cared about were alive and well. Everything had worked out for her mother in spite of her lies and very soon she and Margaret would be needing a ride back to the airport. Blessings all. Even her sore throat had passed.

The Saturday street market in the Hausvogteiplatz was jumping and she joined the crowd of shoppers. The kale and carrots and bell peppers looked jewel-bright, the mushrooms were gorgeous, the neon-green heirloom tomatoes smelled like real tomatoes, and the cheese display tantalized her taste buds. On a whim, she pulled out her phone and called Thor.

"Plans have changed. I'm cooking dinner at home."

"Sounds exciting. Jack and I will bring the flowers."

"Good. Be there by eight. And come hungry."

"Got you. Drop that chocolate bar, Jack."

"And Thor?"

There was a pause. "If I'm interpreting that tone correctly, it's the one that precedes an announcement that you want to do something chancy, or you want me to."

"Not at all. But can you bring home your official laptop? The one that lets you access Interpol's databases?"

"Will this be a working dinner?"

"No, no. I just have one pesky little question. Maybe two."

"All right. I'm reasonably sure the Norwegians aren't listening in. Let's hope your N.S.A. hasn't bugged my phone or planted spyware on my computer."

"How could anybody object to you looking at a few old files?"

"I hope I don't find out. See you around eight."

She bought a filet of beef and a mélange of vegetables, thinking she could find a way to tie all the ingredients together after she got home. She couldn't resist the cambozola and she splurged on an expensive bottle of red wine. Inspired, she lugged her purchases the remaining two blocks to the apartment.

She schlepped her bag up the stairs and as she walked through the door, Aphrodite meowed and scarpered toward the kitchen. Dinah followed and saw that her bowl was empty.

"K.D.?"

No answer.

Swell. She spooned out a mound of cold fish and began unloading the groceries. "How come K.D. gets the purring and nuzzling? I feed your mangy ass and all I get are yowls and scratches."

She went to see if anyone else was at home. To her surprise, she had the place all to herself. Neither K.D. nor Margaret had left a note. In the bedroom, she noticed Margaret's suitcase, seemingly undamaged, lying open on the floor. Dinah hoped she was out looking for a hotel, but she didn't rule out the possibility that she'd been lured into another assignation with Hess. People came and left this apartment as unpredictably as gusts of wind.

Before she started dinner, she went into the office, sat down at the computer, and called up Interpol's website. She clicked on the link to Wanted Persons. To her amazement, the photos, nationality, and ages of two hundred and eighty-eight people appeared with a detailed physical description and the crimes for which they were wanted. Murder, fraud, forgery, robbery, extortion, brigandism, abduction of a minor, and illicit trafficking in narcotics. But it soon became apparent that tax evasion didn't land a person on Interpol's wanted list. There was a report of a pan-European investigation of tax evasion and money laundering that involved fictitious VAT invoices and air pollution trading rights, but she couldn't see how that would relate to Hess. Anyway, Thor had other resources.

She hunted up a recipe for raw kale and carrot salad and returned to the kitchen. She browsed an ancient copy of *Bon Appetit* and decided that she had enough of the main ingredients to do a modified version of beef Stroganoff. While she cooked, she tried to replay Farber's slideshow of the powwow in her mind. Had any of the people in those pictures looked like the man who showed up on Baer's doorstep? She didn't think so, but they were all in disguise to a greater or lesser degree.

The room began to fill with the aroma of shallots and mushrooms sautéed in butter. She cut the beef into pieces and dried it in preparation for browning. She took a shortcut with the stock. Who had time to boil bones? She used canned stock, enriched with a generous amount of beef demi-glace. She was pouring in the Madeira to begin the reduction when Thor and Jack blew in.

"You're early," she said, taking a great bouquet of dahlias out of Jack's hand. "And these are beautiful. Thank you."

"You're welcome," he said. "The final race in the Le Mans series is being run today, the Circuit Paul Ricard. May I please be excused to watch TV?"

"Go," said Thor. He gave Dinah a perfunctory kiss and set his laptop down on the table next to the wine. "Grand vin de Bordeaux, two thousand ten. Looks ready to enjoy. Let's have some." He opened the bottle, poured two glasses, and sat down.

She took the mushrooms off the stove and clanked about in the pantry until she found a vase. "That kiss was not one of your finer efforts. Are you annoyed because I want you to contact Interpol?"

"No. I'll contact the Kremlin if that's what you want."

"I don't think the Kremlin or even Interpol is the right agency. Can you access a photo of a German citizen? His national ID card? Or his driver's license or passport photo? Whichever agency will give you a peek at Reiner Hess' puss would be great."

"Simplest will be the driver's license. Give me a few minutes." While he trolled the Net, she arranged the flowers in a vase and wondered what to do if the man she'd seen going into Baer's house really was Hess. Had Baer been hiding him in his underground bunker? Was Baer part and parcel of Farber's art theft ring?

"Here you go," said Thor, turning the laptop screen around.

She saw a gray-haired man with a high forehead, a narrow ridge of a nose, and piercing eyes. It was Hess. She'd seen the mystery man at last. "I know where he was a few hours ago. You'd better call Lohendorf. Even if he's convinced that Viktor killed Pohl, Hess was at Müggelsee that night and he was at the gallery when I broke in. He should be questioned."

"Tell me where you saw him and when and I'll text Jens."

"At Baer Eichen's house. Shortly after three."

He logged off the computer, took out his phone, and sent the text. "Done. Now I want you to do something for me."

"What?"

"Sit down."

She sat, not much liking the look on his face.

He picked up his wineglass, turned it around a few times as if studying the contents, and set it back down without tasting. "How are we doing on our trust problem?"

"Oh, that." She wasn't ready to discuss the long-term fallout from his secret or from hers. "I haven't had time to think about it."

"Think about it now. Do you trust me?"

The question by itself made her leery. "Mostly."

"I know you had the rug pulled out when you were a kid, Dinah. You've been raised on shifting sands and there will always be a tendency to doubt. I'm willing to accept that 'mostly' is as good as it's ever going to be with you. But 'mostly' covers a lot of ground."

The sound of screaming engines blasted from the TV in the office. "What's this about, Thor? Are you trying to tell me you've fathered another child?"

"No, and don't be flip. Sometimes the best defense is no offense."

"What then?"

"We've each kept secrets. Lied, if that's how you want to characterize it. But deep down, I trust you to do the right thing and I'm telling you that you have to trust me the same way if we're going to have a life together."

She didn't know what to say. Trust was an almost religious thing. It had to be more compelling than facts, stronger than fear. Distrust was her defense against the fear of being deceived. "I trust you as much as I can, Thor. In some ways, more than I trust myself."

"Prove it." He took a notepad and a pen out of his pocket and set them next to her wine. "Write down the name and address of that bank in Panama, the account number, the balance, the names of all the employees you've spoken to, the dates you've made withdrawals and the amounts. Everything."

"Kingdom come! You want a confession? Are you going to turn me in?"

"Did you just say that you trust me?"

"I said mostly." She got up and turned the heat on under the frying pan. What the hell was he thinking? Did he have a crisis of conscience and blab to the IRS? Was he trying to arrange some kind of a plea bargain? Was he protecting himself or her? She dropped in the butter and oil, which began to sizzle. She lowered the heat and ladled in the pieces of beef. "Will you at least tell me what it is that you intend to do with the information?"

"Yes, but not tonight."

A drop of hot grease splattered onto her hand. She licked the burn and thought about all those yanked rugs and shifting sands and sinkholes that had opened up under her feet over the years. Without realizing it, had she been waiting for Thor to disappoint her in some way? Had she been subconsciously looking for an excuse to break off the affair and go start another—the way her mother always did?

An old proverb popped into her head. *Ponder the path of thy feet.* Well, she was due for a patch of solid bedrock and if Thor Ramberg wasn't it, maybe it didn't exist. One way or the other, it was time she found out. She turned around and handed him the tongs. "Turn the beef as it sears. I'll write down the information."

The kiss that followed was a vast improvement, a kiss worth remembering if she ended up doing serious time in the slammer. When the kissing was over, while he tended the beef, she sat down and laid out the whole Panamanian enchilada. She didn't need to look up any numbers or names or dates. She knew it all by heart. When she finished, she went to get the key to the safety deposit box attached to the account. She was using a yardstick to winkle it out of its hiding place behind the mirror in the foyer when Margaret walked in the door.

"I've done what you asked," she said. "I've put Reiner Hess behind bars. He trusted me and I threw him to the wolves. It just goes to show."

# Chapter Thirty-two

Margaret's bulletin teemed with connotations. Dinah couldn't unpack them all at once, so she asked the most obvious question. "Has he been arrested?"

"Oh, yes. I called Lohendorf and told him where Reiner and I were having dinner. He wasted no time. He and his men rousted us out of the café before the dessert came. I'll be seeing that *et-tu-Brutus* look in Reiner's eyes on the day I die, which I hope is soon."

Thor had come out of the kitchen to listen. He said, "The man broke the law, Margaret. You did the right thing."

"You get paid for locking people away in prison, son. I've been there and I can tell you it's hell. I don't give a fig that he hid his money and I don't believe he had anything to do with blackmailing Swan or murdering Alwin Pohl. But Dinah means more to me than Hess, more than she knows. I couldn't leave Berlin with her thinking that I'd colluded with him." She rasped a bitter laugh. "Then again, maybe he'll say that I did and stab me in the back the way I stabbed him."

Dinah was touched. "I'd take your word over his, Margaret."

"There are two kinds of people you shouldn't take at their word, kiddo. The ones you know and the ones you don't."

Thor chimed in a little too quickly. "Dinah made beef Stroganoff. Will you join us for dinner, Margaret?"

"Thanks for asking, but I'm not fit for human company."

She unwrapped a new bottle of Monkey 47 and started into the bedroom.

"Margaret, wait." He put out a hand. "Where had Hess been living while he was in the city?"

"The Adlon. He was registered under the name Dobbs." Her eyes gleamed with mischief and her mouth bent up on one end like a tire tool. She held Dinah's stare for a moment. "If any more strangers drop in for a slumber party, I'd prefer to wake up with a good-looking man next time." With that, she retired to the bedroom and shut the door behind her.

Dinah grappled with the ramifications. What was Margaret saying with that look? Did she know that Swan had moved into the Adlon? Did Swan know that Hess was there? Had their paths crossed? Was Margaret making a joke about the convergence or hinting at something else?

"Is that the safety deposit key?" Thor asked.

She flashed to a vision of herself in an orange jumpsuit and cringed.

"What's wrong?"

"Nothing." She dropped the key into his hand and called Jack to wash up for dinner.

Back in the kitchen, she added the beef into the reduced stock and blended in the sour cream and the cream. She whisked the balsamic vinaigrette for the kale salad and set the table.

Thor put out the flatware and the napkins and poured a glass of water for Jack. "Do you think your mother knew that Hess was staying in the same hotel?"

"I have no idea. I don't know if she would have told me if they were sharing a room."

They all sat down at the table, but the Stroganoff didn't stimulate much conversation. Jack provided most of the commentary. He was excited about the fortieth annual Berlin Marathon, scheduled for tomorrow. He asked Thor if he was going to run. Thor said no, he hadn't had time to train. They talked about the Kenyan who was favored to win and set a new world record. Dinah listened with only half an ear. Her thoughts shuttled from

Panama to Georgia to Egypt to the Adlon. How much of what everyone had said was the truth, how much mostly the truth, and how much flat-out lies?

Jack's phone rang. "It's Mom."

Thor said, "Go talk to her in the other room. Be sure to tell her I'm working on your application to the English language school and ask how your granddad came through the surgery."

"Okay."

Thor topped up Dinah's wine and smiled, but somehow it didn't allay her doubts. She said, "You've barely tasted your wine. Does that mean you've changed your mind about running the marathon?"

"No. It'll be a late night. Jack got antsy and I didn't finish my report. I'll help you clean up and then I'm going back to the Embassy to work."

"That's awfully conscientious of you. If I had a pal on the police force, I'd duck out to hear all the poop about his big bust. I'd buy him a beer and get him to tell me what Hess had to say about his relationship with my mother and with Margaret. I'd pump him for everything Hess has said verbatim."

"Don't be sarcastic, Dinah. If you don't believe me, say so."

"Tell me you're not going to call Lohendorf the instant you walk out that door."

"I am going to call him, and buy him a beer if he's willing, and pump him for everything I can get out of him. First, I'm going to the Embassy to finish my report. Like I said, I'll be late getting home."

She supposed she couldn't blame him for doing exactly what she'd do, if she could. She put the food away and washed the dishes. He dried, stacked the plates in the cabinet, ordered Jack to behave himself, and split. Peevish and at loose ends, she carried her wine into the living room. She should try again to prepare for her class, but she couldn't gin up any enthusiasm. If Tuesday arrived and she wasn't in handcuffs on her way back to the States, she'd have to wing it. She picked up the paper and ran her eyes over the day's headlines, but she couldn't concentrate.

The cuckoo flew out and HOO-hooed ten times, exacerbating her peevishness. There was no sign of K.D. She dialed her mobile, but the call went to voice mail. "Get your buns back to the apartment by midnight, K.D. Thor says to tell you, you can't stay if you don't follow the rules." The fact that no rules had actually been set was an oversight. Dinah went to find a pen to put a few into writing.

Margaret had apparently succumbed early to the Monkey. Her snoring rumbled and wheezed, rumbled and wheezed. It was maddening. She was about to pop a CD into the Bose to drown out the noise when her phone jingled. Baer Eichen.

Her forehead contracted. She was still mulling his suggestion of two murderers.

"Hello, Baer."

"I hope I didn't call too late."

"No. I was just relaxing with a glass of wine."

"I don't want you to think I've been trying to mislead you."

"About what, Baer?"

"The man you saw at my front door this afternoon was Reiner Hess."

"Is that so?"

"You seemed alarmed. I thought you might have recognized him."

"I thought it was he who seemed alarmed."

"He was. I don't know if you realized, but it was Reiner. He constantly fears arrest. I hadn't seen him in months. I didn't know until he told me that Stefan has been hiding him in his hotel under a false name. He came to offer his sympathy about Viktor."

She hadn't a clue why he was telling her this. "Since you're Hess' friend, I don't suppose you plan to inform the police."

"No."

"Aren't you afraid that by telling me this that I will?"

"It wouldn't matter. He moved out of the hotel this afternoon and plans to return to Cyprus tomorrow."

She could have put him straight about Hess' altered status,

but why spoil the surprise. "Did he concur with your opinion that Viktor committed suicide?"

"Yes, he thinks it was either suicide or an accident."

"Does he think Viktor was tormented by guilt for killing Alwin Pohl?"

"We didn't speak about Alwin." His delivery became formal and stilted. "I wanted to inform you that I received a letter from Viktor postmarked the day before he died. In it, he stated that Florian had procured certain items that Viktor should have identified as stolen. He asked for my forgiveness."

"For helping Farber fence stolen art or for killing Alwin Pohl?"

"For depriving other cultures of their sacred heritage and, as I choose to believe, forgiveness for what he was about to do, which was to end his life. He said that after your visit, during which you suggested the idea that Pohl was blackmailing Florian, he found certain acquisition documents that had been falsified. He also discovered a number of payments to Pohl, which confirm your suspicions."

She said, "Are you going to give the letter to Inspector Lohendorf and try to clear Viktor's name?"

"No."

"But why? If Florian murdered Pohl, don't you want to see him brought to justice?"

"Alwin Pohl has caused enough grief. Where Viktor is, he will not mind that his reputation has been soiled."

"If you're not going to give the letter to the police, why tell me about it?"

"Think of it as my final contribution to your investigation. Your guesses have been validated. And now I will say goodnight to you, Dinah."

# Chapter Thirty-three

Dinah put Jack to bed on the sofa, dimmed the lights, and after trying twice more without success to reach K.D., she went across the hall and caught Geert just as he was leaving for the club.

"I'm worried about K.D., Geert. Do you know where she is or who she might be with?"

"*Nein*. Before she went to sit with that tiger Lena, she danced with a regular at the Noise, a boy named Dolf. If they come tonight, I will knock heads and send her home."

"Thanks, Geert."

Feeling inadequate on a dozen different levels, she meandered through the apartment and back to the refrigerator. The *Kummerspeck* had zapped her again. Someone had wedged a new tub of chocolate ice cream in the freezer next to the icemaker. She scooped out a dishful and ate it standing up, elbows propped on the counter.

If Viktor had found documents that incriminated Farber, then Farber had as much motive to kill him as he had to kill Pohl. Baer said Viktor found the documents after her visit. Did he remove them from the files in Farber's desk? Oh, God. What if her snooping had gotten Viktor killed? Florian could have noticed them missing the night she broke in. Maybe he assumed Viktor had taken them and staged a break-in to cover his tracks. Hess said, "I'll take care of it," and a few hours later Viktor was dead.

A discrepancy in one of the slides Farber had shown her grated on her. Something had registered subliminally, but what was it? Something out of place or incongruous. She flogged her memory. Maybe if she saw the pictures again, with all she had learned in the interim, the significance would sink in. Those photos had been made immediately before, or just after, Pohl's murder. Lohendorf had made copies and maybe Thor could finagle a way for her to look at them again.

Stuck here with a head full of guilt and unanswered questions was almost like being in prison. She couldn't stand it. She had to do something or she'd go stir crazy.

She went into the bedroom, switched on the overhead light, and pushed Margaret's eye mask off her face. "Margaret, wake up."

She emitted a disgruntled snort and resumed snoring.

Dinah went to the kitchen and put on a pot of coffee. When it had brewed, she poured a mugful and went back to the bedroom. "Margaret, wake up and drink this. I have to go out and I need you sober in case Jack wakes up and needs something." She shook her shoulder and patted her cheeks.

One bloodshot eye bobbed open like a red jellyfish. She lifted the other eyelid with one finger. She seemed to be goggling at Dinah from twenty leagues under. Gradually, she focused. "What time is it?"

"Elevenish."

"Where's Thor?"

"At the Embassy. Working."

"While you stay home with his kid?" She blew a raspberry. "If this is how it's going to be, I'd make damn sure I got a marriage license and a joint bank account out of the deal."

"Come on, Margaret. Jack's asleep on the sofa. He won't be any trouble."

She pushed herself into a sitting position. "The last time Jack and I talked, he asked me what it felt like to shoot a man."

"What did you say?"

"If you shoot the *right* man, it's very satisfying."

"Margaret, please tell me you're joking."

"I'm joking."

Dinah handed her the mug of coffee and went to see if she could find Farber's home phone number. Calling him at this hour was a little over-the-top, but maybe he was a night owl. A lot of thieves and smugglers were. And if he'd heard that his partner Hess had been nabbed, he'd be wide awake and worrying. They were equally strong candidates for the murder, or murders. She didn't intend to accuse either one of them or mention Viktor's letter. But if she could persuade Farber to meet her in a public place and show her those photos again, she felt sure she would have her answer.

She needed a decoy. Somebody who was at the powwow. Somebody whose picture was in the slideshow, but that Farber didn't care about. The schnapps guy. What was his name? It would come to her. She fished out a business card for the gallery with three contact numbers. She dialed the last one first, assuming it was the number of last resort.

A hoarse voice growled in her ear.

"Is this Florian Farber?"

"Who is this?"

"It's Dinah Pelerin, Herr Farber. I apologize for calling so late, but I've figured out who murdered Alwin Pohl."

"Amsel told me the police believe it was Viktor. He killed Alwin, then himself."

"The police are wrong."

"Viktor is dead and the business is over."

He sounded as if he were about to hang up. She revised her plan. "The murderer is a member of *der Indianer* club. Show me those pictures again and I can prove it."

There was a sharp intake of breath followed by dead silence.

"Herr Farber?"

"Who? Who did it?"

"Burning Torch."

"Luther?"

"That's him. Luther Wurttemberg."

"But why? How do you know this?"

"I'll have to show you. I have to see the pictures. I'm sure you want to put this nightmare behind you as quickly as possible. Can you meet me tonight?"

There was a pause during which she could almost hear the cogs in his brain spin and whir.

She threw in a sweetener. "And if you will show me the certificate of authenticity and the price, I know a collector who may be interested in the *katsinam* mask."

"All right. I will meet you in the gallery in a half-hour."

"The FBI Bar on Augsburger Strasse would be more convenient."

"Very well. I will see you there."

The FBI bar would be packed on a Saturday night, but in an excess of caution, she tucked the Smith & Wesson into her purse on the way out the door.

The sunny afternoon had turned into a cool, drizzly night. The humid cold seeped through her raincoat and raised goose bumps on her skin. She opened the garage and hoped that the Golf would start. It hadn't been driven since Pohl rammed it into the bridge. She needn't have worried. The engine started without a hitch. While it warmed up, she reevaluated her plan. The worst thing would be a failure to see the photos again and leave without a clue. She didn't think that would happen. She buckled up, backed out into the street, and got rolling.

The car pulled stubbornly to the right as she tooled along Lietzenburger Strasse. The crash had obviously buggered the alignment. The rational, cautious part of her brain also pulled slightly to the right. At every cross street, a still small voice told her to turn right, back off, go home and wait. But curiosity trumped caution and she had too much momentum to stop.

She parked in an alley three blocks from the FBI bar and walked. There were lots of people milling about, lots of potential rescuers should the need arise. Yellow crime tape decorated the window of the FBI, whose logo featured the barrel of a gun extending from the top of the letter "I." She opened the door and looked around for Farber. All of the tables were full and a double row of people clustered around the bar, but she spotted a free stool at the far end facing the door and claimed it.

Everybody was laughing and talking and the noise made it hard to hear.

A busy bartender leaned across the bar and placed a napkin in front of her. "*Was haben sie?*"

She ordered a vodka martini with a twist and checked her watch. Waiting brought out the bugaboos in her imagination. Had Farber agreed too easily to this get-together? Would he come alone? Had he sent someone ahead to watch her? Every minute that passed amped up the tension. Maybe this was God's way of telling her to get while the getting was good. She stripped off her raincoat and pulled out her mobile to see if Thor had called. He hadn't.

She munched a handful of salted peanuts and sized up the other patrons. Most were male-female couples. There were two tables with only men, but she was pretty sure that one pair was gay. Two plausibly straight guys in business suits sat across from one another in the corner. One of them looked up and caught her staring. He gave a little nod of invitation and she turned away, embarrassed.

The martini came, but she was afraid to drink it. She needed her wits about her. Well, one sip to wash down the peanuts.

And then he walked in the door. He wore a fedora and carried a small briefcase. His eyes didn't so much survey the room as strafe it. She took another sip of the martini and held up a hand. He saw her and threaded his way through the crowd to the end of the bar.

He said, "This place is too crowded. There are no tables and no room to open the laptop on the bar. We must go to another place. My car is outside."

She jerked her head toward the table in the corner and improvised. "My boyfriend came with me. He's having a drink with a friend while we talk. Here, you sit and I'll look over your shoulder."

He shot a suspicious glance at the alleged boyfriend.

"Let me hold your hat," she said.

He took it off and handed it to her, then took the computer out of the case and sat down. The case was in the way and Dinah stuck it under her arm. Farber moved her drink out of the way and opened the laptop on the bar. "This is preposterous."

She smiled. "It won't take long."

He waved off the bartender, moved her martini still farther out of his way, and started the show. "Ask what you will."

The first picture was of Viktor. It was hard to look at his earnest face as he stood beside the bonfire, hard to look at Lena, too. She wore a cheeky smile, unaware in that frame that her life was about to change, or already had.

Farber clicked on the next picture. "There is Hans Oostrum and Luther. What has made you suspect Luther?"

"Hang on. Tell me again the items he brought to the powwow."

"The grill and the lanterns."

"It's a large grill. How did he get it up the hill?"

"Hans has a *transportwagen*."

"A dolly?"

"Yes. It rolls. He also rolled the keg up."

Next up was a picture of Stefan Amsel in his porcupine roach. "What was Herr Amsel doing in this picture?"

"He is trying to set up a folding table for the food, but he is already drunk."

Or pretending to be, she thought. She took another sip of her martini. None of this paraphernalia rang any bells or suggested any bright new ideas.

"What about Baer Eichen?" she asked. He stood apart from the others, his avant-garde glasses at odds with his red-fringed ghost shirt and rows of beads.

"As you will see in several of the photos, Baer helped with every chore as needed. He was friendliest with Viktor, always. They arrived together. Viktor carried the glow logs, Lena carried his drum, and Baer carried the cooler with the sausages and the box with the cups and plates."

She studied the slides one by one as they flashed by.

The door opened, letting in a surge of wet, cold air. She shivered and set the martini back on the bar.

Farber frowned and moved it safely away from the computer. "Is that all you wish to see?"

"Did no one offer to take a picture of you, Herr Farber?"

He gave her a scathing look, but called up two photos from a different file she hadn't seen before. One of them showed Farber assisting Hans Oostrum into the eagle-feather war bonnet. In the other, he was feeding chips into the grill.

"I thought it was the photos of Luther that interested you."

"Yes. They did interest me. Thank you." She had seen what it was that bothered her. She handed Farber back his hat and his laptop case and scrapped her previous assumptions. The pictures didn't prove anything, of course. But she knew in her heart who had killed Pohl and her instinct told her that the reasons were more convoluted than she'd thought.

The guy she'd said was her boyfriend brushed past on his way out the door. Farber gave him a quizzical look. "Your friend is leaving."

"Me, too." She took a last quick sip of the martini and burrowed into her coat.

"Don't you want to see the certificate of authenticity of the *katsinam?*"

"Some other time." She didn't bother to say thanks or goodbye. She left him holding the tab for the martini and hoofed it.

# Chapter Thirty-four

Could there be an alternative explanation for the change of costume on such a chilly night? If she could talk with Thor, he'd help her to work out the sense of it. Maybe what he'd learned from Lohendorf tonight would help to clarify things.

The drizzle had turned to rain. The Golf's wipers were beating like a funeral drum and condensation on the inside of the windshield made it hard to see. She futzed with the climate control and wiped the glass directly in front of her with a tissue.

At a red light, she pulled out her phone to check her voicemail, but before she could peck in her password, the light changed and the driver in the car behind laid on his horn. Why hadn't Thor called? Either he was buying Lohendorf a lot of beers or he had news that he was in no hurry to relay. News that the IRS had picked out the penitentiary where she would be doing time. News that Hess had plopped her mother back in the soup.

She tossed the phone into the passenger seat and drove on, exhausted and strangely queasy. One in the morning. Was she reading the time right? She would have to file a missing person report if K.D. hadn't skylarked home by now. More hassle. More conflict. More distraction. No wonder she couldn't penetrate the fog.

Fingers of bright light fell across the wet street like pick-up sticks. She felt dizzy. Those few sips of vodka had hit her like a bus. She slowed and moved into the right lane. Too far. The

Golf's right front tire sideswiped the curb. She jerked the wheel left. Horns blared and shrieked.

Sweet Jesus!

Everything looked smeared and filmy, but she couldn't stop in the middle of the street. Traffic zoomed past on both sides. She had to stay in the flow. She was almost home. Had to turn soon. Had to get into the left lane. She strained her eyes. Was this her street? The yellow light ahead had a bleary halo. She accelerated and swerved left. Things were just coming into focus when a swell of nausea rolled over her. She clapped a hand to her mouth, lost control, and the Golf jumped the curb. The seatbelt grabbed and she barely got it off in time.

She opened the door, leaned out, and retched. She was sick for a long time. When she was done, she lay her head back against the headrest and drifted away into the darkness.

Somebody opened the car door and tapped her cheeks. "Dinah, are you hurt?"

"Thor."

"Is anything broken? Can you stand up?"

"Mm. Little wobbly."

He helped her out of the car and she realized that she had actually made it all the way to Niederwallstrasse. The car sat jacked at an angle within sight of her lavender garage, its right front tire flatted on top of the curb and its emergency lights blinking.

"Can you walk?"

"Since I was two."

"Good. Then let's walk." He put his arm under hers and semi-carried, semi-dragged her. "What happened?"

"Not sure."

"Did somebody try to run you off the road again?"

"No. I felt sick and blacked out. I still feel a little woozy, but I think I'm okay." That martini had really walloped her. Was it possible that Farber had slipped her a Mickey? Or one of those date rape drugs? She normally had a good head for spirits and she certainly hadn't drunk enough to make her sick. "What time's it?"

"A little after one."

"Then I wasn't out long."

"Did you hit your head?"

"No."

"Say something that persuades me not to take you straight to the hospital."

"I think I'm okay, Thor. Really."

"Did you have too much to drink? Are you lit?"

"If I'm lit, I didn't do the lighting. Somebody served me a bad martini." She balked. "I forgot my phone and my purse in the car."

"I'll get them when I go back to move the car."

"Better do it now. The Smith & Wesson's in my purse."

She felt the muscles in his arm knot and braced herself for a bawling out, but he curbed it and they turned back. He propped her against the street sign and reached inside the car for the phone and purse. He put the phone in his pocket, slung the purse over one shoulder, hooked one of her arms around his neck, and continued walking her toward the apartment.

He said, "Talk to me."

"I'm too tired. You talk to me. How did you find me?"

"I was turning the corner on my way home and saw the car half-blocking the street. You scared me."

"I scared myself. Note to self. Never drive after a martini."

"Did anyone I know happen to share this martini with you?"

"I'll tell you the whole story in the morning. Right now, we have to find K.D. If she's not back, will you call Geert at the club to see if she's there?"

"She's probably asleep in the sleeping bag." He opened the security door and helped her up the stairs to the apartment.

Jack hadn't budged from his berth on the sofa. Margaret sat in the armchair in the corner. She looked up from a book as they came in. "One of you will want to go get K.D. She was picked up a few hours ago along with a group of animal rights protesters and thrown in the pokey for trying to liberate a bear from a bear pit in Köllnischer Park."

Dinah's capacity for surprises had maxed out. "A live bear?"

Thor looked as close to exasperation as Dinah had ever seen him. "I'll take care of K.D." He went over to the cuckoo and toggled a switch on the underside of the house. "No more noise from that squawker. Drink some water and rest. Keep an eye on her, Margaret. Use your judgment. If she gets sick again or starts to sound delirious, call an ambulance."

"Will do." Margaret handed him a piece of paper. "Here's the address of the jail."

"I'd better hurry before streets start being closed off for the start of the marathon." He gave Dinah a last, concerned look, set her purse down on the foyer table, and left.

"You don't look sick to me." Margaret felt her forehead. "You don't have a fever and your color's good."

"I feel much better. I think the man I went to meet drugged me, but I got it out of my system. I'm going to wash my face and brush my teeth and zonk out for a few hours. I'll need all my powers to deal with K.D. in the morning."

"You can have the bed, Dinah. I've slept on the floor before. I'll be fine."

"Thanks, Margaret, but I'd rather be with Thor."

"So would I, but I don't think he'd enjoy himself as much as I would."

Dinah laughed and headed off to the bathroom. When she came out, she felt revived. Whatever Farber had put in her drink must have metabolized quickly. She couldn't think why he would have drugged her, especially if he thought that her boyfriend was only a few feet away. Had he meant to kill her, but she hadn't drunk enough of the cocktail? He surely must know that she had already shared her suspicions about his gallery with the police, so what was the point?

And bears? Bears. Weary as she was, her brain wouldn't shut down and now, incredibly, she felt ravenous. She went to the kitchen to forage for a snack.

Margaret sat at the table with her book and a bowl of leftover Stroganoff.

"You'd better not eat that, Margaret. In retrospect, maybe it was the beef that made me sick."

"I'll chance it. It's delicious. You're a pretty good cook."

"I like to cook when I have time." She took a wedge of Cambozola out of the fridge and warmed it in the microwave. "Since I quit smoking, I'm hungry all the time, especially these last few days. It's the stress. Geert calls it *Kummerspeck*. The literal translation is grief bacon."

Margaret stuck a forkful of Stroganoff into her mouth and gave her a speculative once-over. "When was the last time you had a visit from your Aunt Flo?"

"What?"

"The curse, honey. When was your last period?"

Dinah's thoughts unspooled. Dear God, had the patch failed? It was beyond comprehension. She grabbed the calendar off the wall, dropped into a chair, and did her best to deny the evidence in front of her eyes. "How could this have happened?"

"In the usual way, I suspect." The microwave beeped and Margaret took out the Cambozola and handed Dinah a knife and a box of crackers. "Accidents happen."

"To teenagers. Not to anyone my age. Not to anybody with half a brain."

"Getting yourself knocked up isn't the worst thing in life. Babies can bring a lot of happiness. It's usually fifteen or twenty years before they break your heart."

Dinah put her head down on the table and whimpered.

# Chapter Thirty-five

It was after ten when she woke up—alone in the big bed in the bedroom, if a woman in her condition could be considered "alone." She could no longer laugh off her symptoms as some psychosomatic reaction to stress. She was well and truly pregnant, bushwhacked by Fate and the effing transdermal contraceptive patch. If the bathroom was occupied, she thought she might take the Smith & Wesson and shoot her way in.

After a dismal quarter hour communing with the toilet bowl, she clumped into the kitchen, infuriated with herself. She rinsed out the sludge of overcooked coffee still in the pot and made fresh. While it was brewing, she canvassed the apartment to see who was in. No Jack. No Thor. No Margaret. Just K.D., innocently asleep on the air mattress in the office with Aphrodite curled against her back. Dinah rubbed her temples. In her arrogance, she had expected to be ragging on K.D. for getting pregnant. The turnabout served her right. The repercussions from liberating a bear seemed simple in comparison.

She went back to the bedroom to find something to wear. If she took this pregnancy to the end, none of the clothes in her closet would be wearable for a long time. Big if. Big dilemma. She deferred the decision to another day and squeezed into her skinniest jeans. Carpe diem.

Margaret's suitcase was still lying open next to the bed. She should write a letter to the manufacturer describing how it had survived a grenade attack. Maybe the company would feature

Margaret and her hard-sided Pullman in an ad and she could earn a bit of money. Dinah lifted up one side of the case to look at the singed exterior. Something thunked. She pushed aside a roll of shirts and tees to reveal a Taurus .22 with gold accents and a rosewood grip, the gun that had been stolen from Swan's room.

Carefully, she took it out and just as she'd been taught, turned it to the side, pulled back the slide, and looked into the ejection chamber. Loaded. When did that happen? Swan had said it wasn't loaded when she went to the tower to meet Pohl. Another lie to assimilate, but who was the liar? She carried the pistol back to the kitchen, poured herself a mug of coffee, and sat down to cogitate. How had Margaret come into possession of Swan's gun and why?

K.D. scuffed into the room and launched her defense. "Before you jump all salty on me, I hope you know that keeping a bear penned up in a tiny pit is cruel and inhumane."

Dinah knew that the bear was the symbol of Berlin. There were hundreds of painted Buddy Bears in public squares all over the city. This was the first she'd heard of a live bear outside of the zoo. "What were you planning to do with this bear after you freed it? Bring it home with you? Because in case you hadn't noticed, we're oversubscribed for beds."

"Hahaha. How do you expect me to tell you stuff if you don't take it seriously?"

"Okay, K.D. Seriously, what was the plan?"

"Dolf and his Bear Alliance friends were going to walk her through the park as a kind of protest. They are positively heroic for trying to free her. They just want Schnute to live out her old age in a natural sanctuary. Anybody who watches her even for a minute can see that she's totally depressed after so many years in captivity. Her daughter Maxi died last month and she's all alone with nothing but a few old barrels and tires to look at. When Dolf broke open her pen, she followed him out like a lamb."

Dinah cut to the chase. "And then the cops came and you and the bear people followed them to the station like lambs. How much did it cost Thor to spring you?"

"It wasn't a big fine and I'll pay him back. I'll get a job. Or I can do stuff for you. I'll stay with Jack when you need me to." The defense rested. She helped herself to a cup of coffee, took her phone out of her pocket, and began texting her friends.

Dinah's circuits were overloaded with matters of life and death. She couldn't get too worked up about Schnute. The coffee tasted brackish and she got up and grubbed through the pantry for a box of tea.

"Whoa!" K.D.'s eyes zeroed in on the gun. "That's creepy. Hey, you didn't—?"

"No. To whatever you were thinking."

"You shouldn't have a sexy little toy like this lying around with Jack in the house." She picked it up and fondled it.

"Put it down, K.D. Now."

"I'm not the child, you know."

Dinah wasn't so sure. "Have you talked with your mother since you got here?"

"Why would I? She doesn't care where I am as long as I'm out of her hair."

"We all have our faults, K.D. You should lighten up on your mom. Try to see things from her perspective and be a little less judgmental."

"Like you are with Swan?"

"Our mother problems aren't comparable."

"Why's that? They're both narcissistic nits."

Dinah's phone plinked. She hadn't noticed, but Thor had plugged it into the recharger for her. She looked at the name on the caller ID. Swan. She blew out a breath.

"What?" demanded K.D.

"Private call. Do you mind?"

She rolled her eyes and scuffed out, back to her texting.

Dinah dipped a teabag up and down in a cup of hot water. "Hi, Mom. How are you this morning?"

"Couldn't be better. Klaus took me to the most fabulous restaurant last night. You simply wouldn't believe the chandeliers. The menu was thick as a Sears catalog. Good gracious, everything you could imagine and all of it simply out of this world. And that rude Mr. Amsel never came back to bother me. I'm still at the Adlon."

"That's good." Dinah went deep into her reservoir of tolerance and asked in a non-judgmental voice, "Did you know that Reiner Hess was also staying at the Adlon?"

"Reiner here? You don't say!"

"Don't lie to me," she snapped, tolerance depleted that fast. "Was that another of your secrets?"

"You sound like you're spoilin' for a fight, baby. Is something wrong between you and Thor?"

"Something's wrong between you and me and has been. Don't lie and don't stonewall, Mom. I'm past the fairy tale stage now."

"I didn't know Reiner was here, Dinah."

"That's thin."

"It's true. It sounds like Mr. Amsel uses his hotel like a private guest house."

Dinah couldn't argue with that.

"I'd like to talk to Reiner," said Swan. "What's his room number?"

"He traded his hotel room for a jail cell. Margaret ratted him out to Inspector Lohendorf and he was arrested last night. Incidentally, did Margaret know you had moved to the Adlon?"

"I told her where I was going when I went back to the Wunderbar to pack up my things after she threw me out. That afternoon after we'd been to the morgue and seen Polly."

Dinah rethought the timing. "But you knew the gun was missing before our lunch that day. When did you notice it was gone?"

"The night of the murder. I put it in the drawer and went down to the bar for a bourbon to steady my nerves. I decided I should hide the gun in a better place, but when I went back to the room, it was gone. It was almost like I'd dreamt it."

"Are you sure Reiner never visited you in your room at the Adlon?"

"Not when I was here. After what you told me about Margaret and Reiner, nothing would surprise me."

"I wouldn't be too sure of that."

"Well, I can't wait to hear all of your news at our family dinner tonight, but listen here, baby. That thing you asked Klaus to find out for you, the whatchamacallit. I had to call you while it was fresh in my mind. Wait now. He wrote it down for me on this napkin. *T-o-t-s,* gosh his writing is teensy. *T-o-t-s-c-h-l-a-g,* is that it?"

"Yes. That's right."

"Well, there's more to it than that. Are you ready? *Fahrzeug Totschlag.* I'll spell it. *F-a-h-r-z-e—*"

"Just tell me what it means in English, Mom."

"Vehicular homicide. It was a terrible car accident at *Nür-burg-ring*, which Klaus says is a famous racetrack southwest of Berlin. They call it the 'green hell,' the green on account of all the greenery it winds through, and the hell on account of the curves—a hundred of them in thirteen miles. They hold lots of races there during the year, but they also let tourists drive the course on certain days."

Dinah felt a pang of premonition and regret. "What happened?"

"I was coming to it. In April, two-thousand-and-three, Alwin Pohl was driving the track drunk in the middle of the day. He spun out and skidded broadside into another tourist's car. Polly wasn't injured, but the driver of the other car was badly hurt and his wife was killed."

"Did Klaus get the name of the dead woman?"

"Sabine Eichen. Poor thing. The accident report Klaus read to me says a piece of flying metal came through the windshield and took the top of her head clean off."

# Chapter Thirty-six

There could be no doubt now. Baer murdered Pohl. The photo Farber took of him as he arrived at the powwow showed him wearing the red-fringed ghost shirt. It must have been saturated with blood as he knelt over Pohl's body and inflicted a wound that in the context of all the Indian mimicry, seemed like a scalping. In reality, it was meant to mirror the wounds Sabine Eichen sustained in the car crash. When Baer greeted Dinah at the powwow, he was bare-chested and strung with beads. He must have buried the bloody shirt in the woods or hidden it under the ice in the cooler he carried. Had the police searched the cooler? She didn't recall seeing them search any of the picnic tackle.

"I brought you a tester," said Margaret, placing a small *Apotheke* sack on the table in front of her. "No sense fretting if it's a false alarm. Took me a while to get it across to the pharmacist what I wanted. She couldn't believe that a woman of my vintage would need such a test."

"Thanks, Margaret."

"What are you going to do?"

"I don't know. One thing or the other." She pushed the gun across the table toward Margaret. "You want to tell me how you came to have this in your suitcase?"

"Not really."

"Tell me anyway."

She poured a cup of coffee and sat down heavily. "When the police came to our door on the night of the murder, I wasn't sure who'd been killed, but I was sure as sunup in the east that Swan had killed him. When she showed up at the Wunderbar, she tried to act sassy, but her voice was reedy and her hands wouldn't stop quaking. It was petty of me, but I confess I enjoyed watching her tap dance around Wegener's questions. I thought, she's killed a man. She's no better than me."

"How did you know about the gun?"

"Reiner had mentioned it when he drove me out to Müggelsee. He knew Swan had a room at the Adlon. His friend Amsel is a big cheese over there. He told Reiner that Swan had received a package in advance of her arrival. Amsel steamed it open and found the gun."

"Mom had it with her the night of the murder. She says she dropped it off at the Adlon before returning to the Wunderbar, but somebody took it while she was downstairs in the bar. Did Amsel filch it, give it to Hess, and then Hess passed it on to you?"

"Yes."

"Loaded?"

"Yes. He thought Swan killed Pohl and this was the murder weapon."

Dinah sifted the devices and designs, still waiting for some sense to fall out. Setting aside the question of who loaded the gun, nobody but Baer knew the caliber of the real murder weapon. "If Hess thought it was the murder weapon, why didn't he leave it for the police to find?"

"I asked him to take it. I asked him to give it to me."

The fact that Hess would do Margaret's bidding so meekly passed Dinah's comprehension. But she could think of only two reasons why Margaret would ask for the gun. She said, "Either you wanted to frame Swan for the murder, or you wanted to protect her, and neither reason makes sense."

"I did it to protect you. With all your other doubts, it would be tough knowing that your mother killed a man, especially in that way."

"She didn't do it, Margaret. This gun isn't the murder weapon."

"You're sure?"

"I'm sure." Dinah couldn't attest to whether she would have killed him if she'd gotten to him before Baer did. She put the mysteriously loaded gun in a Tupperware container and hid it behind a crockpot on the top shelf of the pantry where Jack couldn't see or reach, a precaution that wouldn't have occurred to her if K.D. hadn't mentioned it. Thor always locked his gun in his desk drawer when he came home. She had thought it was just his nature to be prudent.

"I still don't believe that Reiner had anything to do with Pohl's murder," said Margaret.

"You're right. He didn't." Dinah reflected on Margaret's change of heart toward Reiner. "You said you gave Hess up to the police because you didn't want me to think you'd colluded with him, but you didn't feel that way two days ago. Did something happen to cause you to change your mind?"

"At our last meeting, I told Reiner that Pohl had been black-mailing Swan for something or other, but I didn't think she had enough money to make it worth his while. He said Pohl was probably after the money Cleon cached in Panama."

"So he knew."

"Not from me. He had to have learned about it from Cleon. His knowing made me realize that he'd been buddies with Cleon long after he led me to believe they'd gone their separate ways. I thought Reiner had crawled out of the slime. My dear old friend was dirtier than I thought."

"Did you ask if he had given Pohl the information, or did the two of them cook up the blackmail plot together?"

"I didn't ask. I didn't want to know. I went to the john and called Lohendorf."

Dinah felt bound to call Lohendorf to tell him her news about Baer Eichen, but there was no longer a sense of urgency and for once, she felt like waiting. She had other, more pressing things on her mind and she needed a time out. "Tonight, we're all going to smoke the peace pipe and exorcise the demon spirit of Cleon Dobbs once and for all. You, me, Mom, K.D."

"It'll end in a cat fight."

"No it won't. Thor can referee. Anyway, I want you there."

"I'll think about it."

"Be there, Margaret. I'll be making an important announcement." She picked up the *Apotheke* sack and forged into the bathroom for her appointment with Destiny.

She came out a half-hour later, deniability down the drain, and cloistered herself in the office. She lay down on the air mattress and stared up at the ceiling. She had shied away from committing to a long-term relationship out of fear she would replicate her mother's fickle behavior. Living with Thor had diminished that fear, but motherhood was magnitudes more serious than living together. And if she had cause to fear that she'd replicate her mother's child-rearing behavior, shouldn't she do what she could to avoid the accident? She wondered if Jack had been an accident. Thor loved him, but no man wants to make a habit of begetting accidents, and she would be a much worse mother than Jennifer. She couldn't even relate to a cat.

Aphrodite squalled like an angry infant and scratched at the door, wanting out. There were no answers written on the ceiling, and Dinah got up as undecided as she was when she lay down. The one thing she knew was that she wouldn't tell Thor until she had made up her mind. Regardless of any views to the contrary, this was her decision, and hers alone. She was still waiting to find out what Thor intended to do with her confession. Under no circumstances would she give birth behind bars.

She opened the door and Aphrodite streaked through the living room and into the kitchen. K.D. and a young man with dark hair and artless blue eyes sat on opposite ends of the sofa.

"Dinah Pelerin, this is Dolf Kugler."

"The man who took you into the bear pit with Schnutes?"

"Yes, Frau Pelerin. But Schnutes was very gentle and I did not mean to get K.D. in trouble."

"Do you have a gentling effect on women as well as she-bears, Dolf?"

The question flustered him. He looked helplessly to K.D.

"Never mind," said Dinah. "Are you busy tonight or have your parents set a curfew?"

He shook his head.

"Excellent. Our family is gathering for a special dinner and I'd like for you to join us. K.D., this is not a request. Big issues will be on the table. Be there. I will let you know where and when. And will you animal lovers please feed the cat?"

She tapped on the bedroom door. "Margaret?"

"Come in."

Dinah looked in. The Monkey 47 was open on the bedside table and a glass poised at her lips. "Taper off, Margaret. I need you on your best behavior tonight."

"You're pretty high-handed, aren't you?"

"Yes, if that's what it takes to get my life in order. And I'll ask you not to refer in any way whatsoever to my condition. Is that clear?"

"All right. But isn't your condition the important thing you're going to announce?"

"No."

Thor and Jack walked into the apartment, Jack talking a mile a minute. They had seen the Kenyan Wilson Kipsang shatter the men's world marathon record as he crossed the finish line of the marathon at the Brandenburg Gate. Jack was giddy with excitement. Thor, not so much. He greeted Dolf with grudging civility and the air between him and K.D. was decidedly frosty. He couldn't have slept more than two or three hours after his run to the jail to bail her out, and yet he'd gotten up early to take Jack to the finish line.

Dinah took him aside. "You look tired."

"I'm okay. You?"

"Much better. I want to hear about Lohendorf's interrogation of Hess and I've learned some things I need to tell you about. Maybe Lohendorf should be present. Nothing's urgent now.

If you're beat, we can wait until this afternoon and invite your friend Jens to join us for the debriefing."

He laughed. "You sound like a spy back from some secret mission."

"Dinah! I have to show you something." Jack grabbed her hand and pulled her toward the office.

"Don't interrupt," said Thor. "Dinah and I are talking."

"But this is important, Dad. You've got to come see this."

The seriousness in his eyes made Dinah relent. "What is it, Jack?"

"In here."

He led them into the office. His fleet of model cars were lined up on the floor next to the TV, the red Ferrari GTO that Baer had given him out in front. He picked it up, popped the hood, and took out a tiny microcassette. "What do you suppose it is?"

She took the cassette out of his hand and examined it. The first possibility that hurtled through her mind was that this was the tape Pohl used to blackmail her mother.

"You think it's an interview with Stirling Moss?" asked Jack.

"Who?"

"You know, the Formula One driver who raced the car."

"Oh, right. Yes, that's probably what it is."

"Do you think Baer wanted me to have it?"

She forced a tight smile. "I'm sure of it."

"Can we listen?"

She crossed her fingers and prayed that the answer was no. If this was the tape of Swan's conversation with Cleon on the day he killed two federal agents, if it was the smoking gun that could send Swan to prison, then Dinah wanted to be the first person to hear it. "Do you own a microcassette recorder, Thor?"

"No."

His eyes transmitted a ray of suspicion, which made it hard for her to hold the smile. But she did. "I'll just hold onto it until we can find something to play it back on."

# Chapter Thirty-seven

No one had a cassette recorder. Thor had a digital voice recorder, and everyone's smartphone doubled as a recorder. But tape technology didn't exist in the Ramberg-Pelerin household and this being a Sunday, the shops were all closed.

"I guess we'll have to wait to hear Stirling Moss," Dinah said, trying to sound cool and composed, knowing full well that the voice on this tape would not be that of the racecar driver. She didn't believe for an instant that Baer hid the tape in the car and forgot about it. He had to know that Jack would find it eventually and show it to her. He had given her the tape deliberately and for cause. But if the tape was the one Pohl had used to blackmail Swan, if Baer had taken it off Pohl's body after he killed him, it was evidence of his crime. In giving it to her, he had tendered his private confession. Why? A very special car, he'd said.

"Before I call Jens," said Thor, "let's hear what it is you're going to say at this debriefing."

"Oh, the usual stuff. The name of the murderer. The motive. The modus operandi."

"Are you kidding?"

"Only a little. I'm going to take a walk and work out some things in my head and you need a nap or you won't be able to keep your eyes open while I'm giving you the lowdown. And later tonight, you'll have to be referee at the exorcism."

"What?"

"The family dinner Mom wants us to have."

"Where are you going?"

"I don't know. I'm just going to walk."

He looked worried. "I'll go with you. In case you have a relapse."

"No. I need some time to myself. Set up a meeting with Jens for late this afternoon and will you make a reservation at Café Aigner for tonight? With Dolf, there'll be seven of us." She thought about her mother's penchant for fresh romance and wondered if Klaus was in line to become her next stepfather. "Better make it eight."

"What time?"

"Seven o'clock. We could all stand an early evening for a change." She donned her jacket, settled her Wayfarers on her nose, tucked the tape inside her purse, and headed for the metaphorical banks of the Rubicon.

She had reached the street, when she remembered seeing Geert with an old analog Rolleiflex camera. He was a retro sort of guy. Maybe he had a cassette recorder, or had a friend who had one. She ran back upstairs and knocked on his door with no consideration whatever for his sleep schedule.

When he opened the door, she held out the microcassette in the palm of her hand. "Sorry to bother you, Geert. But do you know anyone who has a player?"

He squinnied his eyes as if examining a tiny fossil and blew a plume of cigarette smoke toward the stairs. "Who uses these things anymore?"

"Just me, apparently. I need to hear what's on it as soon as possible."

"My papa has an old recorder, but not a mini. Like K.D. says, you are SOL."

"Right. Thanks anyway, Geert."

Stymied, she went back downstairs and out into a perfect fall day, the cusp between fall and winter. She had the sense that her life was at a cusp, the divide between past and future. She walked in the general direction of the Tiergarten, thoughts of the past thrashing around in her head. If this tape contained a conversation between Swan and Cleon, she needed to know what her mother had said. She didn't blame her for her shortcomings as a mother, or her intrinsic inconstancy and unreliability. But there were limits. She had to know if Swan had encouraged or condoned her father's murder.

A sickening what-if wormed into her brain. What if there was something more incriminating on the tape than Swan had admitted? What if Pohl had threatened to give it, not to American federal agents, but to her daughter? Baer had obviously listened to it. Was he trying to warn her? Help her? What? In some inexplicable way, giving her the tape constituted a declaration of friendship. What danger would there be if she called him and asked him to bring his cassette player and meet her for coffee someplace?

The sunshine and the marathon had brought thousands of people into the streets. Soon she was caught up in a throng of cheering spectators. There were still runners on the course and probably would be for several more hours. As she drew closer to the finish line at the Brandenburg Gate, the driving beat of techno music and cheering rocked her.

She should tell Thor about the tape, but if she did, he would insist she turn over the evidence to the police. But it wasn't just evidence against Baer. It could be evidence against Swan. It could prove that she knew Cleon killed federal agents. It could prove she knew he'd killed Hart Pelerin. It could be empty, garbled, or subject to myriad interpretations. It might have nothing to do with Swan at all. How mortified would she be if it turned out to be Stirling Moss reflecting on his racing career, or Baer reading his recipe for Leberwurst?

The driving electronic music pounded in her ears. She picked her way through the crowd to the corner of Dorotheenstrasse and Wilhelmstrasse. The Marshall Bridge was just ahead. She took out her cell. *Riddle me, riddle me, riddle me ree.* Even if Baer was a cold-blooded killer, he had no reason to harm her. He liked her. He liked her a lot. And anyway, he couldn't very well shoot her on a sunny Sunday afternoon in the midst of all these people. She succumbed to impatience and dialed his number.

The phone rang five, six, seven times. Of course he wouldn't be inside on a day like today. For all she knew, he was out here watching the end of the marathon and couldn't hear his phone ring with all the noise. She was about to end the call when he picked up.

"Hello, Dinah. I've been expecting you to call."

She said, "Jack found the tape."

He was silent for a moment. "The car was for Jack. The tape was my gift to you. You have deduced the meaning?"

"You took it from Pohl after you killed him."

"Yes. After I listened, I understood better why you were so personally involved."

"What did you think it was before you listened?"

"I thought it had something to do with Florian's criminal enterprise. Pohl was extorting him. When I realized what it was, I wanted you to have it. There's been too much collateral damage. No need for more."

"Thank you." Had she thanked him for murder? There was no point in parsing a conversation this weird. "How do you know Pohl was extorting Florian?"

"Viktor heard things, which he repeated to me. I listened between the lines and understood what Viktor did not."

"What things?"

"Since Reiner's legal problems began, his ability to move around has been hampered. At the same time, the art market was mushrooming. Reiner brought Pohl to Germany to assist Florian in dealing with the less savory elements of the business. Pohl had been on the fringes of the business in America. When he saw how lucrative it was, he wanted a larger share of the profits. He threatened them with exposure if he didn't get what he asked. I had other reasons to hate Pohl."

"Your wife's death."

"Yes. It's never easy to see the wicked flourish. I stayed my hand as long as I could. And then I thought killing him would be more than revenge. It would be a gift to Viktor."

A man who conflated murder and gift-giving wasn't a man to trifle with. She fingered the "gift" in her pocket and decided she could wait until the stores opened in the morning to get a tape player.

"I'd like to talk with you again, Dinah. I'd like to tell you about my wife. I would like to explain myself."

In the background she heard the doorbell.

"Will you hold please?"

There was a pause, followed by the sounds of a muffled argument, as if the shouts were coming from inside a thick wool pocket. Somebody grunted and grunted again. There was a heavy thud and the crack of gunshots.

"Baer?" But the line was dead.

A cavalcade of horrors flashed through her mind. She took a deep breath and dialed Thor.

He picked up on the first ring.

"I think someone shot Baer Eichen. Meet me at his house off the Schiffbauerdamm as soon as you can. Hurry."

"Dinah, wait."

"No time." She clicked "End" and started running.

# Chapter Thirty-eight

The corridor down to the river was empty. She looked up and down the street, expecting to see Thor's car careening around the corner, or a squadron of police cars, or to hear the sound of approaching sirens. But there were no cars and no sirens, just an invisible bird cheeping and flittering somewhere in the hedge.

She took the Smith & Wesson out of her purse and rubbed it against her jeans. Just breathe normally, she told herself. The cavalry will be here any second. She held the gun in front of her with both hands and started toward the house. She wouldn't go inside until the pros arrived. She wasn't that foolhardy. She would simply keep watch outside the door and ID Baer's attacker if he tried to flee.

As she drew closer, she saw that the front door was ajar. Of course. What had she been thinking? From the time she heard the shots, it had taken her what, seven, eight, minutes to get here? The shooter wouldn't have stuck around. He was probably long gone while Baer lay dead or wounded inside. She edged around the porch and peered into the dark vestibule. Impossible to make out anything from down below. She'd have to climb the steps to see inside.

She licked her lips and looked back down the path. Where were the police? Thor would have called them immediately. What was taking them…him so long?

A motorboat thrummed by. A man hung over the side and pointed toward the house. A cop? She lowered the gun and waved for help, but the boat speeded up and scooted out of sight. Whoever they were, they were probably reporting a gun-toting lunatic to the police at this very moment.

Gingerly, she stepped up onto the porch and with her left hand, eased the door open wider. Something stopped it halfway. Something squashy. She held her breath and peeked inside. A body, crumpled in the fetal position with face to the wall, leaked a slow stream of blood across the wood floor.

She turned and leaned her back against the outside wall. He might still be alive, but she couldn't make herself step into that gore and if she did, it would just contaminate the crime scene. She slid down onto her butt and was digging out her phone to call for an ambulance when she heard the sirens. A minute later, Thor was loping down the path with Jens Lohendorf and Sergeant Wegener hard on his heels. She buried the gun in the bottom of her purse and tried to stand, but her knees were like foam rubber.

Thor bounded up the steps and pulled her to her feet. Without looking, she pointed to the body behind the door. He glanced inside. "If you didn't look so green, I swear to God I'd smack you, Dinah. Why do you take such chances?"

Lohendorf and Wegener arrived.

Dinah said, "It's not Eichen, Inspector. It's Florian Farber."

Wegener fastened a disapproving stare on Dinah. "What business brought you here?"

"Later, Sergeant," said Lohendorf. "Frau Pelerin, you will please remain on the scene until I have a chance to speak with you."

"We'll be here," said Thor. He dragged Dinah off the porch and walked her to the riverbank. "What *did* bring you here? Is it about that tape? What were you thinking?"

"Those are pretty guilt-inducing questions, Ramberg."

"They're the same ones Jens will ask. You may as well practice your answers on me."

"I didn't intend to come to his house. I called to ask him if he'd meet me. When I heard the shot, I just came. Instinctively." She had a catch in her throat. "I thought I'd find Baer dead."

Thor put his arms around her. After a minute, he backed away and looked her in the eye. "Why did you want him to meet you?"

Either she trusted him or she didn't. "The tape Jack found was in Alwin Pohl's pocket when Baer killed him. Pohl had been using it to blackmail my mother. Baer listened to it and, for whatever reason, decided to pass it on to me."

Thor's eyebrows skewed up and she felt a flash of doubt. She had placed her own fate in his hands by owning up to the Panama account. Now she'd placed Swan's fate in his hands. "What's that look supposed to mean?"

"You knew he was a murderer and you called him anyway? Why?"

"I wanted to borrow his cassette player. To play the tape."

"If you'd told me what the tape signified, if I'd known you were that desperate to hear it…" he broke off. His eyebrows returned to their natural line. "Tell me about your conversation with Eichen."

"He was saying he wanted to explain himself to me when the doorbell rang. He went to answer. There was an argument, but I couldn't make out the words. It sounded like they struggled and then I heard two shots."

"Do you have any idea why Eichen killed Farber?"

"Maybe. Pohl was also blackmailing Farber and his partner Hess about their shady art acquisitions. Viktor lived in a world of his own and was late to figure out what Farber was up to, but he mailed a letter to Baer the day before he died. Baer may have told Hess what was in it and Farber came either to buy it back, or take it by force."

An ambulance came to a stop on Schiffbauerdamm at the entrance to the path and a pair of medics walked toward the house, no hurry. That could mean only one thing.

"Stay here," said Thor. "I'll go and brief Jens and see if they've found the murder weapon or any evidence of a motive."

"Thor, about the tape—"

"Why were you in such a hurry to play it?"

"I need to know how to feel about my mother. I need to understand how far she was willing to go. Toward the dark side."

"You can't understand anyone by listening to a secret recording, Dinah. That's the Stasi way." He looked back toward the house. Lohendorf and Wegener were standing on the porch talking with the EMTs. "Fill me in quick. Did Eichen admit to you on the phone that he killed Pohl?"

"Yes. It was revenge. Pohl was responsible for the death of his wife ten years ago in an auto accident. Pohl was driving drunk."

"That's all Jens needs to know for now. He's got more than enough to keep him busy. Hold onto the tape for the time being if you must." He left her and went to join the police and medics. Everyone slipped footies over their shoes, pulled on gloves, and went inside.

She turned away and gazed out over the Spree. The river was Baer's front yard. From his living room, he could look across into the heart of Berlin, a checkerboard of memorials to the murdered, art museums, concert halls, and soaring towers of commerce. It was a composite of painful remembering and willful forgetting. Berliners lived with their ghosts, but they plowed ahead into the future. What choice did they have? The future was the only thing a people—or a person—could do anything about.

She took the tape out of her pocket. The police had all the evidence they needed to charge Baer with the murder of Florian Farber, and when they found him, she didn't think he'd deny that he murdered Pohl. So what was this little relic of history worth to her? Would it tell her how her mother felt about her father, or about his death? Would it prove that she had known what Cleon did?

More police trooped down the path. They cordoned off the house, but didn't bother her. She climbed over the retaining wall and moved a little closer to the water. Life at this point seemed to call for multiple decisions, all of them irrevocable. How freeing it would be to sail this tape out into the Spree. Could she live with the everlasting doubt of not knowing? Thor was probably right. She wouldn't understand her mother any better by listening to a few words spoken years ago in unknowable circumstances.

"Dinah, I've been called away." Thor stood on the bank above. "Jens has gone back to police headquarters to organize a man-hunt, but he'd like you to remain here with Sergeant Wegener for an hour or so, until he gets back. He wants to question you, himself."

"Should I demand a lawyer?" She held out her hand for a boost up the bank.

"Not yet. It'll be a friendly talk. Either he or the sergeant will drop you off at the apartment after your interview. I'll try to get home in time for the 'family dinner,' but nothing's sure."

"Tell me about it." They walked together back to the porch. "I hope Wegener lets me wait upstairs where I can sit down. I feel as if I'd run the marathon."

"I'm sure she will. The house has been searched and guards posted around the perimeter."

"I know it sounds perverse, but I wish I could talk with Baer again before he's hauled him off to jail."

"The way you say his name makes me think you actually like the man."

"I think I did like him. I've known someone very much like him before."

"I'm on my way, *kjære*. Can I trust you not to pull any more death-defying stunts?"

"Absolutely. I've learned my lesson."

# Chapter Thirty-nine

Dinah averted her eyes from the bloody area where Farber had fallen and followed Wegener up to the sitting room. She paused to look at the shelves where Baer displayed his model car collection. He probably had a replica of the car he'd been driving when Pohl crashed into him. She wondered if some of the hate he felt for Pohl was displaced guilt for taking his pregnant wife for a spin around the "green hell" racetrack. Not that being pregnant turned a woman into a fainting flower. Sabine might have craved speed and adventure as much as Baer.

"You are free to sit if you like," said Wegener.

"Thanks. Is it all right if I get a glass of water?"

"Yes, of course." She couldn't keep the tone of disapproval out of her voice, or didn't try.

Dinah went behind the bar, found a glass, and held it under the tap. There was a staircase on the far side of the bar. From the outside, the house appeared to be four stories. This room was the second floor. The bedrooms, bathroom, and kitchen must be on the upper floors.

Wegener unfolded a large map and spread it open on the coffee table. She studied it minutely, apparently lost in thought.

"Where's the bathroom, Sergeant?"

"On the floor above."

"Am I permitted to go alone?"

"The rooms have been searched. So long as you do not leave the house, you may go as you please."

The carte blanche gave Dinah an instant infusion of energy and curiosity. She drank her water and sallied off to explore the rest of the house.

The third level consisted of one large bedroom with a small adjoining bath. Like the room below, there was a huge window, although this one was shuttered. Photographs of a young woman with dark hair and eyes and a faintly mocking smile covered one entire wall, almost like a shrine. This had to be Sabine, the dead wife. In one or two of the photos, Dinah saw a resemblance to herself. It made her skin crawl. Baer had been flirting not with her, but with the ghost of his wife.

The room was furnished simply—a bed, a side table, a chair, and a dresser. She couldn't help thinking about Viktor's letter, in which he admitted that Farber had bought and resold stolen art. Baer said he didn't intend to give it to the police. Maybe that was because, after reading it, he began to suspect that Farber and/or Hess had something to do with Viktor's death. Had he used it to lure Farber here and carried out another act of revenge? If he hadn't destroyed it, he'd probably hidden it somewhere in the house. The police had been over the place with a magnifying glass and fine-point tweezers or Wegener would never have turned her loose to mouse around, but had they looked specifically for the letter?

She gave the dresser a cursory search, glanced inside the drawer of the bedside table, and did a double take. A Sony microcassette recorder nestled on a blank notepad at the back. She slipped it in her pocket and proceeded to the fourth floor.

On one side, modern stainless steel appliances attested to Baer's interest in the culinary arts. There were two ovens, two refrigerators, a marble island with sink and beside the sink, a fancy espresso machine. She opened the refrigerators. One held fancy mustards and condiments. The other was well stocked with eggs and cheese and sausages. A mahogany dining table sat in front of the huge window overlooking the river. She wondered if he had entertained *der Indianer* club up here, or his many banker friends. His metamorphosis from bon vivant to murderer seemed paradoxical. Usually it was the loners who cracked.

She prospected in the buffet and under the flatware drawers without success and returned to the sitting room. Wegener was behind the bar, her back to the mirrored panels, talking on her cell. Dinah drifted toward the bookcases on either side of the mantle. Hanging across the arm of the chair where she'd sat and noshed Leberwurst, was the bolo tie with the big hunk of turquoise. She picked it up and the polished stone felt cool and smooth. Idly, she began to roll it between her palms as she read the titles in the first bookcase.

Philosophers lined the top shelves. Kant, Schopenhauer, Schiller. The middle shelves were devoted to history, the world wars, and biographies of famous generals and politicians. Titles by Karl May dominated the bottom shelves. A book about Winnetou would be a fitting place to bury Drumming Man's last words. She hung the bolo tie around her neck and felt about, between and behind the books. At random, she took out *Im "wilden Westen" Nordamerikas* with a cover showing an Indian chief standing defiantly on a rocky precipice gazing across a desolate plain. A cowboy, presumably the chief's faithful German sidekick Old Shatterhand, lay on his belly and aimed a long rifle into the distance. She flipped through the pages, which were in German, when a question percolated out of the sediment of her brain. "Did you search the bunker?"

Wegener was still gabbing on her cell. She looked up with a start. "What bunker?"

"Downstairs in the entryway. Behind the coat rack."

She spewed a salvo of German into the phone, including quite clearly *der bunker*, and signed off. "Show me."

"You'll need a flashlight," said Dinah.

She took one from her utility belt and charged downstairs.

Dinah followed, careful to step around the place where Farber died, and pointed. "Behind the coat rack"

Wegener rolled it aside and pulled on the iron ring.

"You have to wrench it hard to the right," said Dinah. "The door slides right."

Wegener grabbed the ring and wrenched. Nothing happened. She looked chagrined, set her jaw, and tried again. The door opened. She drew her gun out of the holster. "Have you been down there?"

"No. Baer showed it to me when I visited. He said the original builder preserved it as a possible tourist attraction."

Wegener shone her light into the pit. She looked back in frustration, as if Dinah held her on a leash. "I have my orders to remain with you and guard you until the Inspector returns, but it is also my duty to capture Eichen if he is down there. You will follow me and do exactly as I say. Is that clear?"

"As the sky over Berlin. But I'll need a light. My phone has an assistive light app. I'll run back upstairs and get it."

"Hurry."

She ran upstairs, took her phone out of her bag, and turned on the mini-flashlight. It wasn't big, but it was bright. She hung the shoulder bag with her gun over her neck and shoulder and went back downstairs.

"Shine this light on the ladder for me as I go down," said Wegener. She grabbed onto the ladder, and descended into a well of darkness.

Dinah aimed the light on her feet, but Wegener had trouble holding onto the ladder and the gun at the same time and several times she missed a rung and almost fell. When she got to the bottom, she said, "Drop the light down to me. The floor is earthen. It won't break. I will shine the light for you."

Dinah dropped it. She heard it hit and Wegener picked it up and shined it on the ladder for Dinah. Descending wasn't easy with the phone clutched clumsily in one hand. Even with the light, her feet groped for each rung. The smell of dust and mold grew stronger and the temperature dropped. At last, one foot found the floor.

"You stay here," ordered Wegener. "Do not move until I call you." She took the flashlight and vanished into the darkness.

Dinah shined her puny beam around and tried to get her bearings. The only thing she saw was a painted phosphorescent arrow on the wall in front of her. It pointed through what looked like a tunnel. Tunnels were among her least favorite things and this one looked particularly ugly.

A minute ticked by, and then two. Two minutes in this black hole was a long time. If Wegener didn't call soon, should she go back up the ladder to the house? Should she go forward and see where she'd gone? Maybe she'd called and Dinah hadn't heard. Hell, what was one more misdemeanor in a lifetime of insubordination?

Fighting her dread, she bent her head and crouch-walked through the tunnel. When she touched the wall on either side, her hands came away with a texture she didn't want to think about. The tunnel had to open into a larger area somewhere. This place had to be cavernous if thousands of soldiers and civilians had sheltered down here during the Allied bombing.

As if reality had taken a cue from her thoughts, the tunnel gave way to an enormous room with twenty-foot ceilings. She straightened her back, wiped the grit off her hands, and looked around. The floor and walls were blackened concrete and the air felt heavy and dank. A scaffolding of military bunk beds had been affixed to one wall and a gauze of ancient cobwebs, seemingly undisturbed for the last seventy years, covered the bunks like mosquito netting. A miscellany of artifacts littered the floor—an old boot, a helmet, a rotting blanket, a scattering of spent shell casings. A message in German had been printed on the wall opposite the bunks and another phosphorescent arrow pointed the way to the next room.

"Wegener? Wegener, where are you?" Her voice pealed, like the acoustics in a cathedral. If Hell had a cathedral.

She took the gun out of her bag and walked on. Stalactites of filth and cobwebs dangled from the ceiling and tiered down the walls like those shelf-like mushrooms that grow on decaying tree trunks. This hidden netherworld was a time capsule and the time it encapsulated must have been horrific. She imagined she could hear the bombs screaming down on the city, feel the crash and jolt as they landed, smell the fear of the people huddled in this man-made purgatory, between life and death.

She didn't have to imagine the gun that prodded suddenly against her back.

"I was hoping you had forgotten about my underground sanctuary, Dinah." He took her gun out of her hand.

She blenched at his touch. "Sergeant Wegener is down here. She's armed, so you'd better let me go."

"The Sergeant has met with a small accident. More a blow to her pride than her person, I assure you."

She could feel his breath in her hair. If she whirled, she might catch him by surprise and knock him down. She turned her head and saw him tuck her gun away behind his hip at the small of his back.

"Don't test me. I wouldn't stick at one more casualty."

The barrel of the gun gouged into her back. The naïve assumption that he wouldn't hurt her evaporated. She said, "Wegener told the others about the bunker. They'll be here any minute."

"Then we'd better hurry." He prodded her again. "Walk please. Use your little light."

She'd read that some of the old bunkers had been linked with underground train stations, but the nearest U-Bahn to this house was the Brandenburger Tor on the other side of the Spree. The bunker must run parallel to the river, and very close. Pools of standing water began to appear. "Where are you taking me?"

"To a place where we can talk. I have something to give you."

Jesus, Joseph, and Mary. Another "gift" from a double murderer.

A rat scurried along the wall. How much farther, and for what purpose? She edged around a pool of water from which two arms of a crudely painted swastika emerged. The floor sloped and river water washed in through cave-like holes.

"To your left." He prodded her again.

"You want me to walk into the wall?"

He moved ahead of her and pushed. The wall opened and they walked into a tiny cubicle, like a dungeon cell. Two LED lanterns emitted a harsh light that hurt her eyes after being in pitch darkness. He pulled an iron ring that closed the wall behind them.

There was a card table and a chair. Wegener lay on the floor, eyes closed and hands bound behind her.

"Sergeant Wegener?"

She didn't speak or move.

"She can't hear you. I daresay she won't wake up for a while yet."

"Give me your shoulder bag, Dinah."

She lifted it over her head and handed it over. He tossed it into a wooden wine crate with Wegener's gun and holster.

"Sit down," he said.

The gun pointed at her middle was persuasive. She sat. "You've got this place tricked out like a medieval castle. How many movable walls and secret rooms are there?"

"This is the only one you'll see." He took a green hardcover book off the table and handed it to her, *Winnetou, die Apache Ritter.* "A *Ritter* is a knight. A noble man, like Viktor was. Go ahead. Open it."

She did and a brown envelope fell out. "Is this the letter you used to bait Farber into an ambush?"

"Naturally, he wanted it."

"That sounds like premeditation. I can understand why you hated Pohl, but you had no cause to kill Farber. He hadn't done you any harm."

"He killed Viktor, or conspired with Hess to kill him."

"What happened to your suicide theory?"

"They would have made it look like suicide, of course, and gotten away with it. I'm sure they had similar plans for me. Florian attacked me when I opened the door. He punched and kicked my legs, thinking to detach my artificial limb. Fortunately, I was armed and able to give him the death he deserved. I had hoped that Reiner would be with him, but Farber said he'd been arrested."

"You were going to kill Hess, too?"

"When both the law and God fail, someone must be concerned with matters of truth and justice."

If that was his twisted translation of the Einstein quote, he was a psychopath. She wondered if there was a chink in his hubris. "Did Florian not understand that all he had to do was offer you money for the letter?"

His face reddened with rage. "It disappoints me that you, of all people, would think me so crass."

"You've murdered two men. Crass isn't the first word that springs to mind. You're a megalomaniac with a sick, inflated sense of your own omnipotence."

He raised the gun to her face. Her courage wicked away in an instant.

"You're a brave woman to speak so boldly," he said, spectacularly mistaken.

"A female Winnetou," she said, worrying the turquoise on the bolo tie she'd hung around her neck. She took it off and held it out to him. "You forgot your tie."

His rage seemed to dissipate. He actually smiled. "Keep it as a souvenir of our brief acquaintance. I wish I had time to change your opinion of me."

Out of the corner of her eye, she saw Wegener's head move. She didn't think Baer had noticed. His eyes were riveted on her face. She tried to keep them there. "What about Sabine? What would she think of her charming husband's gross brutality?"

"The dead don't think, Dinah. It is what the clergy call heaven." He jabbed his index finger on Viktor's letter, lying on top of the open book. "I had intended to mail this to you once I was away and safe, but here we are. You seem to have strong feelings about the Native American heritage. I want you to make sure Viktor's information reaches the proper authorities, whether in Germany or America. He has provided valuable information about the sources and methods of some of Florian's trading partners."

"If you care so much, why don't you send the letter to the authorities, yourself?"

"I can hardly do so without being apprehended and getting the people with power to take meaningful action will require a good deal of nagging."

She looked down at the Winnetou book to sneak a peripheral glance at Wegener. She was holding her head an inch off the floor. She was conscious. To distract Baer, Dinah moved the letter off to the side and began reading at random. "*We came to the spot where I had killed the two buffaloes, but I saw that the body of the old bull was gone.*" She snapped the book shut. "You won't get away, Baer. The police have the house surrounded."

"The police are easily outwitted, Dinah. Pohl outwitted them. Florian outwitted them. Reiner outwitted them. His lawyers have probably already engineered his release. I have no doubt that I will escape. I have a motorized skiff tethered on the riverbank. I can be far away very quickly. And now I must leave you."

He reached across the table as if to touch her face and she stood up, knocking over the chair behind her and upending the table. At the same time, Wegener kicked her legs straight out like a battering ram and clipped Baer hard on the side of the knee. He lost his balance and staggered back against the wall. Her hands somehow free, the sergeant scrambled to her feet and dived at him. Baer fired. The sound was deafening, and the shot ricocheted off the concrete wall.

Wegener wrestled the gun out of his hand. It dropped to the floor and she snaffled it up in an instant. "*Sie sind verhaftet. You are under arrest,*" she said, her eyes shining with triumph.

Dinah's fingers had been clutching the turquoise so tightly, they felt fused. She loosened her grip and let out an immense sigh.

Baer righted himself and massaged his knee. Holding the gun on him, Wegener moved the card table out of her way and reclaimed her gun and holster from the wine crate. "Go back to the house, Frau Pelerin, and guide my colleagues back to this place. I will hold Herr Eichen here for the Inspector."

Dinah edged around the table and pushed open the wall into the outer bunker, pointing her cell phone light into the darkness.

She threw a last glance over her shoulder. Wegener stood on one side of the room looking at Viktor's letter and holding the gun. Baer stood against the opposite wall, elbows out, palms against his back as if rubbing at a pain. One arm moved forward and a synapse fired in Dinah's brain.

"My gun!" she cried, and flung the turquoise at his head.

The stone bonked him hard in the face. Blood gouted from his nose onto his shirt front. His wooden glasses broke and the Smith & Wesson hit the floor behind him as his hands flew to his face.

Looking somewhat abashed, Wegener retrieved the gun, pushed Baer into the chair, and secured her prisoner. She picked the turquoise stone off the floor and bounced it up and down in her hand. "That was a lucky shot."

"Not really," said Dinah.

The Sergeant smiled. "Like Annie Oakley," she said, with nary a trace of irony or disapproval.

# Chapter Forty

Before WWII, Potsdamer was the poshest section of Berlin. During the war, the Allies bombed it to smithereens and after 1961, when the GDR erected the Wall, the square was cut in two. A wide swath on both sides of the divide became an urban wasteland of filth and debris. All that changed when the Wall came down and capitalism triumphed. Sony, Daimler, Nike, and a horde of international corporations moved in and transformed the area into a futuristic complex of hotels and businesses. Many Berliners deplored the "Disneyfication" of the historic square. Dinah sympathized, but as she sat down on a bench under the so-called volcano—a dramatic, tent-like canopy of glass modeled on Mt. Fuji—there was no denying that the new Potsdamer Platz was a wonder of renewal and the power of money.

She had read about the supernatural amplification of power and energy that resulted from meditating under a pyramid. She closed her eyes and tried to focus her thoughts. The clock was ticking on her big decision and she vacillated from hour to hour. Once decided, there could be no do-over. And there was another decision hanging fire, one that was equally irrevocable. No supernatural power whispered in her ear and after a minute, she concluded that meditating under a phony volcano didn't confer the same benefit as a pyramid. She got up and headed to the family dinner, which for a host of reasons had been postponed, downsized, and moved to Lutter & Wegner's here in the Potsdamer Platz. Inadvertently, she had chosen the perfect location to discuss renewal and money.

Margaret, Swan, K.D., and Thor were already seated when she arrived. Jack was off at the movies with a group from his new English language school.

Thor stood and pulled out a chair for her between him and Swan. "How did your first class go?"

"It was great. I dropped all the introductory stuff and had the students tell me what drew them to the course and what books they'd read about Indians. Their interest is more academic and less romantic than *der Indianer* club. It will be a challenge to teach them anything they don't already know."

"Well, I think it's grand, you gettin' yourself a teaching job in a hifalutin university," said Swan, her smile radiant. "Pour her a glass of that delicious Riesling, Thor. We should make a toast."

Thor picked up the bottle, but Dinah put a hand over her glass. "None for me, thanks."

Margaret raised her eyebrows. "You can give me her share, Thor."

"Pathetic," snarked K.D.

In a level voice, Thor said, "Tell me when you can't stand our company any longer, K.D. We're only a half-hour from the airport."

For once, K.D. looked impressed. She simpered an apology. "I'm sorry, Thor."

He said, "It's Margaret who deserves the apology."

"Sorry, Margaret."

Under the table, Dinah squeezed his hand. She panned around the table and cleared her throat. "I wanted you all together tonight because I have an announcement that will concern you all."

"I knew it!" Swan clasped her hands to her breast and gushed. "You and Thor are gonna make it official! 'Little Joey Jingle, he used to live single.'"

"No, Mother. No!" Her voice shrilled. She took a breath and tried to put a damper on her emotions.

"Goodness sakes, baby. I'm sorry if I upset you."

"I'm not upset. As a matter of fact, I'm relieved. I've reported Cleon's money to the powers that be."

"Good God, why?" Margaret seemed stupefied. "The IRS? The DEA?"

"The relevant powers." Dinah hadn't an inkling which agency Thor had consulted or how it would be handled. He had told her only that the matter was in process. She said, "It will probably take the authorities a while to figure out what to do with me. I hope they'll show leniency. But it's entirely possible that I'll do jail time. The interest and penalties will be stiff and I don't have nearly enough money to pay."

The three women stared in stunned silence.

Swan found her voice first. "But Thor will help you, won't you, Thor? With the fines, or what-have-you."

Dinah said, "It's not Thor's place to buy me a get-out-of-jail card."

He answered Swan in a low-key, general way. "Dinah knows she can count on me for whatever she needs."

"There," chirped Swan. "You see? That's what I call true chivalry."

"That was my money," said K.D., her eyes shining. "Daddy left it to me. You had no right."

"I had every right." This was the speech Dinah had been building toward, and K.D. had given her her opening. "I never thought I'd meet another man like Cleon Dobbs. But I recently had the misfortune of spending several hours in the company of another man with a God complex, someone who thought it was his privilege to mete out rewards and punishments. In truth, he was a stone killer with a veneer of charm. Just like your daddy, K.D."

"I know that he loved me, and I loved him," said K.D.

Dinah could have disputed the first part of that assertion, but she didn't. "You're the only good thing he left behind in this world, K.D. But the fact that you hate Margaret, and Margaret hates Swan, and Swan hated a man she barely knew—hated him enough to think about killing him—that's all Cleon's legacy. He hung your mother out to dry, manipulated my mother in ways I'm sure I'll never know, and he used my confusion and my sense of obligation to you and your brother to stick me with that damned dirty money. Now it's out of my hands and I'm done with the Cleon saga. After tonight, I never want to hear his name again."

Nobody said anything for a long time. The waiter came and they ordered food and another bottle of Riesling. K.D. seemed to lapse into a brown study. Dinah was done with the money, but she wasn't done worrying about how K.D. would fare without it. She thought about that bump key and hoped that her own effort at renewal didn't catapult K.D. into a life of crime. "I don't know how, K.D., but I'll do what I can to help you come up with tuition for college. If you'll go."

"Tell the IRS it was my money," said Margaret. "I'll give them an affidavit, or whatever they want. With my record, they'll believe me. I'm serious, Dinah. Do it."

"You'd go to jail for me, Margaret?"

"K.D.'s right. I drink too much. It'll be like a vacation at the Betty Ford Center, only free. Anyway, I've got nothing better to do with my time."

K.D. raised her eyes. "I'm not a plank, Dinah. I know what you've done for me. The only reason I cared about the money was because it stood for Daddy, for how I thought he had loved me and thought of me with his dying breath. I know it was a thorn in your side and I don't blame you. If you let me stay, I can lace up and earn my own way." She laughed. "Maybe Thor will hire me to look after Jack if you have to 'go away.' I promise I wouldn't teach him to pick a lock."

Thor said, "I don't think Dinah will go to prison, but it has to make her feel good that her family is willing to stand by her, come what may."

"It does make me feel good. Thank you all. Thank you, K.D. and Margaret. I wish I had a token of appreciation for everyone, but this is all I have tonight." She turned to Swan. "I brought you a present, Mom." She handed her a little box tied with a red ribbon.

"Goodness, what can it be?" Swan slipped off the ribbon and lifted the lid. Her eyes misted over. It was the microcassette tape and Baer's player.

"I don't know what's on it," said Dinah, pre-empting speculation. "I'm not the Stasi, or the N.S.A. As you say, if a woman can't trust her own daughter." She left the vice versa unspoken.

Swan covered Dinah's hand with hers. "We haven't understood each other as well as we should since your father passed."

"You mean, since Cleon murdered him," said Dinah. "For you."

Swan appeared less shocked than she'd been when Dinah confronted her the first time. "I know how close you were to your father, and whatever it was that Cleon said about his death unsettled you. But the police determined Hart's death was an accident."

"An accident Cleon caused to happen," said Dinah. "Please don't insult me by denying it. I don't really care what you choose to believe, Mom. I choose to believe that you didn't conspire with Cleon because to think otherwise would make me hate you and I refuse to let his shadow darken one more day of my life."

"You're angry because you think I should have spent more time mourning your father instead of taking up with a new husband."

"Several new husbands," corrected Dinah.

"I know that seems shallow to you. If you could have designed your perfect mama, I guess it wouldn't have been me. But nobody gets a perfect mama. Yes, I loved Cleon and I also loved your father. I've loved all of my husbands. I'm sorry you've gotten it in your head that I did something wrong or that I let you down." She acted as though she were the one who was owed an apology and it was her prerogative to bestow forgiveness. Blithe as a lark, she smiled and rolled out the old charm. "This is all just a rigmarole. You're got this jail thing hanging over your head and it's made you crotchety. You need to see Klaus and let him do the worrying for you. And baby, if you have to go to jail, I'll bring you a hacksaw."

There was a sort of amazed silence and then Thor laughed, mostly to break the tension, Dinah thought. He said, "I hear you're a natural smuggler, Swan. Maybe you can give N.C.I.S. a few pointers that'll help us spot the criminals."

Dinah listened to the outpouring of charm that followed, and marveled at Swan's automatic nonchalance. She might be a pathological liar and a narcissist, but she was the mama Fate had given her. As there was no cure for narcissism or Fate, Dinah had budgeted the rest of her life in which to fathom the mysteries of the mother-daughter relationship.

Thor put his arm around her shoulder. "You look tense. Are you sure you won't have a glass of Riesling?"

"No thanks. I'm on the wagon since my episode with the bad martini."

Margaret drained her wine and her face split into a smile that made her look almost young. "You put on a top-notch exorcism, Dinah. I can almost hear the pitter-patter of little demon feet running for cover."

# Chapter Forty-one

Dinah and Thor sat together at the kitchen table. He pecked away on his laptop. She watched the steam rise off her morning mug of tea. Coffee didn't taste right to her anymore and she had bought a box of Tranquil Dream chamomile to see if it went down any better. Her life had changed radically during the one short month she'd been in Berlin. She felt like a victim of future shock.

She hadn't told Thor yet about the failure of the patch. Margaret had sworn up and down that she hadn't spilled the beans and Dinah was angling for a way to break the news. She'd made up her mind to throw the dice and have the baby, but she didn't want him to feel locked in if he didn't want a second child. She feared she might weaken and change her mind again if he didn't, and she was having a hard time thinking how to broach the subject. It would help if he looked up from his damned computer.

"Thor, there's something we need to talk about."

He finished whatever he'd been typing. "Sure, but first there's a news article you should see." He turned the computer screen toward her and clicked on the English site for *Der Spiegel International*.

She rested her chin in her hands and read.

> "The German Government has apprehended one of
> its most wanted tax evaders, Reiner Hess, and charged
> him with felony fraud under the German Criminal

Tax Fraud Law. More than 26,000 German tax evaders have come forward voluntarily and disclosed their undeclared assets. Hess did not and fled instead to Cyprus. His hidden accounts, some in Switzerland and some in Cyprus, will be seized and he faces up to ten years in prison. New information may subject him to further prosecution. Documents found in his possession reveal that he also maintained a multi-million dollar offshore account in Panama…"

She looked up and met Thor's eyes. "Panama?"
He shrugged. "Small world."
She took a sip of tea and resumed reading.

"The bank employee who managed Hess' Panama account has disappeared and local authorities are investigating Hess' prior association with an American drug dealer, Cleon Dobbs, who was shot to death in Australia in 2010. Panamanian and American authorities have been alerted to the possibility that the funds came from a drug cartel that operated worldwide. An investigation has been launched and, if ties to drug smuggling are proved, Hess may be extradited to the U.S. The German court has denied bail on the grounds that he is a flight risk."

"Holy Moses." Dinah could scarcely believe it. "You must have sailed awfully close to the wind to bring this off, Thor. How many laws did you have to break? How many legs?"

"No broken legs. I called in a couple of favors, planted a few clues."

"You could lose your job if anyone finds out."

"I was careful. I didn't leave any fingerprints."

"What about the banker?"

"I gave him a chance to get out of the country before the shit hit the fan. He took it."

"But when he's caught, he'll drag me into the mess all over again, and you along with me. We could both end up in jail."

"That won't happen. It's over, Dinah. I promise."

She had a feeling he wasn't telling her the whole truth, but lately, she'd come to understand that truth and honesty weren't the same thing. The truth depended very much on point of view and it didn't always coincide with justice. "I thought you would give the information to the IRS. I thought you'd play by the rules."

"I usually do."

"You've gone rogue, Ramberg. And I'm extremely, extremely grateful." She pulled his face down to hers and kissed him.

He answered her kiss in a way that suggested a fast return to the bedroom. And then he said, "I've been thinking about your mom's idea."

"What idea?"

"The one about us making it official."

She pushed him away and eyed him doubtfully. "Have you been chitchatting with Margaret?"

"No, why?"

"No reason." Was he lying?

"I'm asking you to marry me, *kjære*. Now. Today."

He was definitely lying. She said, "Getting married in Germany is more complicated than showing up at the Bureau of Vital Statistics with stars in our eyes."

"Neither of us is a German citizen. We could skip the red tape and the waiting period and get married in the Norwegian Embassy this afternoon. Jack can be my best man and K.D. your maid of honor."

"Marriage is a big deal, Thor. There's a lot to consider."

"I've considered." He handed her a ring box. "There's no diamond. It's a simple band with a Sami motif."

She took out the ring and held it up to the light. "What do the markings mean?"

"They're to protect you from the goblins."

"It's too late for that."

"What do you mean?"

"If Margaret hasn't told you already, my protection failed. I'm pregnant."

He looked surprised, or pretended to. "That's wonderful news. I mean, it's great by me, if it's what you want."

"I've never wanted a child. Never imagined it. I don't know when the maternal feelings that people talk about are supposed to kick in, or if they ever will. Maybe I'll be as airy and unreliable as my mother. Yet in spite of my unpromising qualifications and my best efforts not to multiply, it seems that I'm 'on the nest' and I can't come up with a good reason to buck Fate."

"You'll get the hang of it, Dinah. It'll be a collaboration."

She said, "I've heard that babies put the kibosh on sex and romance. Is that what happened to you and Jen?"

"Actually, Jen was certain from the start that she wanted a child. It didn't take long before we both realized that she wanted the child more than she wanted me."

"That's definitely not the order of preference in the present case." She slipped the ring on her finger. "Last chance to reconsider, Ramberg. Marry me and it's 'til death do us part. And that's worse than a threat. It's a promise."

He grinned. "On the way home from the wedding we can stop by a real estate office. I've been thinking for several days that we need a bigger apartment."

To receive a free catalog of Poisoned Pen Press titles, please provide your name and address through one of the following ways:

Phone: 1-800-421-3976
Facsimile: 1-480-949-1707
Email: info@poisonedpenpress.com
Website: www.poisonedpenpress.com

Poisoned Pen Press
6962 E. First Ave. Ste 103
Scottsdale, AZ 85251